THE BONNIE DEAD

ANDREW RAYMOND

HUNTERHILL
BOOKS

CHAPTER ONE

IF MAITLAND FERGUSON had known what was going to happen to his son later that night, then he would never have spent their last five minutes together before bed reading *We're Going on a Bear Hunt* for the seven hundred and fifty-third time. Not that Maitland was paying much attention to the story. He knew it inside out. While his wife Fiona took her turn reading pages with an incredulous intensity like she was discovering the story for the first time, Maitland would rhyme off entire pages without looking.

Everything about the story irritated him. Something he did a poor job of hiding.

Fiona scowled at him. Not for his lack of attention, but for the series of staccato vibrations coming from the phone in his trouser pocket. It was the rhythm of someone messaging in anger, smashing "Send" after every short sentence.

Finally, Fiona broke off from the story to implore Maitland, 'Can't you put that on silent?'

He   d to be making a point of not checking his
phone,   he either already knew who it was. Or didn't
want   w. 'Sorry,' he mumbled in reply.

        s texting you so much anyway?'

        y,' he repeated, stealing a quick glance at who the
    se   was before shoving his phone back into his pocket.
          aded further by gesturing at the dad figure on the page.
    hat's with this guy anyway? He takes his whole family out
    the countryside, not for a picnic, or a nice walk, but to
  hunt for a fucking bear...'

Fiona combined a roll of the eyes with a grimace.

Maitland didn't have to wait for her to explain – yet
again – about not swearing in front of five-year-old Jack. 'An
effin' bear, then.' He gestured further. 'The three kids aren't
properly dressed for the outdoors. He gets them all to wade
chest-high through what must be a freezing river. Then, once
everyone's soaked to the skin and caked in mud, he takes
them into a dark forest, and then into the teeth of some Baltic
blizzard. Which is bad enough. But the dad then continues
with this bear-hunting shit–'

Fiona couldn't be bothered calling him out this time.

Meanwhile, Jack's attention had long since drifted from
what should have been a peaceful bedtime story, munching
his thumb obliviously as Maitland ranted on.

'–and then, when they actually *find* a bear, what does he
do? He shites it, and tells them they have to run away! The
bear then *follows them back home*, and they end up locked
upstairs in the bedroom, hiding under the bedcovers. All
because this arsehole wanted to go on a bloody bear hunt...'

He broke off as another three vibrations went off. Anticipating Fiona's annoyance, he made a show that he was dealing with it.

Jack, used to hearing them bicker in front of him, now had his entire fist in his mouth, bored out of his box. He looked off towards his bedroom window, where late-evening sunlight was fighting its way around the edges of a blackout blind that swayed in a slight breeze.

The window had been cracked open to try and break the heat. It had been pushing thirty degrees earlier, and even stripping Jack down to a pair of Spiderman underpants and a white vest he still felt warm to the touch.

Fiona, seeing Maitland's frozen expression, pressed him, 'Is everything alright?' She kept staring at him. 'Well?'

The blood had drained from his face, eyes lingering on the last message that had been sent:

"you're about to enter a nightmare unlike anything you've ever experienced...Just remember, you could have stopped this..."

Maitland simply repeated, 'Sorry,' then turned his phone off completely. He lifted his hands to demonstrate that the phone had been dealt with properly now, but he couldn't wipe the shaken expression from his face.

Fiona knew that something was wrong – and that she would never get the truth out of him. She never did.

On the surface, Maitland and Fiona Ferguson had it all. A traditional red sandstone townhouse in Glasgow's sought-after Dowanhill area. They were both partners in a thriving law firm with offices across the central belt, and made a small fortune – enough to cover four major holidays each year, and fill their house with the best of everything. Money wasn't something they had had to think about for a long time. They were the sort of couple that when they shopped online, they filtered their searches by *Price - High to Low*. They had two cars out front – an Audi TT for Maitland, and a white Range Rover for Fiona.

Maitland cared about all that stuff, but for Fiona it was all window-dressing compared to the one thing they treasured more than anything: their smart, funny, and miraculously polite five-year-old son, Jack.

WITH JACK ASLEEP IN BED, his covers pushed down towards his feet, Maitland retired to the ensuite bathroom while Fiona sat up in bed holding open a book but reading none of it. She noted him casually pocketing his phone from the bedside table on the way to the bathroom.

His phone was an enigma to her. He always made sure that it was never left in her presence. Unlike Fiona, who was always leaving hers lying around. She didn't even keep a screen lock on. Maitland could scroll through her photos and messages any time, while he guarded his like it had nuclear codes hidden inside.

As soon as the bathroom door closed behind him, he paced around in front of the his-and-hers sinks, contemplating the phone that he'd placed on the edge of the bath. It sat there now like an unexploded bomb he didn't know how to defuse.

He leaned over his sink, staring down the plughole that seemed to have become a metaphor for his life at that moment. He lifted his head to consider himself in the mirror.

A handsome reflection stared back – the symmetrical features that had made him attractive to almost every female he'd encountered since his university days; the once-chiselled jawline now sagging slightly from a dearth of recent gym visits; his hair grown out to floppy salt-and-pepper waves.

He'd come from a family of wealthy estate agents, but he had far exceeded his parents' success. Plus, he'd gone to Hutchie Grammar and his name was Maitland. Guys like him, with names like Maitland, didn't tend to end up unemployed, buying scratch cards at ten in the morning.

The world, it seemed, had only success in store for Maitland Ferguson.

But all that was about to disappear.

CHAPTER TWO

MAITLAND PICKED UP THE PHONE, now able to reply to the text that had left his stomach churning for the last forty-five minutes. He had spent most of it in silence beside Fiona on the couch, considering how to respond. All he could think about was the last line of her last message:

'*Just remember, you could have stopped this...*'

Free to scroll through the full savagery of what he'd been sent, his hand started to tremble as he read the earlier messages.

'*If you come home to find a pet bunny boiling in a pot, you'll sigh with relief at it being a good day compared to what I've got cooking for you. You should never have crossed me, Maitland.*'

He swallowed hard.

Many people couldn't admit to themselves that they were bad people, but Maitland had long since accepted it about himself. He would take whatever he had coming.

He looked away from the mirror and started typing.

'*Whatever you're thinking of doing, do it to me. Please. Leave Fiona out of it.*'

He waited for a reply that didn't come at first.

He typed on.

'*Karen?*'

Thirty seconds passed.

He had no idea how long thirty seconds could feel like, until he found himself staring at a phone screen for that long, praying that the woman you've been having an affair with isn't about to detonate your entire life.

Karen finally replied with what Maitland had feared most.

'*It's too late. It's already done.*'

He backed away from the sink and looked at the ceiling in despair. He tried to catch his breath. He wanted more than anything to let out a cry. A sob. A wail. Something. Any kind of release.

Fiona called from bed, 'Are you nearly done?'

He closed his eyes, trying to remove the tension from his vocal cords. 'Be right out.'

MOMENTS EARLIER, Fiona picked up her phone and texted: '*Has he replied yet?*'

The recipient – Fiona's closest friend – Veronica replied, '*Are you sure you want to know?*'

Veronica worked for a cyber security firm, and was technically proficient enough to arrange for a SIM card clone that Fiona had put in Maitland's phone a fortnight ago. Since then, the evidence had been stacking up, monitored at Veronica's end where every message and keystroke and screen tap was logged in preparation for the inevitable divorce.

'*I need to know,*' Fiona typed.

Reluctantly, Veronica shared the mirror of Maitland's phone screen. Now Fiona was seeing everything as if she was standing over his shoulder.

She felt sick as she read the exchange from Karen. Whoever she was.

Fiona could barely move from anger. He was just a matter of twenty feet away, running the tap as if everything was normal behind that door. Betrayal felt somehow much worse when played out in such close proximity. Normally, cheating involved illicit nights in hotels. Car park meet-ups far away from either of the injured parties. Travelling. Distance.

To have it taking place right under Fiona's nose – in the confines of their own bedroom – made it all somehow much worse.

She was going to confront him. She had decided. She threw the covers off and swung her feet down off the bed.

Then she saw Jack stirring in his bed on the video monitor on her bedside table.

It was a reminder that as soon as she confronted Maitland with the truth, it would be the beginning of the end of everything she really cared about. No more lazy breakfasts together listening to Ken Bruce on Radio 2. No more family Christmases or birthday parties. It would be all tense silences and forced levity to make sure Jack didn't suspect that anything was wrong.

That was when she felt it. A sudden sharp prick at her ankle, like an insect bite or a wasp sting.

She recoiled, pulling her foot up to inspect it. A tiny pinprick of blood appeared under her ankle bone.

'What the hell...' she muttered to herself.

Her foot felt heavy. Like it was filling with sand. It was a struggle to get it back on the floor.

Then her vision turned glassy.

Feeling her entire motor system faltering, she called out to Maitland, 'Are you nearly done? I don't feel well.'

'Be right out,' he replied again.

By the time he emerged, he found his wife hanging off the end of the bed, doubled over, reaching for the floor. A string of drool leaked from her gaping mouth, her eyes rolling around in their sockets.

Maitland rushed to her side, pulling her up from under the arms. 'Hey, what's wrong? What's happening?'

In her head, Fiona explained clearly. But what came out was nothing but a string of vowels.

Maitland fumbled with his phone to call 999, only to have the phone spill out of his hand onto the carpet. It wasn't from panic or fright. It was a reaction to the sharp prick now jabbing into his ankle.

He yelled out, but was quick to dismiss any thoughts of what the pain was. Fiona was the one in trouble. At least, that was what he thought until he leaned down to grab his phone and found himself face-planting the carpet, arms stuck by his sides.

Fiona lay helplessly on the bed, face turned towards the bedroom door. She was paralysed, now a mere passenger in her own body.

Maitland was headed the same way. His vision was cloudy and quickly turning into dark – the room vignetting from the sides.

There was just enough time for him to see the bedcovers ruffling above the valance.

The mattress shifted slightly from underneath.

Then the sight of a hooded figure crawling out from under the bed.

Maitland's mouth hung open in horror, his eyes wide with shock and terror. He knew what he was seeing. He just didn't understand how it was happening. The front and back doors had been locked hours ago.

His brain was still operating on some basic survival mode, and realised that they must have been under the bed for hours.

A stranger. Hiding. Waiting. Listening.

Now they had made their move.

Maitland groaned as he managed the last few inches of movement from his body. He was now prone on the carpet, face turned towards the bedroom door where the hooded figure was now moving.

Fiona was still able to lift her head off the mattress. She

had no concern for her own wellbeing or survival. She had only one thought now...

Jack.

Her eyelids fluttered at the thought of him, finding some deeply embedded strength that allowed her to shift a leg. Then to push herself forward across the bed.

The hooded figure stopped and looked back at her.

He smiled.

The terror of the moment gave Fiona a jolt of adrenaline. Although nothing came out, inside she was screaming. Louder than she'd ever screamed in her life.

Because the hooded figure was making his way out of the bedroom. Across the hall.

Opening the door to Jack's room.

Fiona found another gear, and crawled across the room at a snail's pace. Her eyes were the size of planets, eyeballs throbbing at the thought of harm coming to her only child.

Through gritted teeth, leaving a long string of drool behind, she grunted and snarled all the way across the bed, falling to the carpet on the other side. Now there was only smooth wooden flooring between her and the intruder. She wasn't going down without a fight.

Through her snarls she heard some kind of incantation coming from Jack's room. A song? A nursery rhyme?

The hooded man emerged, cradling Jack in his arms. He was singing him a lullaby.

Fiona's entire body came out in goosebumps. She could tell from Jack's expression that he wasn't sleeping. He had been knocked out. His head dangling over the man's forearm.

The man wore black from head to toe. A balaclava underneath his hoodie. Then, piercing out, two bright white eyes.

His balaclava lifted slightly from the upwards motion of his cheekbones as he smiled.

He stopped in the hall to take in the desperate sight of Fiona. His voice was soft. Unthreatening. 'Don't worry. He'll be safe. Like the others.'

He stepped over her and opened the front door.

Fiona willed herself to grab his leg. To call Jack's name. Neither of these things happened.

The man casually exited the house. Fiona caught one last sight of Jack's face. His expression frozen.

In vain, she tried to yell her husband's name – for him to do something. To stop it.

But Maitland couldn't do or say anything. Like Fiona, all he could do was watch as his son was taken away.

CHAPTER THREE

DETECTIVE CHIEF INSPECTOR John Lomond closed his front door behind him, taking in the sight of his tiny dismal flat, before dropping his suit jacket on top of a pile of unopened junk mail and takeaway menus. He hadn't needed the jacket since leaving at half-five that morning. The arms and chest were heavily creased from carrying it scrunched in his hand all day like a cheap bunch of petrol station flowers, taken from car to office to Greggs to office to home again.

He cursed the infernal summer heat. After all, it was Scotland in July. It wasn't as if summer was an actual thing there. Summer was something that only ever happened down south. Any time the news reported heatwaves, showing hoards of beach-goers, sunburnt by lunchtime on English beaches, the BBC would report it as if it was happening everywhere. Meanwhile, it would invariably be tipping it down all across the central belt.

But for once, Glasgow was in the middle of a heatwave that was now in its seventh day.

Like any senior officer who had put in time at many stations through the years, Lomond had acquired a number of nicknames. While at London Road station working for Major Investigations he was known simply as Big Yin – on account of his six-foot-three frame. As well as Lurch and Bigfoot. One of the more literary minded sergeants had christened him the Long Dark – also because of his height, and his often broodingly dark personality. His wife, Eilidh, had often remarked that his inability to make nice chat at work drinks or functions was the main reason he had languished at Chief Inspector level for so long, while much less talented officers than him had climbed the greasy ladder at Police Scotland's Dalmarnock headquarters.

When in the company of fellow police, all Lomond wanted to do was talk about enquires. And no one *ever* talked about enquiries at work functions. They talked about football or TV, or who might be secretly shagging who. Those senior officers in Dalmarnock were there because they had a talent for talking about themselves. Always lobbying. The only lobbying Lomond had ever done was for increasing prison sentences on murderers, rapists, and paedophiles.

Lomond sighed as he entered the living room. 'You little arseholes...'

He had left the windows open all day, and now three serious-looking wasps were having a major scrap in the middle of the room. Getting them out required a feat of coor-dination, for as soon as he had cajoled one of them out by flapping a small cushion, another had come buzzing back in. Getting them all out took up another fifteen minutes of his time, and left him sweating even more than before.

After a cold shower, he returned to the living room wrapped in a towel, refreshed and chilled.

The room was sparsely furnished. Books on forensic science, Scots law, and true crime were piled in loose stacks on the floor.

Judging on furniture alone, a stranger might have surmised that Lomond had just moved in, or was on the cusp of leaving. There was a TV stand in the corner that the previous tenant had left, but Lomond hadn't brought a TV with him. He hadn't had one for years. In the place of a TV was a hi-fi and turntable. Currently playing was The Blue Nile's 'The Downtown Lights'.

He hadn't exactly pushed the boat out when it came to decoration. He was renting rather than paying a mortgage. He might have been earning over sixty grand a year, but his move to Paisley was only supposed to be temporary. It had seemed pointless buying somewhere in 'Scotland's biggest town' – which was another way of saying it was close to being Scotland's smallest city. Resale in Paisley could be a nightmare, and Lomond had no intention of acquiring a financial anchor in Paisley. Renting made more sense.

That was five years ago.

Since then, he had covered the plain magnolia walls with newspaper clippings, police records, witness statements, various maps of Glasgow, and suspect mugshots. At the centre were five young faces. All of them under ten years

old. The youngest was four. Their eyes glowed with innocence. Gap-toothed grins and rosy cheeks. School ties
knotted clumsily and pulled aside for official primary school
photographs.

They had started as the missing.

Then they were the dead.

And, finally, christened by a *Glasgow Express* reporter as
'*THE BONNIE DEAD.*'

The headline had been pinned to the centre of the wall.

For Lomond, those five faces were what it was all
about now.

Justice. The truth.

He changed into jeans and a t-shirt, then he opened up
the hall cupboard which was completely rammed. As soon as
the door opened, a Tetris construction of different-sized
boxes tumbled out towards him. Among them was a collection of flatpack boxes for a baby crib; a pram; a baby play
mat; a slightly used car seat (whose box was the size of a Fiat
500); and the coffin-like Baby Box sent to every new parent
in Scotland containing dozens of essential items and clothes.

Hands on hips, Lomond surveyed the mess. He had put
the job off long enough.

He took the boxes one by one to the living room. With
the boxes arranged next to the sofa, he changed the vinyl
playing to The Beatles' *Abbey Road*, then opened up eBay
on his laptop and set about the laborious task of listing the
items one by one.

Instead of auctions, he chose Buy It Now and selected
prices far below the suggested. He wasn't interested in

maximising profits. He just wanted shot of it all as quickly as possible. They had all followed him from his previous flat in the west end of Glasgow. Some items like the car seat had since been superseded by newer models, but such were the rip-off prices of baby gear, he would still be able to get close to the original cost back – particularly as none of the items had been used.

As George Harrison's twangy guitar opening to 'Something' came on, Lomond found himself thinking of Ernest Hemingway, and the possibly apocryphal tale of his penning a short story that consisted of just six words:

For sale: baby shoes, never worn.

Lomond had said much the same in his eBay listings:

Brand new, never used. No time wasters.

When he was done with the listings, the Beatles album had reached the closing medley, beginning with the plaintive piano of 'Golden Slumbers'. He sat back in the sofa in relief and closed his eyes.

Lomond wasn't the crying kind. But something about how the evening sky looked from his second-floor window – a radiant orange and burnt umber – and the weight of what he had been carrying for five years now, washed over him as fresh as he had felt for a long time.

He had started the process of saying goodbye. Getting rid of the last traces of his expectant fatherhood. And even now, he wasn't sure that he was ready to let go.

There was no time to wallow. The day job might have been over – his current case a tedious investigation into a till operator who had been skimming from a local supermarket –

but he was still a DCI. He wasn't done with work yet. Not by a long shot.

He cleared the living room of the boxes and set about doing what had become his nightly ritual: unloading boxes of evidence and reading. Lots and lots of reading. All of it on the same case. The case that had loomed larger in his career than any other.

The Sandman.

CHAPTER FOUR

THE NAME HAD COME about when it emerged that the killer
was leaving piles of sand on the eyes of his young victims,
and in the beds he had taken them from. The details had
been kept under wraps upon the discovery of the first victim,
Keiran McPhee, who had been snatched from his bed in a
tiny semidetached house in Possilpark in the middle of the
night while his parents attended a house party next door.
They had only left the party when the police appeared after
a complaint about hours of pounding trance music and
reports of arguing and fights in the street outside. When
Keiran's mum checked on him, she found his bed empty and
the covers pulled back. Where her son should have been
sleeping was now a small pile of sand.

The sand had baffled the local CID who investigated the
disappearance. They found Keiran's body five days later,
lying in reeds at the edge of the canal near the Possil Road
aqueduct. Sand covered six-year-old Keiran's eyes.

The hysteria around the killings really started seven months later around the discovery of the second victim, Leanne Donnelly. Lomond and the Major Investigations Team that were working the case had tried desperately to keep the sand part out of the papers. But the dog-walker who had found Leanne's body at dawn in the middle of Paisley's old Racecourse – a field of a dozen football pitches next to the M8 flyover near Glasgow Airport – had spoken to the press, and Lomond couldn't hold back the tide any longer.

The press revelled in the strange detail, which elevated an already tragic serial killing to something almost mythological. What did this killer want? What did it mean?

The children were snatched from their homes – mostly in deprived areas until the third victim, Blair Forbes, who was taken from a comfortable suburban street of expensive villas in Mount Vernon. Then it became clear: no one was safe.

The children were kept alive, but drugged heavily with a paralysing agent. Then five days later, their bodies dumped.

The papers needed a name. A catchy title to hang their speculation on. The *Glasgow Express*'s Colin Mowatt had been first to print with the name after hearing it from a young detective sergeant from the Helen Street station in Govan, where the Major Investigation Team was based.

Mowatt knew that the name would stick. And it did. The *Express* outsold their rivals two to one the day they ran the front-page headline: "*SANDMAN KILLER STRIKES AGAIN.*"

Once the moniker had gained traction, morbid speculation grew to fever pitch after the third victim was found. It was undeniable proof that a serial killer was at large. Two near-identical murders of children between the ages of five and seven, found in the same way: dumped in a public place, with piles of sand on their eyes.

There seemed to be no pattern to when the killer would strike. Sometimes there were months between murders. Or in the case of victims three and four, a year and a half. Regardless, parents weren't willing to take any chances.

Some took it in shifts to stay up all night, watching their children sleep from a chair in the corner of the room, with various weapons for defence sitting by their feet.

The discovery of victims three and four marked the apex of Sandman hysteria. Years later, it was easy to forget how intense it had all been at the time. How scared the public was. For their own children. Their nieces and nephews. Family friends. Neighbours.

Despite the commonality of victims being taken from their beds, the terror of abduction carried over into the daytime.

Any instance of a lone child spotted walking the streets, people watched over them from their living room windows, waiting for any sign that someone might be coming for them. It led to a rash of strangers approaching children, offering them company home to keep them safe. One man had ended up beaten to a pulp after word spread around an estate that he'd attempted to drag a child into his car. It later emerged that he was simply the child's parent who had been attempting to control an unruly eight-year-old who had been refusing to get into the car for a dentist appointment.

There were similar stories across the city.

On buses and trains and the subway, it was all people talked about and read about, and wrote about on social media.

One paper christened it "Sandmania". Any child under ten who went missing and wasn't found within hours was instantly feared to be the next victim, regardless of whether there were any traits of a Sandman abduction. Parents of the missing resigned themselves to fate by as early as day two, hope abandoned, awaiting the inevitable discovery of a body come day five. The pattern grimly familiar and predictable.

Yet, despite the safeguards – the massive police presence scouring the streets at night for lone males, residents locking their windows and installing motion detector alarms, still more victims fell.

Colin Mowatt was the first major reporter to publicly criticise the police investigation. What had started as full support and cooperation from the public soon shifted when third victim Blair Forbes was found in a tenement back garden next to the rubbish bins.

Constables faced outright hostility on their beat. The public's ire directed at the uniform cops who were there to keep them safe. Doing the thankless, working around the clock, for little fanfare. The days between the abduction and the discovery of the body were the worst. Shouts would ring out on a crowded Sauchiehall Street:

'The Sandman's no' here! Forget about shoplifters and go find that missing wean...'

There always seemed to be some blow-up or confrontation over what was happening. When tragedy now seemed a lot more like incompetence. Which wasn't helped by certain officers leaking unintentionally misleading information that had been passed from station to station, until the whispers turned the truth inside out. Rumours spread through communities about anyone who didn't fit in. Who kept to themselves. Who just didn't seem 'right'.

By the time victim four, Mark Whitehouse, was found, the word had come down from Mordor – aka Police Scotland headquarters in Dalmarnock – that the case was to be controlled from there. Lomond would be the face of things at Major Investigations, but Dalmarnock was running the show now.

Lomond took the blame for the lack of transparency with his own team, having to lock them out of certain details to stop any further leaks. Which only alienated him further from his team, who gossiped that Lomond had purposely shut them out as a means of glory-hunting and beefing up his public persona. Which couldn't have been further from the truth.

It was impossible to run an investigation under such conditions. Dalmarnock seemed more concerned about bad PR than another dead child. It was no longer just a murder case. It was damage control for the police's image. Every year brought the same media circus. And Lomond had become the face of it, reduced to a mouthpiece for his superiors.

Until the night that everything changed for Lomond.

Five years ago.

A night he would never forget, and after which nothing could ever be the same again.

CHAPTER FIVE

He kept a column of faces and names of possible suspects that covered the living room wall almost from floor to ceiling. Night after night, he carried out deep dives on every single one. Refusing to move on and place them in the column of cleared suspects until he was satisfied beyond all doubt that they were innocent.

He had prison records for every suspect that fit the profile of their killer. Crimes against children. Paedophilia. No suspects whose crimes had involved random spontaneous violence. That wasn't their guy. The Sandman didn't do spontaneous or lack of control. Lomond had never encountered a more disciplined killer in his career. Few had.

One name at a time, Lomond cross-referenced against his old suspect list. Every name that ever came up in anonymous phone tips, or was ever mentioned in a witness statement in door-to-doors. Absolutely no one was ruled out unless it was certain.

By year three, Lomond had a list of three hundred and twelve names that had all been ruled out. Now he was going back through them all from the start. He was sure of it: somewhere, someone had messed up. Missed something. A killer like the Sandman must have thrown up a red flag to someone through the years. Normal people kill all the time. But they never did it quite like the Sandman.

Sometimes it took hours, sometimes days or weeks, to clear a name. He did it all in his spare time, now that the Sandman case had been passed on to another DCI. As far as they were concerned, the case was colder than the River Clyde on a winter morning.

Like the city at large, by the third year of no murders, the police thought it might be all over.

It was in Glasgow's nature to move on. People forgot how scared they had once been. Children grew up, getting too old to be likely victims. Memories fade. Like when terror attacks happened. There was blanket coverage for a week, then when the headlines stop and something bigger or more urgent takes over, people forget.

But not John Lomond. He couldn't forget those faces. What those children had looked like in person at the crime scenes.

That awful sand piled over their eyes. Covering where such beauty and innocence had once glowed.

The fourth year without any further murders brought speculation that maybe the killer had died, or been imprisoned for some other crime. No longer free to continue their twisted, demonic 'work'.

Life returned to normal. Parents slept in their own beds again. Playgrounds were full. Children roamed freely with balls and bikes, fearing nothing and no one. The Sandman was something horrible that had happened to other children, and now he was gone.

By the third true crime book on the subject, public appetite for Sandman material waned. Everyone wanted to move on.

John Lomond didn't have that luxury. What he had were failed promises to grieving parents. Promises to find the bastard who had killed their children and lock him away forever. To make sure that no one else ever suffered the cruel fate of those five bonnie kids. When everyone else could look away from the horror, he stuck with it. Because it was in his nature. His programming. That he couldn't turn away and move on.

Lomond's superiors and the senior officers still dipping their toes into the cold cases of the Sandman killings, thought it was over because they wanted it to be. It was more comfortable for them to believe that. They wanted to live in a world where people like the Sandman didn't exist.

But Lomond knew that a killer like that couldn't just stop.

It wasn't over.

LOMOND COUNTED down the time to midnight, the same way he always did: in quiet contemplation, with a healthy dram in his hand, standing in front of the wall of evidence that dominated the living room.

He checked his watch again. Nearly there. Nearly another day safely gone. That was the only consolation, that at least no other child had died at the Sandman's hands.

It was still impossibly hot for the late hour. Lomond wiped away a layer of sweat on his upper lip before taking another sip of whisky. He ran his hand over his completely shaved head. At the first slight sign of thinning hair at age thirty-two, he'd gone to town on his scalp with a number one clipper blade. A cut that he performed weekly. It made him look older than his forty-three years, but appearances were not terribly important to him – although he had noted with concern his growing paunch, how much noise he made getting up off the sofa, and the alarming rate at which his nose hair was growing.

He had on a live version of 'Summertime' by Ella Fitzgerald on YouTube, recorded in Berlin in 1968. Gone was the studio version's familiar hazy mood and lush strings, replaced by a brooding jazz quartet that played the song at half speed. Rather than the studio version's romanticism, Ella's voice was now that of love lost for good. The perfect soundtrack to a heatwave at night.

Lomond had heard it dozens of times, but it still found ways to surprise him. Every note meant something to Ella, deep in her bones. The cameras showed Ella dabbing sweat gently from her neck, crooning softly before launching into a sudden change of pitch, a stunning vibrato that appeared like a bolt of lightning that was so powerful it made the pianist behind her visibly jump on his stool. The moment gave Lomond goosebumps.

He went to the window, looking down on the street. A lone ned stalked along, buzzing from the bottle of Buckie in his hand, still shirtless from earlier in the day. His back and shoulders were scorched neon pink with sunburn. At each passing car, he unleashed a volley of abuse. About what was unclear. It was no mystery to Lomond how someone could be so angry at everything. He had encountered so many lives that had been chaotic from birth, all that mattered to them as young adults was getting as wasted as often as possible. They had seen and heard things by primary school age that most adults couldn't even imagine. Years on the streets had taught Lomond to always see the core of who they would have been as children. No one was born bad, were they? What always stumped Lomond, though, was the Sandman. How could someone become so evil? What made a person want to do those things to children? What explained that? What explained *evil*?

He checked the time again...

Only another three minutes had gone.

It was so close to another day without incident.

He woke up his phone to check his messages. What friends he had at Helen Street promised to keep him in the loop if any murders had been called in for the division. They owed him that much at least. To keep him informed.

At two minutes to midnight Lomond turned the music off. He took a seat on the sofa, watching time tick by on his phone.

He even allowed himself the thought that everyone else was right. The Sandman was gone for good. He might not have been caught. He might have got away with it. But bad people got away with terrible things all the time. Lomond knew that all too well.

He also had instincts. And instinct told him five years ago that the Sandman wouldn't stop. Not until he was caught. They weren't satisfying some wild bloodlust. It meant far more to them than that. Which meant that they wouldn't stop without a reason.

Lomond's phone screen lit up. The ringtone cut through the silence of the room, giving his heart rate a jolt.

The ID said "Linda Boyle".

Detective Superintendent Linda Boyle.

Lomond held the phone out, dreading what she would have to say. He no longer worked under Boyle, so any call at such a time could only be bad news.

He answered, 'Linda?'

There was a pause.

As soon as he realised she was outside somewhere, he knew what had happened.

She said, 'You were right. It's happening again.'

CHAPTER SIX

LOMOND WAS in his car ten minutes later, ripping up the short drive from Paisley on the M8 to the Clyde Tunnel, then across the west end to the leafy streets of Dowanhill. He felt strange being back there. He had tried to avoid the area whenever necessary, reminding him of a time in his life that had long since passed.

Finding the Ferguson residence among the winding, rolling streets didn't take long. It was in Kensington Gate, among an S-shaped terrace of red sandstone houses, which were currently illuminated by blue flashing lights from multiple parked police cars. An hour earlier there had also been the lights of two ambulances that had since sped away to the Queen Elizabeth Hospital, carrying Maitland and Fiona Ferguson, who were both paralysed and incapable of speech.

Most of the neighbouring windows were occupied with residents who had been woken by the sirens and lights. It was the biggest event to happen there since the pre-summer clean-up in the communal garden. The contents of Kensington Gate homes might have appealed to burglars, but their one way in/one way out main front doors did not. The residents' WhatsApp group was lighting up with messages every minute as fears grew for little Jack Ferguson: his parents had been spotted on stretchers, but there had been no sign of the child anywhere.

Constables and detectives were canvassing the neighbours, but so far no one had seen anything: everyone had been in bed, or watching TV. There had been no audible disturbances, crashes, or bangs. Nothing suspicious at all.

Lomond showed his ID lanyard and gave a purse of his lips to the constable dutifully guarding the cordon at the end of the Ferguson's front garden. The constable recognised Lomond's face but couldn't quite place him or his name. He knew that he'd heard it around the station, though.

While Lomond inspected the soil in the front garden, he asked the constable, 'Superintendent Boyle?'

The constable leaned back to see towards the hallway, through the open front door, around which several large moths were buzzing around the white exterior security light. 'Last I saw she was downstairs, sir.'

Without a word, Lomond handed him a bottle of water. He had spent many lonely nights on cordons in his career, and knew that a little professional courtesy went a long way for a constable on a hot night in uniform. DCIs and DSs got all the glory and the press, but constables did all the really hard work, pounding the pavement, out on response, kicking in doors, and a tonne of specialisms that often left them better qualified for certain roles than the officers in charge of them.

Once Lomond was inside, a young detective sergeant who had been trying to listen in from a few doors down approached the constable.

He flicked his chin up. 'What does he want?'

The constable shrugged innocently. 'He said he wanted the super.'

'You know who he is, right?' the sergeant asked, desperate to show off his insider knowledge – to show that he was important enough to know gossip about a chief inspector.

The constable had met a few junior detectives like him already in his brief career. They were as much in love with the idea of poncing about looking important in plain clothes as they were getting the job done.

The constable let the sergeant go through his little routine anyway. 'I've never seen him.'

'God, you *are* new,' said the sergeant. 'That's John Lomond.'

'Yeah, I did actually look at the badge he showed me.'

'The badge doesn't tell you he ran the Sandman case. For a while.'

'Why was he taken off?'

'I never found out. The press had been caning their arse for close to five years already. They used to say Lomond was on his way to Linda Boyle's position now. Had to take six months leave, and when he came back he was sent to Mill Street. Couldn't hack it in the city anymore.'

The constable looked clueless. 'Mill Street?'

'The main station in Paisley,' the sergeant said. 'Massive grey seventies monstrosity. Looks like something out of East Germany.'

'Is going to Mill Street really that bad?'

'After heading up Glasgow MIT, that's like going from number nine at Real Madrid to sub goalie at Cowdenbeath.'

The constable considered this, then pushed out his lips. 'Don't really follow football.'

Dissatisfied at the response, the sergeant set off towards the next door to chap.

Lomond set off through the front garden, observing two senior officers in the hallway. The woman was Detective Superintendent Linda Boyle. The male, who was making a hasty exit at the sight of the approaching Lomond, was Chief Superintendent Alasdair Reekie of G Division, Greater Glasgow.

Like most senior officers, Reekie had a nickname he knew nothing about, passed about from station to station. It started the same way it had for Reekie in primary school. Even a small child's limited vocabulary could get them to 'reek' from Reekie. Then from reek to smell. From smell to shit. Then from shit to shithead. Not exactly Oscar Wilde, but as far as accuracy went, it was spot-on. And what had been good enough in the playground to taunt a short, bespectacled Reekie was more than good enough for the constables and sergeants of Police Scotland that Reekie had pissed off –

and there were plenty of them. In another life, Reekie might have been a bishop in the church. The sort who loved nothing more than putting on the fancy purple robe and the jewellery and ornaments.

As Reekie passed Lomond on the concrete slabs, he said simply, and without eye contact, 'John.'

Lomond had to remind himself not to say, 'Arsehole.'

Shithead. Arsehole. Or sometimes the Grand Arsehole. When it came to Reekie, imagination wasn't as important as capturing the sheer contempt that everyone on the force had for him. And sometimes the simplest was the best.

Lomond said, 'Sir.' He looked over his shoulder, and noted Reekie going out of his way to greet a young detective sergeant – the same one who had gossiped with the constable at the cordon.

Boyle greeted Lomond at the front door, and said to him with typical sarcasm, 'You took your time. What, were you parked around the corner?'

He replied, 'The motorway wasn't exactly busy.' He motioned at Reekie driving off in his Porsche 4x4. 'What's The Grand Arsehole doing here?'

'He's shitting it, isn't he. That it's starting again on his watch.'

'He seemed pleased to see me. He didn't plunge a knife into my back or anything, so I must be on the up-and-up. What have we got?'

So far, all he knew was that a boy aged five had been abducted from his home, and the parents had been rushed to hospital.

Boyle said, 'Same as the others. Mostly. Home invasion. It looks like the boy was snatched from his bed.'

'Sand?'

'In the bed.'

'Shit. Why do you say "mostly" the same?'

'The parents were found passed out on the floor. They'd been drugged.'

'That's different. I mean, we know the children in the past were drugged, but never anything with the parents.'

'They're still KO'd. Only faint feeling in their limbs and neither of them can talk. The doctors say it's some kind of paralysis agent.'

Lomond squinted. 'Why the parents?' he wondered aloud. 'Why something new?'

Boyle said, 'You don't need me to tell you that this might not be our guy. But I wanted your opinion anyway. I don't want to take any chances.'

'So he drugs them to get to the kid...' Lomond said to himself. 'How did he manage to drug the pair of them? Our guy doesn't do physical confrontation. Now he's taking on two adults in a house he's unfamiliar with?'

'That's not all,' said Boyle. 'He didn't fully knock them out.'

'What do you mean?'

Boyle indicated the constable watching the cordon outside, the first officer at the scene. 'The FOS said that the parents were wide awake, but they couldn't move or speak. Totally paralysed from the neck down. The doctor reckons they might have been conscious through the whole thing.'

Lomond wondered aloud, 'If drugging is purely to make taking the kid easier, why not knock them out altogether? Better yet, why not just hit them over the head with something? Faffing around with needles?'

Boyle waited for him to complete his thought.

'This one wasn't just about taking the kid,' he said. 'He wanted them to see the kid being taken. It was about making the parents feel powerless.' He shook his head, trying to see past the details that confirmed what he was already thinking. He clicked his tongue rapidly, assessing the totality of what they were looking at. 'We've never seen any evidence that our guy cares about that.'

'Go on,' said Boyle.

'It's a change in pattern.'

'I know how much they drive you crazy.'

The corner of Lomond's mouth turned up slightly in appreciation. Quoting one of his mentors, he said, 'Changes can't be ignored because they're inconvenient to your theory. And this drugging is definitely inconvenient.'

BOYLE LED the way to the kitchen at the rear of the property, pointing out a door still locked from the inside. 'I'll tell you what else is inconvenient. The kidnapper was already in the house when the alarm was tripped. Both external doors, front and back, were locked.'

Lomond said, 'No sign of tampering.'

'The alarm company said Maitland Ferguson entered his

pin at quarter past eight tonight. The alarm was tripped at ten forty-two at the front door. The suspect used the key and walked straight out the front door with the kid then locked the door behind him.'

Lomond nodded slowly. The break in conversation allowed him to take in as much of the plush surroundings as possible as they returned to the hall. He undid the top button of his shirt and loosened his tie a shade. *How can it possibly still be so hot this late at night?* he thought. He said, 'He was calm. Didn't panic and break the door down. Took the time to find the house keys.' Lomond was distracted as the detective sergeant from outside called out from the garden path.

'It's not him. He doesn't do risk or complication. His snatches are clean, out of sight. He doesn't take the time required to research a job, a family, like this. And he doesn't take the risks necessary to pull something like this off. It feels too...' He searched for the right word. '*Personal.*'

He swaggered over, dripping with attitude. Everything about him said *I reckon I'm destined for big things.* He was on the short side – tall enough not to worry about height restrictions at fairgrounds, but nowhere near troubling six foot – and was wearing a matching tweed waistcoat and trousers, having discarded the jacket on account of the heat. His white shirt was a size too small for him to accentuate his physique (though he wasn't nearly as muscly as he thought), and his hair was pushed back and long on top, and shaved at the sides into a classic undercut. Lomond wasn't sure if he was looking at polis, or someone about to go clubbing with the lads.

Boyle introduced him. 'John, this is DS Ross McNair. Ross, John Lomond. Paisley CID.'

Lomond smirked. He'd met plenty like DS McNair in his time. Under ten years in and thought they knew it all. 'Ho, Peaky Blinders. You got a license for that swagger?' he asked.

Boyle stifled a laugh.

His air of superiority punctured, McNair produced an evidence bag containing a mobile phone. 'The paramedics found this on the bedroom floor.'

Lomond switched it on pressing the side buttons through the bag. 'How did we get the call in the first place?'

Boyle answered, 'The alarm company got an auto response when the front door was tripped.'

Lomond pondered the numerous sensors hooked up wirelessly around the property.

'What is it?'

Lomond said, 'It's pretty serious security, even for a west end pad.'

'Allow me,' said Ross, taking the phone from Lomond. He opened the alarm app, bringing up camera footage from the front door. 'Watch this.'

It showed a hooded figure, unmistakably male, carrying a small body out the front door through the garden.

'I suppose it's too much to ask for any images of a car or a van driving away?' asked Lomond.

'Yep,' Ross said. 'Far too much. He just walks out of view

to the left. There's an alley around the side under some trees. He probably parked there. It's only used for bin collection lorries. The residents park at the front.' He tapped out of the app and opened the messages. 'I was wondering if you think that maybe this warrants further investigation.' He held the screen up to Lomond, showing the last message received.

"you're about to enter a nightmare unlike anything you've ever experienced...Just remember, you could have stopped this..."

Lomond pointed at the sender's phone number. 'Who is this delightful ray of sunshine?'

Ross replied, 'It's a burner, so it's going to take some time. We're working on it.'

'What about the neighbours?'

'No one saw or heard anything unusual.'

'What about–'

'No one suspicious seen walking around in the last week. I've spoken to all twenty-four households with eyes on the front door.'

Surprised and impressed, Boyle said, 'You've spoken to twenty-four already?'

Ross said, 'Yeah, I mean...first hours are crucial, right?'

Lomond kept wandering the property, looking for the one detail that didn't look right. 'Detective work's a marathon, not a sprint, Ross. You race through witnesses that fast, you might miss something.'

Not appreciating the unsolicited guidance and showing the first signs of irritation, Ross turned to Boyle. 'Sorry, am I missing something? Shouldn't DCI Sutherland be hearing this too? Because, with respect,' he gestured to Lomond, 'this is a Glasgow MIT job, not Paisley CID.'

If Lomond's closest pal on the force, and a senior officer, hadn't been standing there, he might have considered laying the cheeky bastard out. Being on friendly terms with the CSU had given the young DS an inflated sense of where he was on the ladder of Police Scotland's rank.

Boyle said, 'John's giving us some perspective on what we're dealing with.'

Ross replied, 'I can help you with your perspective, DCI Lomond. It's not your serial. I don't care about that pile of sand in the bed.'

'Are there any other facts you'd like to ignore?' Lomond asked.

'I'm not ignoring them. I'm disqualifying them. There's a difference. I think someone's gone to lengths to make us *think* this is the Sandman.'

'You think the mystery woman on the phone is behind it?'

'Using publicly available details about a serial killer is a good way of hiding your work.'

Boyle deferred to Lomond.

'It's possible,' Lomond conceded.

Ross added, 'I know a lot of this isn't the Sandman's style, so we also can't discount the possibility of a copycat.'

Lomond's body language did a good job of displaying exactly what he thought of Ross's idea. 'Someone who goes to the trouble required to make this sort of scene isn't interested in being a copycat. This person's got something to say.

And we should listen. Even if that might be uncomfortable for you, Detective Sergeant. But even if this isn't him, our chances of finding little Jack alive after the first week drop to about seven per cent. Seventy-five per cent of abducted children are murdered within three hours of abduction.' Lomond checked his watch then held it up to Ross. 'We're currently fifteen minutes out from three hours.'

CHAPTER SEVEN

To EMPHASISE THE URGENCY, Boyle said, 'We've got until dawn to build something promising before the media descends on us. We need something. Anything. An eyewitness. A car plate. CCTV. Dashcam footage. Something we can investigate and chase down.'

Lomond looked out to the street with concern, as a souped-up Ford Focus rumbled into the parking space vacated by CSU Reekie. 'Oh, for–'

Boyle craned her neck to see who it was. 'Who is that?'

Lomond puffed. 'Colin bloody Mowatt.'

'How the hell are the press getting wind of this already?' asked Ross.

Boyle gestured at the abundance of windows snaking around the street, all with a clear view of the police presence. 'We're not exactly running incognito here.'

Lomond warned, 'If Mowatt's here, he knows something bigger than an average burglary is up.'

Boyle called to the constable by the cordon. 'Get rid of him.'

A baby-faced thirty-year-old man with floppy red hair and bright freckles dashed around the front of his car, and threw his hands up in the air in defeat. 'Oh, come on! I'm a good half hour ahead of the pack on this one.' Getting as close as he could to the cordon, he called out, 'John! Is it happening again? Is he back?'

Lomond wouldn't even look at the bastard. 'Ah, it's Ron Weasley. I see you never bothered your arse to use that gift voucher I got you for Dignitas. Shame, that.'

He took out his notepad. 'Can the *Glasgow Express* quote you on that?'

Lomond was held back by Linda, and, out of professional loyalty, Ross.

Lomond started to wriggle out of his suit jacket. He seethed, 'You can quote me on *this*, Christopher fucking Robin–' He made a sudden move towards Mowatt.

Boyle and Ross wrestled him away, while two other constables ran over to keep Mowatt back.

'Let's not do that,' Boyle warned Lomond, leading him back into the house.

'Prick,' he spat, his blood still up.

Boyle told Ross, 'Get onto Dalmarnock about that phone. Maitland Ferguson could be under for another six hours, and we need to know who he was messaging earlier.'

As Ross disappeared into the back of the house, phone clamped to his ear, Lomond managed to calm down. 'What's his story?'

'DS McNair?'

'Hang on. Let me guess.' It only took him a moment. 'Took the sergeant exam as soon as he could. Now he's working towards Organised Crime.'

Boyle was taken aback. 'How did you know?'

'That's where all the young guys want to go. All that glamour and swaggering around Dalmarnock in their tight t-shirts. They're worse than Anti-Terror. One psycho sets himself on fire at Glasgow Airport, and they spend the next ten years walking about the city carrying M5 submachine guns like they're the last line of defence. Organised Crime are even worse. I tell you, *Line of Duty*'s gone straight to these boys' heads.'

'Don't underestimate him, John,' said Boyle. 'He's one of the best I've got.'

'And he's pals with Reekie, eh? Not bad having the Greater Glasgow CSU in your back pocket.'

'Trust me,' said Boyle, 'Ross has earned his spot.' She lowered her voice conspiratorially. 'Word is, before he applied for the entrance test, Reekie was in his ear about direct entry as an inspector.'

'That scheme's minging. You can't do the job without coming up through all the shit.'

'Hey, you don't have to convince me.'

For an instant, the pair had flashes of the worst that they had seen in the force down the years. For DSU Boyle, the stuff that really lingered – that really haunted her – wasn't the murder investigations or random acts of violence. It was callouts to terrified pensioners living in rough schemes surrounded by grade-A psychos. Or the dreaded callouts to an unexplained smell and finding a six-month-old dead body. It wasn't the ones with gore and pools of blood. It was the small, tragic human stories behind a teenage runaway, or a parent's suicide. Without seeing all that stuff, as far as Boyle and Lomond were concerned, you could never truly understand what the officers below you are going through.

Boyle went on, 'But Ross wouldn't have it. He went through his entrance exam, detective training programme, his accreditation for all his core competencies. He's a worker.'

Lomond turned towards the front door where there had been a knock.

'Evening, Linda,' said the Crime Scene Manager, reluctantly buttoning up his white forensic suit. It had all the breathability of a medical-waste bin liner. In such heat, Scene of Crime officers had a true understanding of the fate of boil-in-the-bag rice.

There were four SOCOs carrying metal cases and dressed in their full whites standing behind him.

The sight of their white suits always prompted a Pavlovian sense of fear in Lomond, as the severity of what they were facing came starkly into focus.

'Evening, Terry,' said Boyle, gesturing towards the stairs. 'It's up here.'

'What have we got?'

'Not very much that I can see, at least.'

Lomond followed them all upstairs towards little Jack's

bedroom. With the mum and dad out of commission, the room had been perfectly preserved since the abduction.

Forensics set up their gear according to Boyle's direction, while Lomond held back at the bedroom doorway, taking in the scene.

It had been lushly decorated, no expense spared. The two exposed walls were covered with large murals of rainbows streaming over a cute woodland scene, as well as a clear patch of white wall where Jack's height was being marked every few months. Lomond kept his eyes fixed on the most recent line. How the hell could someone hurt anyone as small as that, he thought. Even after all this time on the force, he found himself searching for answers even though he knew that there weren't any.

On top of a pristine white chest of drawers was a row of cuddly toys, their oversized eyes blank and innocent to the nightmare that had taken place earlier. Jack's old paintings from nursery were hung on the wall, etched with his crude signature. It was a room that told you Jack was well loved and nurtured.

Lomond got a sudden vision of his wife dressed in paint-stained denim dungarees, singing to the radio as she rolled light-mint paint across the wall of the spare room in their old Broomhill flat – at least, what they had always called the spare room, but had since changed to the 'baby's room'. In slow motion, Lomond saw his wife turn around, pausing in profile which highlighted the roundness of her pregnant bump at seven months in. She smiled at him. *'What is it?'*

Lomond paused for a moment. '*Nothing. It's just...I didn't know I could love someone as much as I love you.*'

Her smile widened, and she turned up the volume of the radio and started singing as she danced her way gingerly across the room to him. When she reached him, she dropped paint onto the end of his nose then kissed him.

'*This is going to be the cutest baby room ever,*' she had told him.

Coming back to the scene in front of him, Lomond thought that his wife would have approved of the decor. The personal touches. The warmth on display.

All that was missing was the child.

The only hint of something wrong was in the bedspread: the duvet peeled back like the corner of a book page, where Jack had been hoisted out. A handful of sand sitting on the mattress. Lomond got a chill whenever he looked at it.

He retreated to the parents' bedroom, which showed a similar lack of a struggle. He crouched to inspect the carpet, which was scuffed underneath the edge of the bed. Putting on his shoe covers, he came closer to the bed, observing thick drag marks in the carpet pile, from knees or feet.

He called out to one of the SOC officers who was taking prints from door handles for elimination. Lomond pointed to the carpet. 'Can we get a sample of this, please?'

The officer stopped what he was doing. 'The carpet?'

Lomond looked at the scuff marks again, getting a sense of how it would have gone down based on what Boyle had told him. 'They were in the house for hours. Hiding under here.' He did a quick three-sixty of the room. 'There was nowhere else to go. They would already have been wearing the hoodie. The central heating thermostat says the temperature in the bedroom didn't go below twenty-four all night. It would have been stifling under the bed in all that gear for that length of that time. That means sweat. Maybe a hair sample.'

The SOC officer flashed his considerable eyebrows up at the scale of what Lomond was asking. 'How much do you want me to take?'

Casually, he said, 'There's no way of knowing exactly where they were lying, so take it all.'

The officer paused. 'That's a kingsize bed.'

'What's your point?'

'Do you have any idea how long that's going to take to analyse?'

Lomond got to his feet. 'I don't have a bloody clue, and I don't really care.' On his way past the officer, he told him, 'Cut it and bag it.'

Boyle was waiting for him in the hallway. 'What do you think?'

Lomond rubbed at his stubble. It was time to make a call. 'I think it's him. I think he's back. But it's different this time. He's changed.' He turned to face her head-on. 'I want to be lead on this, Linda.'

She seemed to flinch at the suggestion. 'Reekie wants Sutherland for it. He says you bring too much baggage with you.'

'Sutherland? He cuts more corners than a Black and Decker, and Reekie knows it. Come on, Linda. You know

I'm the best chance Jack Ferguson has. And if the Sandman has lifted his head for the first time in five years, then we owe it to the parents of Keiran McPhee, Leanne Donnelly, Blair Forbes, Mark Whitehouse, and Taylor Clark to catch this guy once and for all.'

Her defences slipping, Boyle said, 'Let me deal with Dalmarnock and Reekie. But I can't promise anything.'

DS McNair appeared at the foot of the stairs, holding his phone up. 'Ma'am, that was the consultant at the QE. Maitland Ferguson just woke up. He's able to speak.'

All Boyle had to do was look at Lomond.

He told McNair, 'Tell them we're on our way.'

'We're?' asked McNair.

'Yeah. You're coming with me. If Linda can spare your towering intellect.'

Boyle said, 'Like a tree misses Dutch elm.' She paused. 'Fine. But Ross?'

He hung back excitedly in the main doorway. 'Ma'am.'

'I don't care if you're taking statements from the centre of the fucking sun. Put your jacket on.'

Once Ross had set off towards his car, Boyle asked Lomond, 'You're sure you want him?'

'Yeah,' he answered.

'Why?'

'Because he knocked on twenty-four doors. He might look like he's been booted through the clearance aisle of H&M, but he wants the right thing: to get Jack Ferguson home to his parents.'

CHAPTER EIGHT

THE DRIVE from the west end to the Queen Elizabeth University Hospital on the edge of Govan was just a quick blast along Great Western Road through Anniesland and the Clyde Tunnel. During the day, it was one of the busiest sections of road in the city. This late at night, only the odd taxi and Deliveroo rider provided any company to the two detectives.

Lomond could feel DS McNair assessing the inside of his terribly average saloon car. There wasn't much to hang a judgement on. The inside was spotlessly clean, leaving no clues as to what Lomond was like. No giveaway sweetie wrappers or crisp packets. No fag packets or ash. No forgotten paperwork or police kit or Personal Protective Equipment. Which, in itself, told Ross a *little* something about Lomond.

Worse still, Lomond could sense Ross about to make conversation.

'I didn't mean to step on your toes back there,' Ross said.

'It takes a lot to make me cry, Ross,' Lomond replied. 'If you've upset me, you'll know it.'

'Do you really think he's come back?'

'The only things I know for certain in life, Ross, is that Billy Connolly is the funniest man who's ever lived, and Partick Thistle will never win the Champions league. Beyond that, it's pretty much all up in the air.'

'One thing I always wondered about the Sandman case... why the sand?'

'In Scandinavian folklore, the Sandman sprinkled sand into the eyes of sleeping children to bring on sleep and dreams. The act is too calculated – too specific – to be the work of some bog-standard paedophile or psycho snatching a kid at a bus stop. I expect there's religious background in their childhood, but somewhere along the way it got badly skewed. Some propensity to see meaning in a life, a world, beyond this one. The world of dreams. Somewhere far removed from our reality.'

Trying his best to pretend that he understood a half of what Lomond was talking about, Ross nodded. 'Yeah, I mean...I guess that makes sense.'

'Why he keeps them alive for five days is anyone's guess. Probably keeps them drugged so that they're docile. Compliant. He wants to enjoy his time with them. It's a meditative thing for him. Five days is about the limit he can risk keeping them somewhere without getting caught. It's about ritual. Iconography. The lack of sexual or physical abuse in the victims, and the deliberate, careful placing of the bodies, suggests that the killer doesn't see himself harming the children. He thinks he's liberating them.'

'From what?' asked Ross.

Lomond gestured at the rapidly passing landscape of semi-detached houses, takeaway food joints, and hairdressers. 'All this. Life. Regular existence. Don't you ever wonder, why did we choose this? Cities. Buildings. Roads. We used to live in forests. In the hills. On crofts. Work the land.'

'We also used to club each other over the head for food.'

'Then what changed?' asked Lomond. 'Why is this better for us? Our killer doesn't want any part of this. He wants to transcend it. The act of abduction and murder is his way of removing himself from the herd.'

'By killing kids?' Ross said, clearly unconvinced.

'It's all speculation, of course, but I've put in the time. Done the reading. It didn't make me any happier about the world, but it's important to understand what human kind is capable of. If you know that, then you can understand where a killer comes from.'

'And where does the Sandman come from?'

'I would expect there's something deep lodged in their childhood. Something changed them at a crucial stage. Changed how they saw the world. Turned it into a place that was cruel. Ruled by bad people.'

'It sounds like a great theory, sir, but whatever happened to crazy? You don't think the guy's just crazy?'

'It's a mistake to dismiss his methods as crazy.' Lomond

kept his eyes on the empty road. 'He might be evil. But he's not crazy.'

In the pause that followed, Lomond counted down in his head from five. When he reached one, Ross said, 'It must have been rough trying to find someone like that.'

'Show me a murder enquiry that's easy and I'll show you a unicorn that farts rainbows. But at this time of night and at the speed I'm driving, we're about five minutes from the QE. We can do *This Is Your Life* another time, alright.'

'*This Is Your Life?*'

Lomond rolled his eyes. 'It was a TV show. Michael Aspel. He'd go through this big red book filled with stuff about your past, and they brought out all these people from—' He could see Ross's eyes glazing over. 'It doesn't matter.'

'I was surprised you asked the Det Sup to bring me along. I kind of got the impression that we weren't on the same page back there.'

'We're not.'

Ross gave a snort of disdain. 'Then why bring me along for this?'

'Because you chapped on twenty-four doors tonight instead of leaving it up to uniform. If we're going to find Jack Ferguson alive, I need hard workers like you.'

Ross wished that Lomond hadn't felt it necessary to add the 'alive' part. But it had the intended effect of reminding Ross of what was at stake.

Lomond went on, 'A lot of young detectives think cases are solved by deep creative thought, or brooding in dark rooms with a bottle of whisky. They're about teamwork, talking to as many people as you can, putting in the hours. And chapping doors.'

Lomond slowed as their run of straight green lights came to an end and they approached the vertigo-inducing, MC Escher of crossroads: Anniesland Cross. Even lifetime locals could end up looking like lost foreigners navigating the spaghetti overlap of merging lanes and filter lights. As your brain desperately tried to make sense of the chaos, you could almost hear Glasgow City Council cackling somewhere nearby, 'Aye, good luck dealing with *this*, ya bastards.'

Ross said, 'Barely five per cent of applicants make it into the ranks. I've been proving people wrong my whole life, Detective Chief Inspector. I'll happily add you to my list.'

Lomond kept his eyes impatiently on the red light ahead, his foot purring the engine. Silently impressed by the way Ross had stuck up for himself, he conceded, 'You did okay with the phone. You deserve a chance to follow up on it.'

Lomond hit the accelerator the moment the light changed. He made short work of the Crow Road dual carriageway, then gunned it into the Clyde Tunnel, paying little attention to the thirty miles an hour speed limit. He was in a hurry to get on with the job – but not to see the hospital grounds again.

He had hoped to have seen the last of them five years ago.

———

THE QUEEN ELIZABETH UNIVERSITY HOSPITAL was built

on the site of the old Southern General, and had been nick-named the "Death Star" by locals for its imposing fourteen-storey design, which was topped by an enormous aircraft landing pad, where emergency helicopters shuttled back and forth day and night. Though the interconnectedness between the various wards and buildings might have seemed clever in an architect's office, it left many who visited there baffled as to what building they were even standing in.

Maitland and Fiona Ferguson had been rushed to Accident and Emergency at the rear of the adult hospital, next to the separate Maternity unit – the one place Lomond didn't want to be anywhere near.

Being not long after midnight, A&E was still dealing with the backlog from its peak hours, but the two detectives didn't have to face the ignominy of the A&E car park, where drivers puttered around for ages waiting for the miracle of a space appearing. Plenty of drivers had given up altogether, simply abandoning their vehicles across any free open stretch of pavement.

Lomond parked across from idling ambulances, their rear doors hanging open, the insides being cleaned out from whatever tragedy or mess had befallen the poor sod who'd been lying in there. Paramedics wandered aimlessly under the pillared awning, their green overalls flapping open, trying to create some cool air while they refuelled with the sort of packaged pre-made food you buy at a motorway service station when you're short on options. They wore the looks of people who could no longer be shocked by anything.

They were, after all, used to working Friday nights and weekends in Glasgow.

Fragments of human interest were dotted around the place. Relatives of the sick or injured. The injured themselves, clutching homemade bandages and crudely built tourniquets, taking to the outdoors in search of respite from the heat inside – the air conditioning in the waiting room had burned out hours ago. Two hours in to their waiting times, most of them would still have another two hours to go before even seeing a nurse or a doctor. So notorious were the waiting times, many locals, if they injured themselves between seven and midnight, would resist their family's urging to get to A&E. Better to just take their chances overnight.

A twenty-year-old ned stood near the entrance, loudly giving his version down the phone of a brutal fight that had left him soaked in blood, and lucky to escape a stabbing.

The atmosphere inside was tense, as a drunken group of young men in various brands of expensive sportswear were marauding about the place, apparently incapable of altering their behaviour for a hospital waiting room compared to, say, a nightclub, or a park after dark. Auto-tuned trance music pounded from a phone far louder than any phone had a right to be, and no one dared confront them about it. Everyone else there was injured enough already.

Moving quickly through the place, Lomond said, 'A&E's one of the great equalisers in society. A knife doesn't care if you cut yourself while prepping for an elegant dinner party, or if you were slashed across your face as part of a ten-man gang fight. The bones of the middle class are no less brittle than the working class. Absolutely everyone is capable of total idiocy, or dumb bad luck from time to time. And when it happens, everyone has to come and sit in this room together, waiting for the same length of time. If you want to know what the downside of equality is, come to an A&E.' Lomond caught the eye of the ned blasting trance music from his phone, and showed him his ID. 'Ho, you! Can you turn down the chipmunk music, please? There are enough ailments in this room already without adding headaches and suicidal thoughts to the list.'

Keeping DS McNair in his slipstream, Lomond walked straight up to the receptionist's window, bypassing the queue. He pressed his ID up against the shatterproof window.

'Maitland Ferguson,' he said. 'And Fiona Ferguson, too. If she can talk.'

CHAPTER NINE

LOMOND TRIED to get a read on Maitland, who was sitting up in bed with a haunted look on his face. Lomond's eyes alternated between Maitland and the consultant who was briefing them on the Fergusons' condition.

'They'll both be fine in a couple of hours,' the consultant explained, 'but the drug has been a little slower to leave Mrs Ferguson's system. Absorption rates with a drug of this kind can be wildly different based on the dose.'

'What sort of drug are we talking about, doctor?' asked Lomond.

'You'll need to wait for blood work before I could say with any certainty. But judging by the symptoms when they were brought in, and Mr Ferguson's time to recover, I would say you're looking at a neuromuscular paralysing agent of some kind.'

'How much will they have been aware of? I mean, could they have made out a face?'

'As far as vision is concerned, they will probably have seen everything in front of them, but were unable to move or speak. It's a curious choice.'

Ross asked, 'In what way?'

'If the drugging was done purely to facilitate the capture of the child, there are a million other drugs that could have knocked the parents out much deeper and for longer.'

'You're saying the abductor wanted them to see what was happening?'

'Almost certainly. I gave a sample of both the Fergusons' blood to one of your constables earlier to take to Gartcosh. Your guys will have the drug identified far quicker than we will. But if you're hoping for something exotic so that it's easier to trace, I suspect you're going to be disappointed. Anyone with access to a decent pharmacy could achieve these results.'

Lomond asked, 'Do you think we could be dealing with a doctor or a pharmacist?'

'Or a vet. Or anyone who has a credit card and internet access. The medicine here isn't going to help narrow your pool, Detective Inspector.'

It was late, and Lomond suspected that the consultant hadn't slept in about twenty hours, so he let the casual demotion go.

Ross unfolded his arms, eager to press on. He stole a look at Maitland Ferguson through a gap in the privacy curtains. 'Is Mr Ferguson *compos mentis* enough to take some questions?'

The consultant glanced back at him, then gave a put-upon sigh. 'He'll be able to understand your questions. But you'll need to be very brief.'

Lomond was already pulling the curtain back. 'Thanks, doctor.'

Maitland flinched a little at the sudden swoop of the curtain on the plastic rails. He grimaced from the throb of a pounding migraine that was currently setting up camp.

The consultant stood at the end of the bed. 'Mr Ferguson? The police want to ask you a couple of questions. How are you feeling?'

'I need to get out of here,' Maitland croaked, trying to peel back the bedsheet.

'You need to stay right here,' the consultant told him, pulling the sheet back over his legs. 'You need to rest.'

'Fiona. Fiona, where is she?'

'I told you, Mr Ferguson, she's next door. She's going to be fine.'

Lomond and Ross exchanged a look. Maitland was showing signs of amnesia, which didn't bode well for getting a statement from him. Or anything that might stand up to scrutiny in court.

While the consultant tended to Maitland, Lomond whispered to Ross, 'We need to tread lightly here.'

The consultant exhaled before telling Lomond, 'A few minutes. No more.'

'Yep,' he replied, eyes already narrowing at his target.

This was where he had made his reputation. Questioning. Interrogation. It wasn't common for a DCI to take part in questioning suspects, especially out in the field. But John

Lomond didn't exactly do ordinary, and his interrogation skills were sorely needed in a case where the first few hours were the most crucial.

'Mr Ferguson,' said Lomond, presenting his ID, 'I'm Detective Chief Inspector John Lomond. You can call me John. This is Detective Sergeant Ross McNair. We're here to help find your son. I know that you and your wife have been through a very traumatic event, but there are a couple of things about tonight we need to go over while the details might still be fresh in your mind.'

'I just want him back,' Maitland said, closing his eyes against the pain tightening his temples.

'We're going to get him back,' Lomond assured him. 'First, why don't you talk us through what happened.'

This was how Lomond often started a line of questioning. Liars protect themselves by remembering rote answers and details. They don't stray far from certain phrases or descriptions or adjectives, whether it's the first time they're talking through the timeline of events, or the tenth. It was why detectives like Lomond were fans of repeatedly asking the same questions. He wanted to hear Maitland Ferguson's version and let his natural radar for bullshit start beeping.

He went through the family's routine for Jack's bedtime, which was always the same: bath, bedtime story, lights out. Maitland had argued often with Fiona about the necessity of doing a bath for Jack every single night. When he'd been Jack's age, he only had a bath every other night or if he had got actual dirt on himself.

THE BONNIE DEAD   63

Lomond asked, 'And the routine for locking the house at night – the alarms – all that was the same?'

Maitland huffed, 'I've told you already. I set the alarms at the same time every night. That bastard snuck into the house before. He was hiding under the bed.'

Lomond waited a beat to see whether Ross would jump on it or not.

'You're sure it was a man?' Ross asked.

Maitland stammered, 'Well, it must have been, right? I mean, the physique, and around the eyes...It was a man's eyes.'

'It's incredibly important that we don't jump to any conclusions at this stage, Mr Ferguson. So we're clear: you didn't actually see the suspect's face?'

Patience waning, Maitland relented. 'No. I just felt something plunging into my ankle, then I started to weaken. He had on a hooded top and was wearing a balaclava underneath. Like I said, I caught a glimpse of his eyes. It was a man, alright.'

Ross asked, 'It's our understanding that you could hear and see what was going on, but you couldn't move?'

'Well, yeah...but Fiona managed to crawl across the room at least.'

'Did the man say anything at all?'

'He said something to Fiona, but I couldn't hear.'

Lomond said quietly to Ross, 'Find that consultant and get an ETA on when Mrs Ferguson might come around.'

Once Ross was gone, Maitland said tearfully, 'Tell me it isn't him. Please.'

'Mr Ferguson–'

'Was there sand left in the bed?'

Lomond put his hand out to try and calm him down. 'The best thing you can do–'

'Please! I know that he left sand on the others' beds.'

He tried again. 'The best thing you can do right now–'

Maitland snapped, 'Just answer the question! Is it him?'

Lomond relented. 'It's one of a number of possibilities, Mr Ferguson.'

'I thought that it was all over. I remember when it was happening. I used to see those parents on the news. I felt sorry for them. Of course, I did. But we didn't have Jack then. Everyone tells you when your first is on the way, you've no idea how much you can love someone. How strong the urge to protect them is. I never disbelieved anyone who told me that, but it is true. You can't know until they're there. In your arms. Or you're tucking them into bed.' His voice started to crack. 'How far you'd go to save them...'

Lomond had been told those things too. And like Maitland, he always believed them.

'Mr Ferguson, you said that this man said something to your wife. Was there any particular accent you could identify? Any particular words or phrases that stood out?'

'No, just what I told you he said. The accent was...' he shrugged, 'Glasgow, I don't know. Not especially strong.'

'Well spoken? Rough?'

'No, I...' Maitland rubbed his temples. 'I don't know, I just don't know...'

Ross returned, telling Lomond, 'He says it could be minutes, or it could be hours.'

'I want to see my wife,' Maitland declared.

'Soon,' Lomond said. 'But first, we need to clear something up.' He turned to Ross, hand held out for the phone in the evidence bag. They each steeled themselves. The next part had the potential to get very messy.

Lomond produced Maitland's mobile phone in an evidence bag. 'The first officer on scene found this on the floor. I'd like to ask you about some messages you received earlier tonight.' He handed the phone to Maitland, who had turned as white as the sheets that were covering him. His hands were already shaking before he got to the end of the first screenshot. Lomond pointed at the phone with conviction. 'I need to know who that person is, Mr Ferguson.'

After scrolling through a few messages, Maitland handed the phone back. He didn't need to read anymore. 'She has nothing to do with this,' he said dismissively.

'With respect, it's up to us to rule anyone in or out of this investigation. You received a very stark threat hours before your son was taken in a calculated and deeply methodical attack. An attack designed to inflict maximum emotional damage on you and your wife.'

'But...what about the Sandman? You're not saying she's—'

'I'm not saying anything right now, Mr Ferguson, other than I'm exploring every possibility to give us the best chance of finding Jack.' He put his hand up to stop Maitland interrupting. 'But there are also a lot of things that are very much *not* like previous cases. This attack seems personal in a way that we've not seen before, and we wouldn't be doing our job if we didn't rule them out. The parents have never been targeted in such a way, and the attacker has never hidden themselves inside a home before. Now, we have limited time to establish if this is related to previous cases, or whether someone might be using it as a smokescreen. Or we could even be looking at a copycat–' He managed to stop himself saying "killer". 'Offender.' He showed Maitland the phone screen again. 'So if you don't think this text conversation is pertinent, I need to know why.'

Maitland raised his trembling hands to his face and took a long, shuddering breath. 'I need assurances that anything I tell you will be handled confidentially.'

Ross said, 'Mr Ferguson, we're the police. We're not exactly in the habit of posting sensitive criminal evidence on our Facebook pages.'

'Not you,' he replied. 'I mean from Fiona. She can't know about any of this.'

Lomond said, 'I'll do my best.'

Maitland muttered to himself, 'She wouldn't...I mean surely she would never...'

'Who would never?'

'The woman in the messages. Surely she can't be involved in this.'

'That's going to be for us to decide. We're going to need more information, Mr Ferguson.'

With little choice but to disclose everything, Maitland said, 'It started as the stupidest thing. Two married people at a bar during this work thing.'

'You're a lawyer, is that correct?'

'Yes. Criminal defence mostly, specialising in motoring law.'

'Motoring law?'

'Speeding charges. Drink driving. A lot of my clients are celebrities, sports figures. I find the loopholes that keep them out of jail. Fiona and I started the firm together, but she's stepped back from things a bit the last few years.'

'Tell me about this woman. How did you two meet?'

'We were at a function one night in Edinburgh. We couldn't get a sitter for Jack, so Fiona had volunteered to stay at home.' Maitland's mouth twisted into different shapes from tension, replaying that simple moment where everything changed, and how so much could have been avoided. 'We'd been making eyes at each other all night. I'd told myself in the bathroom, don't do it. Don't pretend that you're twenty-five again and single, just to get that rush, you know? That excitement when someone starts flirting with you. But I couldn't help myself...' He shook his head. 'It should have been little more than a stupid little flirty chat. Instead, she gave me her number and we started messaging each other the next day.'

'She initiated swapping numbers?' asked Lomond.

'Yeah,' Maitland replied.

'Who messaged first?'

He paused, already seeing the angle Lomond was working. 'She did. First, during the day. Just chat. Then at night. That was when the chat got more...intense.'

'You started an affair with this woman?'

His head dropped. Weighed down by the shame and guilt. 'Yes. Until, you know, she wanted more.'

'And you didn't?'

'I'm a happily married man. What she wanted was impossible.'

Ross asked, 'Do you think this woman is capable of being behind this attack on your son, Mr Ferguson?'

Maitland exhaled sharply, almost trying to convince himself. 'She wouldn't do that. You don't understand. This isn't some random crazy person. She's...' He broke off.

'She's what?'

Looking to press home the evidence in front of them, Lomond quoted from the messages. '"You're about to enter a nightmare unlike anything you've ever experienced. Just remember, you could have stopped this." That sounds pretty clear to me.'

Maitland was panicking – the idea that his affair was the catalyst for his son's abduction was too much to comprehend.

Lomond could see him slipping further into denial. 'What about work, Mr Ferguson? Have there been any cases recently that might have put you in a vulnerable position?'

'You're asking have I been blackmailed?'

'Yes.'

'No. I haven't.'

Ross added, 'What about someone with a grudge or–'

Maitland threw his head back in exasperation. 'Will you just get out of here and find him, for crying out loud! You're wasting all this time on me. Meanwhile, Jack's out there somewhere...' Something caught in his throat. It was the realisation that the police might be right. And that it might actually all be his fault. 'Do you really think this could be why Jack was taken...Really?'

Lomond pulled a seat up beside the bed and inched it closer. 'Mr Ferguson, who is the woman who sent you those messages?'

Maitland's shoulders slumped. He looked broken. 'I can't tell you that.'

'Even if it might help locate your son?'

'You're going to have to trust me that she's not involved.'

'In the circumstances, no, that's not something we're prepared to do. I haven't trusted anyone since about,' Lomond checked his watch, 'nineteen ninety-two. We're the police, Mr Ferguson. We don't operate on a system of who we trust the most. We follow evidence. And so far, the most compelling evidence we've got leads to this woman who might just know where your son is.' Lomond leaned forward on his knees. 'Who is she?'

'I...I can't...'

'Can't what? What's so scary about her that you won't even name her to save your son?'

'I'm not scared,' Maitland said. 'I'm trying to protect her.'

Lomond tried one last time. 'Who is she, Mr Ferguson?'

He gulped hard. 'It's Karen Prodger.'

Ross looked up in surprise. 'As in...'

'Yes. That Karen Prodger.'

Lomond snapped, 'Sorry, have I walked into a meeting of the Karen Prodger Secret Society? Who is she?'

Ross rubbed his eyes in exasperation, knowing the rough road they would have ahead.

'She's an MSP,' said Maitland.

'She's more than that,' Ross added. He exhaled dismally. 'She's the Justice Secretary at Holyrood.'

'Still think she's involved?' Maitland sniped.

Lomond took out his phone, preparing to search the map function. 'I want an address.'

'You can't be serious.'

Maitland's surprise was matched by DS McNair's.

'Sir, could we maybe take five outside?' he asked.

Before Lomond could respond, the cubicle curtain flew open and the consultant appeared with a nurse behind him.

'Detective Inspector,' the consultant began.

Lomond wasn't in the mood for letting it go a second time. 'Detective Chief Inspector, actually, but who's keeping track?'

'I'm sorry. I'm going to have to insist that Mr Ferguson is left to rest now.'

'Fine.' Lomond got to his feet and gestured for Ross to follow him out. 'We've got what we wanted.' He handed a contact card to the consultant. 'I want to be called the moment that Mrs Ferguson can talk.'

'Right,' said Lomond, closing over Maitland's cubicle curtain. 'Edinburgh it is, no doubt. It shouldn't be hard to find out an MSP's address.'

As they marched towards the A&E exit, against a backdrop of drunken arguing and nurses pleading for calm, Ross said, 'Are we really going to wake up a cabinet secretary in the middle of the night – and, what? Accuse them of child abduction?'

Lomond replied, 'Yeah, pretty much.'

'And you still think you'll be leading this investigation by the morning?'

'Oh, I think the chances of that are slim. But I didn't get where I am, Ross, by pulling my punches.'

CHAPTER TEN

THE M8 WAS PREDICTABLY quiet for DCI Lomond and DS McNair's eastwards drive to Edinburgh. Once they had crossed the city's outer fringes, they began the long drag uphill, passing the Eurocentral business park and various warehouses that marked the end of the urban. There were no more motorway lights now as trees and greenery took over on either side of the road. In Lomond's rear-view mirror, the city twinkled with a thousand lights, an immense sprawl cut into the vast surrounding countryside.

'You forget sometimes,' Lomond said, 'that all that behind us used to be just a big field.'

'Yeah,' replied Ross, 'I guess so.' He sounded like a child being encouraged against his will to appreciate a view.

Lomond hadn't left the fast lane in ten miles and hadn't been troubled by any other traffic. He wondered what they were all doing out there in the middle of the night. All those lone drivers in the dark with no one to ever know their stories.

Trying to make conversation, Ross ventured, 'So is it time for our life stories yet?'

Lomond had been miles away. 'What do you mean?'

'You said when we were on our way to the hospital that there wasn't time for our life stories. I thought now might be the time.'

'You don't want to know about my life,' said Lomond. 'There's not much to say. I do the job. I go home.'

'That sounds...' Ross thought for a moment. 'Depressing as hell, sir. Me? I play five-a-sides every week. I don't go in for all this being scared of toxic masculinity stuff. Sometimes it's good to just go run around with some guys and kick the shit out of each other over a game of football then have a pint. Have a laugh. You should try it sometime. The football, I mean. You could sub in for a half.'

Lomond tried to think how he could reply politely. 'Not really my thing.'

'What is your thing? Sitting in a dark room every night reading Dostoevsky?'

'It's not my thing because I have no need. The world needs people like me. Someone who doesn't need all those so-called regular things like companionship. Love. Hobbies. A desire to tend to a garden. Argue online with strangers about inconsequential shite.'

'Everyone needs that.'

'Not me. I know it's hard for someone like you to understand, but I don't consider the way I live my life to be a sacrifice. I used to tell myself that the job made me this way. But the more I think about it, I think I might have been this way all the time. Maybe the job just brought it out.' Realising that he was bumming Ross out, Lomond said, 'Linda told me you've got a wee one at home?'

Ross's face lit up as he reached quickly for his wallet and pulled out a picture of him with a woman his age, and a newborn baby. 'That's my girlfriend, Isla. And the wee man's Lachlann.'

Lomond nodded affirmatively. 'Good Scottish name that. Don't see it much. How old is he?'

'Seven months, two weeks,' Ross replied. He smiled at the photo before putting it away again. 'Have you got anyone at home?' He pointed at Lomond's wedding ring.

'I was married,' he said. 'For a few years. We had a little boy. I lost them both.'

Ross didn't know how to respond. 'Oh my god...I'm...I'm so sorry. I had no idea. And I'm waving my photo about–'

'It's fine, Ross. That's what a dad's supposed to do. I made my peace with it a long time ago. Doing this, I've seen people mowed down under buses. Beaten. Killed for no reason. I remember a guy in Feegie Park in Paisley when I was a constable. Guy was carrying home a pack of nappies. Some psycho stabbed him for the five quid in his pocket. I've never counted myself as any different to anyone else. We're all subject to the same chaos and chance of the universe. That's what happened to my wife and boy. Truth is, the more I see of the world, the more I feel at peace that they're not around. Maybe it's for the best that my boy didn't have to experience this. A world where people are killed for a fiver.'

Ross had met his share of pessimists in his time, but he had never met someone as far gone as John Lomond. Forget about catching the most elusive serial killer in Scottish criminal history. Ross thought it a wonder that Lomond could get out of bed in the morning.

———

They stopped for fuel and coffee at Harthill services. The surrounding area was the closest the Central Belt came to a wilderness, marking the halfway point between Glasgow and Edinburgh. There was something disorienting about the harsh lighting and occasional Doppler effect of passing traffic on either side. Everyone just passing through.

The small Marks and Spencer had long since closed, leaving only the petrol station for the pair to pick from. Lomond grabbed a takeaway black coffee, not requiring an extra cup or outer holder to protect his fingers from the heat. His hands were rough and callused. He made a show of checking his watch while Ross hummed and hawed about whether to opt for crisps or chocolate.

'Pick something, Ross,' he told him, 'or I'll collect you on the other side of the bridge on the way back.'

'Sorry, boss.'

'John is fine,' said Lomond.

Ross corrected himself, 'John.' It felt wrong to be calling

him it. Like calling your primary school teacher by their first name.

They were walking back across the forecourt when Lomond's phone rang. When he saw the caller ID, he muttered, 'Shite.' He told Ross, 'It's the Det Sup.'

'You didn't tell her we were coming this way?'

'It might have slipped my mind,' he said, before answering, 'Linda. What can I–'

Before he could get any further, DSU Boyle bellowed, 'Have you lost your mind? Have you *actually* lost your mind?'

Lomond put his coffee cup on the car roof while he opened the door with his free hand. 'I'm not entirely sure, Linda. But you seem pretty convinced.'

'I've just been on HOLMES and found Karen Prodger's name all over the place.'

After explaining the situation, Lomond hadn't succeeded in calming her down much.

'John,' she said, as if trying to explain to a small child why you can't run out into traffic, 'you cannot show up at the Justice Secretary's house in the middle of the night and accuse them of conspiracy to abduct a child.'

'I'm following the evidence of a direct threat to the child's father,' Lomond replied, getting them back on the motorway. 'Who is, by the way, currently hospitalised. Not exactly an empty threat.'

'You're ignoring decades of established protocol. We have to talk to East Command first for a suspect like this. There's going to be a total landslide of shit on our door if it comes out that we didn't even give the minister a chance to present themselves at a station with legal representation.'

'I've got a thread of text messages that ends with a direct threat against the father of an abducted child. It's not going to be an interrogation. It's merely a conversation with a view to eliminating a potentially time-consuming line of enquiry. It's the verbal equivalent of an elimination fingerprint.'

There was a long pause at Linda's end.

Ross was on the edge of his seat and hadn't so much as sipped his coffee yet.

'I urge you, John,' she said, 'tread carefully with this one. If this gets out…it's going to put me in an impossible situation. Reekie's got Sutherland waiting in the wings, and he's just waiting for an excuse to not give you the lead in the enquiry.'

Lomond asked, 'What do you suggest?'

She replied, 'If this is the one you're swinging at, make bloody well sure you hit it. Because if you leave without something concrete, I can't promise that I can protect you.'

THE FORMER VILLAGE of Morningside was a mile and a half south of Edinburgh's Old Town, past The Meadows public park to the upscale district of Holy Corner. To many, the area was seen as upper class, as caricatured in the 'Morningside accent': an over-refined and affected 'pan loaf' accent. It had become *the* place to be for professionals and artists and creatives with money to burn, with its independent businesses and cafes and restaurants, whilst remaining a largely unspoiled time capsule of Victorian and Edwardian tenements and villas.

For a Member of the Scottish Parliament like Karen Prodger, living in Morningside's leafy surrounds made perfect sense as an antidote to the draining, volatile atmosphere of Holyrood. It was a chance to live in the countryside without ever leaving the capital.

'So this is Edinburgh's Dowanhill,' Ross speculated.

'Something like that,' said Lomond. 'A lot of lawyers and rich hippies that don't mind paying more than a fiver for a cup of tea and a bit of cake. If you shout "Archie" or "Angus" on the high street, about a dozen wee boys with floppy haircuts and wearing rugby shirts will turn around.'

Karen Prodger's house was a detached villa on a quiet street that was too narrow for parked cars, but everyone had their own driveway and garage.

Lomond mounted the pavement to park, then he took out a black backpack from the boot. He looked awkward carrying it on his shoulder, like a mature student on his first day at uni.

He and Ross found themselves on the outskirts of the property, outside a heavy, solid wooden gate. For an embarrassing moment, Lomond worried that if no one answered the attached video intercom they'd be stuck out there. But after nearly a full minute's wait, a female voice answered. 'Yes?'

Lomond showed his badge to the camera. 'I'm DCI John

Lomond, this is DS Ross McNair. Am I speaking to Karen Prodger?'

She could see them, but they couldn't see who was talking inside.

'Speaking,' she replied.

'Mrs Prodger, we need to talk to you as a matter of urgency.'

There seemed to be some conferring going on in the background, followed by the gate buzzing open.

THE MINISTER OPENED the front door, still wearing her work clothes from the previous day. Her husband, Tom, was wearing chinos and a polo shirt that bore the logo of Muirfield Golf Club – a club so posh that it was officially called "the Honourable Company of Edinburgh Golfers" and had only recently begun allowing female members.

Tom remained on the periphery of the hall, like a mouse unsure whether to leave its home in the floorboard in case it gets eaten. When he heard it was the police, his mind immediately jumped to thoughts of "have I done anything wrong? Am I sure I haven't committed a crime recently?"

That they were plain clothes came as a relief. If anyone was to be arrested there would have been uniformed officers too.

Forever the second-most-important person in the house, he tried to assert his authority as the man who was going to 'handle' things, calling out in a reedy voice, 'What's this all about?'

Lomond ignored him and spoke to the minister. 'I'm sorry to come at such a late hour, Mrs Prodger–'

'What is it this time?' she asked. 'Far left? Far right. None of the above?'

'I'm sorry, ma'am, I don't follow.'

'I assume it's more online threats again? If so, this really should wait until office hours tomorrow.'

'No, ma'am. We're here about Maitland Ferguson.' Lomond waited for the penny to drop, fascinated by how the minister would react.

The husband waited for an explanation.

'Tom, this shouldn't take long,' she said. 'Why don't you go back upstairs.'

He did as he was told.

The minister lowered her voice. 'What's this all about?'

The husband took long enough on the stairs to see Ross looking from room to room, then saying, 'It might be best to find somewhere private, ma'am.'

Tom took out his phone halfway up the stairs. By the top, he'd got an answer. 'Fraser, it's Tom Prodger. Apologies for the late hour, but I think Karen has got a bit of a problem here...'

CHAPTER ELEVEN

THE MINISTER SHOWED Lomond and Ross to the study, where evidence of Tom Prodger's late-night crossword and half-empty glass of Lagavulin remained. Bookcases lined the walls, along with photos of the couple meeting prominent people: the First Minister, leaders of trade and business, TV personalities, sports figures. Ross did a couple of takes of the room before he realised what was odd about it to him – there was no television.

Lomond settled on the leather chesterfield couch and opened up his backpack, revealing a battered laptop with scuffs and more than a few dents around it. 'Mrs Prodger, I'd like to apologise again for coming so late, but I think you'll understand our urgency once I've explained. We're investigating the abduction of Jack Ferguson.'

The minister closed the drawing-room door carefully, making sure as little of the conversation as possible leaked out. 'Abduction?'

'That's right.'

She shook her head as if trying to reset her thoughts. 'Hang on. I thought you said this concerned Maitland Ferguson.'

'It very much concerns him, too.' Lomond opened the laptop and navigated to HOLMES – the Home Office IT system where UK police forces could organise and coordinate their investigations. 'You do know, Mr Ferguson, correct?'

To buy herself a little time, she cracked open the window a little higher, then stood in front of it with her arms folded. 'Well, I think I met him at a function a while ago. It rings a bell anyway.'

Lomond said, 'Because back in the hall, it seemed like you recognised the name straight away.'

'Detective...' She lifted her head, inviting him to remind her.

'Detective Chief Inspector Lomond,' he replied.

'I don't know if you realise how many people I meet on average on a daily basis. How many phone conversations, handshakes, and chats I rack up?'

'I'm afraid I don't, Mrs Prodger. I don't really follow politics. Not if I can help it. For the same reason I avoid four-hour subtitled films and anything with James Corden. I prize my sanity too much. But I'm not talking about strangers you encounter out and about in public life. I'm talking about a man you were sending messages to just a few hours ago.' He opened the tab where the evidence from Maitland's phone had been uploaded, showing the phone number that had sent him so many messages earlier in the night. 'Do you recognise that number, Mrs Prodger?'

She stayed standing, putting on her glasses to see as she leaned down for a closer look. 'I...can't say that I do,' she replied.

Ross didn't take his eyes off her. As a police officer, he was used to being lied to, or hearing lies on a routine basis. *No, I was never there, I swear!...I never even hit him. He just fell down...Those aren't mine. I don't know where they came from!* A lot of polis liked to think they could spot a lie as soon as it tripped off the end of someone's tongue, but Ross really did have a talent for it. It was all in the eyes. Shifty. Evasive. Uncomfortable staying put on any spot for more than a second or two. And the minister's eyes were darting all over the place.

He then caught sight of a particular face in a photo on the wall. A scene of three men standing on the first tee at the Old Course at St Andrew's. Two men he didn't know, along with Tom Prodger. But it was the man standing next to Tom in the photo that Ross was focussing on.

It was Alasdair Reekie.

Ross couldn't think of a way to draw Lomond's attention to it.

Lomond went on, 'Earlier tonight, Maitland Ferguson's son was abducted from his home in Glasgow. A few hours after Maitland had received this message.' He showed her the message.

She only needed a slight peek before she shut her eyes. She was giving in. 'Chief Inspector, I can see where you're going with this, but you're terribly mistaken. My relationship with Maitland Ferguson is a private matter. I'm very sorry to hear about his son, but none of this has anything to do with me.' She started towards the door. 'Now, if you have any further questions, I would direct you to my solicitor who will be happy to help you with your enquiries. If you don't mind, I have to prepare for constituency appointments tomorrow morning–'

'No, I *do* mind, Mrs Prodger,' said Lomond, staying put on the couch. 'I've got a missing child, and I've got a direct threat from you to the boy's father the same night.'

Her expression hardened. 'Mr Lomond, we both know that you can't pin that phone number on me. I mean, sure. You might have some circumstantial location data that puts it within twenty metres of this property. But there's no way in hell you can pin me as the person who typed that message and sent it.'

'I've got more than enough for a warrant,' Lomond warned her. 'I'd need to come back here with more officers to carry out a thorough search. Here, and your constituency office. As well as Holyrood. Which will be fine for you, because there isn't a lot of press kicking about there on a daily basis, is there? And I'm sure your husband – who you're going out of your way to keep this conversation from – will be more than willing to corroborate that there's been no long-standing intimate relationship with Maitland Ferguson. He'll give you an alibi, won't he? Unless he's worried about how a perjury charge might go down with the old boys at the club.'

Ross looked on in stunned silence. He hadn't spent any time in the presence of politicians, let alone senior government ministers, but he was pretty sure that you weren't supposed to speak to them the way that Lomond was.

Before the minister could reply, there was the sound of the front door being answered by Tom Prodger, and an as-yet-unidentified male voice who enquired, 'Where is she?'

A second later, the study room door opened, revealing a man in a smart suit and an open-neck shirt, like a politician trying to look casual and 'down-to-earth' on the campaign trail. He was carrying a briefcase and had hurried over from his flat across the city, and his short hair had the slight misshaping of having been on a pillow for a few hours already.

He told the minister, 'Thanks, Karen. I'll take it from here.' He was all business. Unintimidated by the police presence. He held his hand out towards Lomond. 'Detective Chief Inspector Lomond, I believe?'

Lomond shook his hand, wondering how he knew his name already. 'And you are?'

'I'm Fraser Bonnington, Mrs Prodger's solicitor. As her legal representative, I'm calling a halt to this conversation, which is completely irregular as you well know. Mrs Prodger will be more than happy to cooperate with your enquiries at a prearranged time that suits her busy schedule.'

Ross now had a face to go with the third man alongside Tom Prodger and CSU Reekie in the golf photo, and it all started to fall terribly into place.

Lomond's phone began to ring.

Bonnington pointed to it. 'You should take that. It's the Chief Superintendent for Greater Glasgow who's about to find you a desk somewhere bleak.'

Right enough, the caller ID on Lomond's phone said "CSU Alasdair Reekie."

He knew he couldn't ignore the call, but he also didn't want to have to answer it in front of Bonnington and his entitled client and hear him getting a dressing down.

Reekie wasn't just angry. He was on-the-ceiling angry, and spent the next thirty seconds explaining to Lomond all the different reasons he was angry and what he expected Lomond to do about it.

Lomond replied, 'I understand, sir, but I have a missing child and—'

Bonnington led his client away to the hall, much to Lomond's relief.

Reekie concluded, 'You and DS McNair get back to Glasgow. I'm going to be spending most of tomorrow cleaning this up. You're done, Lomond. I've called Linda already. You'll be back in Paisley where you belong tomorrow. I want you back on your outstanding enquiries.'

'What about this one, sir?' asked Lomond.

'While you've been gallivanting across the country, DCI Sutherland has been running things properly in the background. I'm sorry it's turned out this way, John, but I can't afford the headlines. I've got to say, the way you've handled this tonight is beyond reckless.'

Lomond nodded softly to himself. 'Sir.'

'Check in with Linda and make your handover with Sutherland. Okay?' Reekie hung up.

Ross asked with trepidation, 'What's happening?'

'We're done here.' Lomond corrected himself, 'Or should I say, I'm done.'

———

THE DRIVE back to Glasgow was a quiet affair, neither man feeling much like speaking.

Ross was first to break the ice. He shook his head in irritation. 'Did you see the photo on the wall?'

'Yeah,' Lomond replied. 'I caught it before I sat down. I pretty much knew we were toast then.'

'Is that why you went after her so hard?'

'I didn't have much choice.'

'It's bullshit.'

'Yep.'

'*Actual* bullshit.'

'I know.'

'So because some politician's husband is mates with a senior cop, an abduction enquiry stalls?'

'There's a few things in life, Ross, you simply don't want to see how they're made. Laws, sausages, and Major Investigations.'

'The husband calls the solicitor, then the solicitor calls Reekie, right?'

Lomond couldn't muster the same sense of injustice as

Ross. He'd seen so much of it over the years that he was immune at this point. 'Something like that.'

'Now what?' Ross asked.

'Now we check in with the Det Supt, then we go home.'

'It's bullshit.'

'Yeah, you said that already...' Lomond saw a call coming through, flagging on his dashboard.

It was DSU Boyle.

He answered, 'Ma'am, you're on speaker with myself and DS McNair.' They might have gone way back, but Lomond always paid her the respect to address her formally in front of a subordinate.

'Are youse on your way back?' she asked. Her voice was weary, not long off the phone going ten rounds with Reekie.

'Yeah,' said Lomond, checking the time. 'We should be about half an hour.'

'Fiona Ferguson started to talk an hour ago. She wrapped up with a DC from Sutherland's team not too long ago. But I need you to do a follow-up.'

'Follow-up?'

'The DC never went over crime scene photos with her, and Sutherland never sent an FLO with her.'

Lomond sighed in exasperation. 'For fuck's sake. What's he *doing* over there? He doesn't send a Family Liaison to a woman whose son's been abducted, and now this DC forgets...' He would have continued complaining if Reekie hadn't already given him the boot.

'I know,' said Boyle. 'I've sent an FLO over now. They'll be waiting for you at the Ferguson house.'

'She's home already?'

'She demanded it. Her and the husband are being driven back just now. The doctor said that medically there was no reason to keep them in., though he wanted to. It's like an anaesthetic that's worn off.' She paused. 'John, this isn't how I wanted this to pan out. You know that, right?'

'Don't worry about it. But isn't this a bit below my pay grade? I thought this was why we have DCs.'

'Fiona Ferguson asked for you personally.'

'Me? Why?'

'I'm not entirely sure. It's what the FLO at the hospital told me. And you know what FLOs are like. Anything that gets a family member talking.'

Lomond knew that Ross could handle it in his sleep. But he was intrigued by Mrs Ferguson's request. And after all, it would be one last thing he could do for little Jack.

But the task wasn't going to be anything like as trivial as Lomond thought.

CHAPTER TWELVE

THE CRIME SCENE at Dowanhill looked very different to the one that Lomond and DS McNair had left a few hours ago. All the neighbours had long since gone back to bed, the street-facing windows now vacant. Curtains drawn, blinds pulled down. There was still a constable posted at the front door, and forensics were inspecting the garden area for footprints. Everything now scaled down.

Fiona and Maitland Ferguson hadn't been back long by the time Lomond and Ross got there. A Family Liaison Officer answered the front door. If he hadn't, Lomond would have been standing outside for a while: Fiona and Maitland were busy arguing in the kitchen behind a closed door. The words were indistinct, but the tone and volume were unmistakable.

'Detective Chief Inspector Lomond,' said the FLO, extending his hand.

'What's your first name, son?'

It took him two attempts to get it right. 'D-Derek, sir. It's a pleasure to meet you.'

Lomond shook his hand, then gestured to Ross and introduced him.

He knew that it wasn't politically correct, and it wasn't as if Lomond pictured an FLO always as a female officer who had been 'specially trained' to make cups of tea and dole out strategic hugs and consolations to grieving family members. But he had never quite pictured someone called Derek – and looking like Derek – being an FLO. He looked like he belonged behind the wheel of a lorry rather than guiding a family in crisis.

They weren't just there to keep the family company. Primarily, Family Liaison Officers were investigators, and had been that for over twenty years. Of course, sensitivity and communication skills were imperative when dealing with relatives of murder victims or other serious crimes. It was equally important, not just to the family but to the investigation team, that they have a deeply enquiring mind, taking in everything that was said around a dinner table, or in passing during a phone call – something that doesn't stack up against what had previously been told to detectives. Their job was to listen and to observe.

The tragic truth was that a lot of murder victims know or are related to their killer. In that, or any other major investigation, the devil can always be lingering in the detail somewhere. Like an FLO's ability to cultivate open conversations that can fill in gaps that detectives wouldn't otherwise be able to uncover under more direct and official questioning.

It's natural for the public to be intimidated by detectives, even when they haven't done anything wrong. A good FLO gets rid of that fear, and gives the truth a chance to come out on its own.

They were also there to walk the family through the investigation process, to explain procedure to people who were in no fit state to take onboard the *what-is-happening-and-why?*

Their title and public perception might have made them appear the fluffiest of police officers, but many an FLO had blown open major investigations in the past purely by listening and paying attention to the smallest of details behind closed doors.

'What's the deal?' asked Lomond as they entered the hallway.

All three of them had half an eye and ear on the ongoing argument in the kitchen.

The FLO kept his voice down. 'As you might have gathered, the wife knows about the affair. It's been kicking off since they left the hospital.'

'That's actually good,' said Ross. 'One less thing to have to skirt around.'

Derek shrugged in agreement.

Lomond asked, 'Does she know where we've been?'

'Aye,' Derek replied. 'I've told her that it was just talking to someone who was helping with our enquiries. She seems convinced that Karen Prodger's got more to answer to than just sleeping with her husband.'

Lomond told Ross, 'Right. Well, first of all. We need to

get these two separated, or we'll never get anywhere. We need them focussing on the details, not each other.'

Derek added, 'Angry minds don't think clearly.'

The kitchen door flew open behind them, revealing Maitland Ferguson, who stomped up the stairs.

Derek called after him, 'Mr Ferguson, are you–'

Maitland barked back, 'The bedroom's off limits, yeah, I know. Fuck's sake, I can't breathe in here...' He slammed the spare room door behind him.

Fiona Ferguson then appeared, carrying a plastic tub of cleaning products into the living room.

Derek did his best to broker an introduction to Lomond and Ross. She heard him, but she wasn't listening.

Lomond stepped forward, trying to get her attention. 'Mrs Ferguson, I'm Detective Chief Inspector John Lomond. You can call me John. This is DS Ross McNair. I know Derek's explained that we were coming over to ask you some questions, and maybe run through a few photos.'

She set the cleaning products down on the carpet and kneeled by a nest of tables, setting to work scrubbing them with a damp cloth. 'He said.'

He approached her gently. 'Why don't we sit down over here.'

'You can ask me your questions,' she said, knuckles white, face tight with effort. 'I've just got to get this place clean again.'

To Lomond's annoyance, Derek was a little too fast to interject, 'Fiona, why don't you–'

She slammed the cloth down on the table. 'Can you

please...' She took a moment to compose herself. 'Can you give me just five minutes, Derek? Please?'

'Of course,' he said, excusing himself to the front garden.

His removal seemed to calm her down.

'I'm sorry,' she explained, still kneeling on the carpet, looking around the room. 'It's so disgusting. Knowing that they were in here. In my home for so long without us realising. I keep thinking about their hands on Jack. It makes me want to throw up. I want to get any trace of them out of here.' She finally looked up at Lomond. 'The other DCI. Sutherland. He said it was okay with forensics. That they've sealed off Jack's room and our room.'

Lomond nodded. 'That's all. They've got everything else they need.'

She got slowly to her feet. 'It doesn't even feel real. It's like I'm stuck in an actual nightmare. First Jack.' She gulped, her gaze drifting towards the stairs. 'Now this, this *woman* that Maitland–' She broke off, covering her mouth in disgust. 'I knew about it, you know. The affair.' She fumbled with her phone, scrolling to the relevant screenshots. 'I'm not going to get in trouble over this, am I?'

'The SIM card thing?' asked Ross, thinking of the most tactful way to respond. 'It's not something we'll be prioritising right now, Mrs Ferguson. The important thing is doing everything we can to find Jack.'

She looked back through the messages, then tossed the phone aside. 'When you read messages like that. From someone you think loves you. It's like watching them be taken over. Possessed. Like it's not really them. Then the real kicker comes when you realise: maybe that's who they really were all along. You were never really getting them. Just some other version of them.'

Lomond cleared his throat, trying to reset things. 'For what it's worth, Mrs Ferguson. Having spoken to this woman, I'm satisfied that she's not connected with what's happened to Jack tonight.'

'Really?' Her eyes were rigid and searching, holding Lomond's unwaveringly. 'You're absolutely sure?'

Lomond opened his clasped hands. 'She's guilty of having an affair. Not that we're investigating this based on intuition, but suffice to say, I've looked into the eyes of someone capable of abducting or hurting children, and she's not one of them. At this stage, it is a possibility that Jack's case is related to other child abductions in the past.'

'Murders.'

'I'm sorry?'

'They were child murders. The Sandman.' She gulped dryly. 'How many days was it? Before he...' She couldn't bring herself to finish the sentence.

'It was five.' Lomond leaned forward. 'But Mrs Ferguson, we're going to find him before then.'

'How many times have you promised that to other parents, John?'

He didn't reply.

'I'm sorry,' Fiona said, staring with exhausted, haunted eyes.

'No, you're fine,' Lomond replied. 'It's true that I investigated this man in the past. And the reason I went to Edinburgh tonight to talk to Mrs Prodger is because there is nothing I won't do to get your son back. I want you to know that.'

'My husband might have destroyed our marriage, but I trust that he's not the reason that our son's been taken. He knows senior people in Police Scotland. Someone who told him that no one got as close to catching the Sandman as you.'

'I don't know about that. In a murder enquiry like that "close" doesn't really matter.'

'I spoke to DCI Sutherland on the phone at the hospital earlier. I can't say I cared for him much.'

Lomond had to restrain himself from saying something unprofessional. He opted instead for silence.

Fiona continued, 'I've asked around about him as well. I can't say I'm filled with confidence.'

He shook his head, trying to be diplomatic. 'These decisions are really not up to me.'

'Well, I don't want my son's fate depending on people like DCI Sutherland.'

Lomond exhaled, not sure what to do with the direction of the conversation. He couldn't start running down a colleague in front of a crime victim and a subordinate.

'I just don't get the impression that he cares the same way you do,' said Fiona.

As far as he was concerned, he was already officially out the door anyway. Whatever he had to say now wouldn't make any difference. 'Forgive me for asking, Mrs Ferguson. But it's my understanding that you asked for me personally to come here.'

'I did,' she said. 'I was told that you can be trusted. They told me about your handling of the Sandman case. They also told me a little about why you couldn't continue leading the investigation.'

Ross couldn't help but notice that Lomond looked uncomfortable. It was the first time he'd seen any hint of vulnerability in the man so far.

'Ah,' said Lomond, hoping she wouldn't expand too much on the details in front of DS McNair.

She explained, 'I need someone like you in my corner. In Jack's corner. For him to have...' She broke off. 'The best chance of getting home.'

'Speaking of which,' said Lomond, taking out his laptop from his backpack. 'I know your husband looked through these earlier, but someone should have gone through them with you as well. So we're making absolutely sure that we don't miss anything.' He pointed the laptop at the space beside her. 'May I?'

'Of course.' She shuffled down. 'What exactly am I going to have to look at? I don't want to see anything...I don't know...graphic. I don't know exactly what if anything has been found.'

'I've had a good look through these,' said Lomond. 'These are photos of rooms that, according to you and your husband's testimony, the suspect was present in. Myself and DS McNair, we don't know what normal in your home looks like. You do. That's why we ask people in your position to do this. To check that nothing out of the ordinary is there.' He handed her the laptop, then showed her what buttons to press to progress.

Starting scrolling through the photos, Fiona asked, 'What am I looking for?'

Lomond turned to Ross, who said, 'Anything that doesn't look right.'

Lomond gave an affirmative blink. He couldn't have phrased it better himself. It had been the exact phrase that Ross was taught to use for interviewing witnesses.

Fiona was doing a stellar job at keeping it together in the circumstances. She knew that in that moment Jack needed her to concentrate. Although Maitland had already looked at the same photos, she simply didn't trust him to have done a thorough enough job.

Then, her tough exterior faltered for a moment at the sight of Jack's empty bed and the small pile of sand. How wrong the whole scene seemed to her. Any photos she had ever taken in the room featured toys being played with. Smiles. Happy memories. The pictures that forensics had taken were as stark and emotionless as someone in insurance assessing a property for a claim. Pictures of the everyday that it would never occur to a parent to take: snaps of the window frame. Some stray clothes strewn on the carpet. A small pile of books that had been discarded from the bedtime story options.

Lomond could see her confidence draining as each photo went by unremarked, the shaking of her head growing wider. In desperation to latch onto any clue no matter how tiny, she was questioning every square inch of every photo, but nothing seemed wrong with them. It made her feel like her inability to spot something was failing little Jack.

'I can't...I can't tell,' she said. That was when she saw it.

Jack's cuddly toys gathered together.

She stopped.

Her eyes narrowed in confusion.

She zoomed in for a closer look. What she saw there convinced her further. 'Hang on...'

Lomond gave nothing away with his tone, but inside he felt like he'd been given an electric shock. 'Is there something there, Mrs Ferguson?'

She was no longer shaking her head. 'It's the strangest thing. This...' She pointed to a plush toy badger next to an oversize giraffe, and the baby hare from *Guess How Much I Love You*. 'This one isn't Jack's.'

Lomond came closer to inspect it. 'The badger?'

'It's not his.'

'Are you sure? Maybe your husband might have–'

She scoffed. 'Trust me. Maitland never buys things like that.'

'And it couldn't have been a relative?'

'I'm telling you,' she insisted. 'Every night, Jack and I take down all his pals – that's what he calls them – and we say goodnight to each of them before putting them back up on the shelf. Every one of them has a name. I know them all.' She stabbed a finger on the laptop screen. 'That cuddly toy was not there when he went to bed.'

Lomond leaned towards DS McNair. 'Ross, grab one of those SOCOs outside and get them upstairs, pronto.'

CHAPTER THIRTEEN

On the way into the Helen Street police station car park in Govan, Lomond stopped at the secure entrance barrier just as another car stopped at the exit. For a moment, the two drivers were facing each other.

When the exit barrier went up, the driver stopped and put down the passenger window. Lomond did the same. He leaned across DS McNair to be heard. 'Alright, Jim?'

'Awright, John,' said DCI Sutherland, chewing a sandwich that should have been lunch. 'That you back from Edinburgh?' The prick couldn't keep the smile off his face. 'What's your next big career move? Maybe a smack habit? How about a neck tattoo that says "FUCK THE POLIS"? Or you could get one of they Mexican gang tattoos of a teardrop at the corner of your eye to commemorate the day you guaranteed you'd be stuck in Paisley until you retire.'

Lomond replied, 'Actually, we're just back from Gartcosh dropping off vital evidence in your case. After finishing up interviews you never bothered to get your DC to do. You're welcome, by the way.'

'You know your problem, John?'

'I'm sure you're going to tell me.'

'You're like the Tiger Woods of humiliation. Every time everyone thinks you're done, you make another comeback that outdoes the last one.'

Lomond replied, 'And you're a pain in the arse the way Billy Connolly tells jokes: fucking effortless, mate.'

Out of comebacks, Sutherland opted for something more biting. 'You know, folk sometimes ask me: that John Lomond, is he an awright guy? I tell them, "he's a good detective."'

'Better to be right than liked,' said Lomond.

Sutherland scoffed, leaning over to address DS McNair. 'Watch yourself with this one, sergeant. You'll only learn bad habits.'

Ross almost let it go, then retorted, 'Actually, DCI Lomond's helped the investigation a lot tonight, sir. I think you'll see that in the morning.'

Sutherland scoffed, then pressed the accelerator.

THE STATION WAS the most secure in Scotland, used for detaining high-profile arrests and terror suspects. Bilal Abdulla had been taken there after the Glasgow Airport attempted bombing, and David Cameron's former Director of Communications Andy Coulson, when he was charged with perjury in his case against Tommy Sheridan.

From a distance, the station's long orange brickwork border wall made it look like a small, modern prison, contrasted by its large glass frontage that made it look like a rather dingy health club. Inside, there wasn't much that was healthy taking place.

The Major Investigations Team were based on the second floor near the back of the building, which endured the steady white noise of traffic on the M8 beside it. There were MITs throughout Scotland, responsible for investigating murder enquiries, and the most complex, large-scale cases. At any one time there were multiple cases being investigated by single teams. Sometimes it could be days, even weeks or months between leads, and there was far too much crime in the city for its most sought-after investigators to be sitting on their hands. MITs also weren't limited by geography.

The creation of Police Scotland in 2013 merged the eight regional police forces in Scotland. Which meant that an investigator in Glasgow could be sent to an MIT as far afield as Dundee or Inverness – or even beyond. It wasn't always a good thing. A detective from Aberdeen might have been seen by the executive bigwigs at Tulliallan as the most talented investigator. But that didn't always make them the right choice to lead a Glasgow gangland murder enquiry, where working local sources was so crucial to breaking cases.

For a detective of any rank in a Major Investigation Team, Govan was the place to be. Because of its size, facilities, and central location, it got all the biggest cases. It was where Lomond had been stationed during the Sandman murders, when he was granted the rarity of working exclusively on that one case.

Overseeing it all was Detective Superintendent Linda Boyle, whose office was on a small mezzanine above a bullpen of dozens of desks separated by fabric dividers. As the leader in all operational matters of the MIT, she didn't see much sunlight. Or get much sleep. She was often the first one in, and last one out.

She met Lomond and Ross in the bullpen, which still had several CID officers on secondment hard at work gathering evidence to support a charge on a suspect being held in the custody suite before they ran out of time.

Boyle took a quick slurp of coffee from a mug that was so badly stained, just drinking from it deserved a Chief Constable's Bravery Award. 'Thanks for taking that to Gartcosh,' she told Lomond.

'No bother,' he replied. 'They're pretty buried over there as usual, but they'll get to it as quickly as possible.'

'Well, I appreciate that, John.' She gave Ross a lingering dry look.

Taking the cue, he pointed towards his desk. 'I'd better...'

'Thanks, Ross,' said Boyle.

Before he left, he held his hand out to Lomond. 'Thanks for your help tonight, sir. Paisley's lucky to have you.'

Once he was out of earshot, Lomond told Boyle, 'If you had twenty Ross McNairs, the clearance rate in here would double.'

'Don't I know it,' she replied. 'Just so you know, I tried to talk Reekie down tonight...'

'It's alright.'

'I hate to ask you, but would you mind popping back tomorrow morning for a handover with Sutherland? I don't want his fuck-up on this Fiona Ferguson stuff to spiral any further. That FLO with her says she's talking about making a formal complaint against Sutherland. Negligence. Can you imagine if this wee guy shows up dead?'

Lomond perched on the edge of a vacant desk. 'If rule one is don't fuck up, rule two should be don't fuck up with a criminal defence solicitor.' He looked down into his hands. 'Promise me, Linda–'

'We'll get him,' she assured him. 'Go get some sleep.' She turned to DS McNair. 'Ross. You too. Get your head down.' When she spotted him clearing paperwork from his desk, she added, 'Ross. At *home*.' She told Lomond, 'You too, mister.'

'Night,' he said, heading back through the bullpen. Then he stopped. 'Linda?'

'Yeah?'

'Do you think you'll get him this time?'

She took a beat, wondering what their chances were without Lomond onboard. Then, for the first time in all their years of working together, she lied.

'Yes,' she said.

CHAPTER FOURTEEN

LOMOND FELT like he'd barely been through his front door before it was time to leave again the next morning. After getting home from Helen Street, he had sat in front of his wall of Sandman research eating a pie and beans with a can of Tennent's lager, taking it all in – still hoping against all odds that some detail would jump out at him that he could take into Helen Street later on. But nothing had come of five years dedicated work. The idea that something new would reveal itself at the eleventh hour was little more than wishful thinking.

He had always found his best ideas came from thinking intensely hard about the problem for a long time, and then simply walking away from it. His brain had done all the hard work. At a certain point, he had to give it space to run through the calculations, then the answer would suddenly click when he was in the middle of doing something as innocuous as taking his car to a car wash. Or ironing. He had even solved a problem in a murder case cooking a batch of chilli with The Blue Nile's *Hats* album blasting at a deafening volume.

Deep down, Lomond knew that the Sandman case wasn't about one little detail and a moment of revelation. It was about grunt work. Putting in the time. Pounding the pavement. Inches at a time. Talking to people.

As much as the abduction of Jack Ferguson was a catastrophe for his parents, if it was indeed the Sandman that was responsible, it was exactly what the police needed to regain a foothold in the original investigation. It had been running for so long now, finding new witnesses and clarifying existing statements became harder and harder. Memories fade. People forget. And the one thing that a solid murder case needs is certainty. Without it, a defence team would rip you apart.

Before he left the next morning, Lomond took one last look at the wall and resigned himself to being stuck on the outside of the investigation.

The drive to Helen Street for the handover was little more than a quick run down the M8 from Paisley, turning off before the really heavy rush-hour traffic kicked in around Ibrox. The thought of pulling into that drab grey building at Mill Street later on, while a new potential Sandman case started up, was crushing.

When Lomond had played football in school, his dad would berate him for running away from the action. Wee John argued that he was trying to find space, but his dad told him that it didn't matter. 'The best fitballers want the ball, John. Because when it comes down tae it, you cannae trust a teammate to score. All you can do is rely on yoursel.' It wasn't long after that conversation that John quit the football team and took up running long-distance instead. No more teammates for him. No more disappointments. It would all be on him.

Stuck behind a Glasgow Airport bus showing an ad on the back for some idyllic Caribbean island with the tagline 'ISN'T IT TIME YOU ESCAPED?', Lomond thought about what his days in Paisley CID were going to look like for the next while. Building cases against neds slashing each other in parks. Shoplifters at Braehead. Junkies...well, pretty much everywhere. Burglaries. And what the job was becoming more and more: mental health emergency response.

Lomond caught sight of the hubbub as soon as he came off the roundabout onto Helen Street. There were dozens of press outside. And not just photographers. There were three TV-news crews, their vans taking up most of the public parking outside the orange-brick security wall.

'The hell is going on?' he muttered under his breath. He told himself that it must be for a different case. Perhaps a terror suspect being brought in. Or a footballer on a speeding charge.

Then he saw Colin Mowatt. The little ginger weasel

himself. Thumbs poised over his phone as he launched more poisonous rhetoric onto Twitter.

As soon as Lomond pulled up to the entrance barrier, waiting for the anti-terror roadblocks to lower into the road, Mowatt and a few others leapt towards Lomond's window.

He heard his name being called, and he felt like someone who'd staggered into a movie halfway through. He exclaimed to himself, 'What the fuck is going on?'

Camera lenses pivoted towards him. Then more clamouring as the TV crews joined in.

Someone called out, 'Are you back in charge, DCI Lomond?' 'Are there any arrests imminent?'

Then from Mowatt: 'Is this Police Scotland's biggest-ever failure, John?'

Lomond was relieved to reach the relative sanctuary of the interior car park, but his head was still spinning.

There was more of the same inside, although at much lower volume and without cameras. Lomond could feel eyes on him from all directions. The way that people stare dumbly at celebrities when they see them in public. There were whispers. The corridors felt weirdly charged as Lomond walked through them.

He knew that as far as police officers went, he was reasonably famous insofar as most cops would never be interviewed by *BBC News* as he had been so many times. Lomond had featured as part of an evening's lead story for an accumulated total of weeks.

As he held his ID card up to the RFID reader at the secure entrance to the Major Investigations Team floor, in the slit of a window in the door, Lomond spotted DCI Sutherland making his way through the bullpen. He was carrying a large cardboard box and had a face like he'd had nettles for breakfast.

The appearance of Lomond didn't do much to lift his spirits.

'Well,' Sutherland said from several steps away. 'You got what you wanted, John.'

'What are you talking about?' Lomond asked.

Sutherland didn't realise that Lomond wasn't playing dumb. He genuinely didn't know. 'Someone at Tulliallan must really like you.'

'News to me.'

Sutherland took a withering look up towards Boyle's office on the mezzanine. 'They're waiting for you upstairs. Just do me a favour, Big Yin. Don't fuck this up.'

Boyle appeared at her window, waving Lomond to come up.

There was someone else in there, but he couldn't tell who until he opened Boyle's door.

'Good morning, John,' said Chief Superintendent Reekie, legs crossed, picking lint from his trousers to let Lomond know that he considered the task of greater importance than bothering to look him in the eye.

'Sir,' Lomond said, standing in front of Linda's desk.

She remained standing by the window overlooking the bullpen. 'You'll have heard by now, then?'

'I haven't heard a thing,' said Lomond. 'Other than a squad of the great unwashed outside.'

Reekie leaned forward to lift his peaked cap, indicating the copy of the *Glasgow Express* underneath.

The headline read: "THE SANDMAN IS BACK"

'Colin Mowatt's handiwork,' said Reekie, indicating the newspaper. 'But then, it was only ever going to be a matter of time before it got out. Another twenty-four hours would have made things much easier for us. Not to mention the Ferguson family.'

Linda added, 'There's a bigger police presence at their house this morning than there was last night.'

'Sir, forgive me,' said Lomond, 'but I haven't caught any news this morning. And I just passed DCI Sutherland–'

'Sutherland's gone,' Reekie announced. 'Linda's already gone through the details with me. The fact is, I can't have the mother of the victim being dealt with so sloppily. And given the way this has blown up in the media overnight, I've decided to keep you on, John.' He stood up and popped his cap back on. He shook Lomond's hand without a word. 'I've got to say, John. I didn't think any of the DCCs held you in such esteem. I'm almost impressed.' At the door, Reekie said, 'Linda will give you the details. And John...let's nail the bastard this time, eh?'

Lomond was still shaking his head once he was alone with Linda. 'Can you please tell me what the hell is happening?'

Linda walked across the office to close the door. 'Whatever you said to Fiona Ferguson last night must have really landed. It seems that she called in a favour from her old pal, Jim Airey.'

Lomond's eyes widened. 'She's pals with the Deputy Chief Constable?'

'She gave him hell over Sutherland's fuck ups last night with the crime scene photographs. She said you were the only person she trusted to find her son. Which doesn't count for bugger all, of course. Until Airey picked up the phone and spoke to me. He was impressed with your work, John. We nearly missed a vital piece of evidence because of Sutherland.'

'The DCC and her must be pretty friendly for him to get involved.'

'Less to do with friends,' said Linda, 'and more to do with the outstanding favour he probably owed her. Maitland Ferguson got Airey off a speeding charge last year.'

'That's the first I'm hearing of it.'

'It happened down south during the summer. It was hushed up as a favour. Seems like Airey leaned on Reekie pretty hard this morning.' Linda pursed her lips with an encouraging nod. 'You're in the hot seat, John.' She pointed to the clock on her wall as she marched across her office. 'And that also means you're doing the eight o'clock briefing in fifteen minutes.'

CHAPTER FIFTEEN

THE MURMUR of conversation died down a little when Lomond emerged from Linda's office. She clapped everyone to attention to neuter the remaining chatter. There was a sense of anticipation in the air. By now, word had got around that Jack Ferguson was looking like a potential new Sandman case. The fact that the Major Investigation Team would be dealing solely with the enquiry was a clear indication of how seriously Linda was taking it – and how scared the executive branch at Tulliallan were of the mounting press coverage, which, so far, had been unremittingly savage on Police Scotland.

A new Sandman case was going to be a lead news story every day until either a body was found or the killer was caught. It wasn't every day you got to work a case like that, even at the thick end of things in Govan.

The twenty-strong team all stood to attention around the bullpen, watching Lomond with a mix of intrigue and intimidation. Only DS McNair and DSU Boyle had worked with him in any capacity, but word of his exploits in the Sandman case had travelled far and wide through the years. To have such a DCI helming their case was a big deal.

'Good morning, everyone,' Linda announced, taking up a spot in front of a long whiteboard. 'For those of you who have been living under a rock for the last ten years, or for the little ones we still have running around here in their Pampers pull-ups, this is DCI John Lomond. He's going to be leading things from the ground here.' She looked to Lomond. 'John. All yours.'

Lomond took up a position in front of the whiteboard that ran for several feet at the front of the bullpen, which DS McNair had diligently filled with the details of Jack Ferguson's abduction as they knew it so far.

Lomond paced slowly from one side of the board to the other. 'Keiran McPhee, Leanne Donnelly, Blair Forbes, Mark Whitehouse, Taylor Clark. Before last night, those were the known victims of the serial child-killer we've come to know as the Sandman. Now, we may well have a sixth name to add to that list in a few days' time: Jack Ferguson.

'Jack was abducted from his bedroom after his parents had been drugged by a home invader that had hidden in the bedroom for hours beforehand. Jack has been missing since about half past ten last night. So far, we have no clear leads. No meaningful eyewitnesses. No physical evidence. And as you might have noticed outside, the press are all over this already.'

There was silence across the bullpen – everyone listening with rapt attention.

Lomond went on, 'Why, then, am I encouraged? Because I know that standing in front of me are twenty of the best officers in Greater Glasgow, which puts you high in the running for best in this entire police force. Helen Street is the thick end of the wedge. We are in this room because we have passed gruelling selection processes. We have studied and passed exams, and put in hundreds of hours on the sort of core competencies that are going to solve this case, and find Jack Ferguson.' He stopped pacing, coming to a halt in front of the centre of the board. 'I've investigated a lot of abductions and murders. I've had to sit down with the families of the abducted and tell them that their children have been found dead. In previous Sandman cases, there were a few things in our favour. The abducted children were kept alive until the fifth day. It's not a lot, but it's something. It means we have a *little* time. But we're also seeing details that suggest we could be dealing with a Sandman killer who's operating slightly differently this time.' He paused, wanting the point to sink in. 'It means that we should prepare ourselves for absolutely anything.'

There was silence, as everyone wondered whether the briefing was over or not.

Lomond's gaze panned across the room at the unfamiliar faces. 'Today, we get our fundamentals right. Where is DS Whyte?'

A hand went up in the middle of the bullpen.

Lomond said, 'Your team is on eyewitnesses in the streets

around the Ferguson property. DS McNair ran down loads of statements last night while eyes and memories were fresh. I want more doors chapped today. We have these images to distribute now–' he pointed to the images of the suspect captured on the Fergusons security camera '–which might jog some memories. If your people are talking to multiple-occupancy properties, which most of these are in Dowanhill, I want everyone in the property spoken to. Not just mums and dads. I want kids who were up late playing video games, or smoking fags in the back garden when they thought everyone was in bed.'

Whyte gave a firm, 'Yes, sir.'

Lomond looked elsewhere. 'DS Hutchison?'

A voice called out, 'Hutchinson, sir.' Followed by a hand in the air.

'Apologies, Detective Sergeant,' said Lomond. 'You're on vehicle identification, and for my money, this is where we get the most bang for our buck. So I want you teaming up with DI Dagley and DS Johnstone. We need all our manpower directed to finding whatever car or vehicle the suspect used. It wouldn't have to be big, of course, so check everything from tiny Fiats to minivans.'

DI Dagley announced, 'I've already got my guys combing through traffic cameras from a square mile out.'

DS Johnstone added, 'We're looking through night bus camera footage, external property cameras, restaurants and bars. Anything for suspects that match the description we have.'

Lomond was shaking his head before Johnstone had even

begun. 'Guys, a square mile out is too far. There's no way this suspect walked as far as a mile with a five-year-old child that late at night. It draws attention. The suspect could not have been parked more than a few streets away. We need to focus on going door to door. Every car that we know was in or near Dowanhill within ten minutes of the time that Jack Ferguson was taken.'

DS Johnstone made the mistake of doubling down. 'Our thinking was that the bigger a picture we have, the more comprehensive–'

Lomond could tell that he wasn't getting his point across. He felt a frustration boiling up that no one else in the room except DSU Boyle could understand. 'There's no *time* for that! We have to focus all of our efforts on the jobs we can get done in the time that we think we might have.' He marched towards the board and wrote in black marker as big as would fit, "5 DAYS". He pointed to it. 'That's what we have, people. If we're working off what's happened before. That's all we have. And trust me when I tell you, that when I led the charge for Mark Whitehouse and Taylor Clark, we did exactly what you just suggested. We lost an unconscionable amount of time. I've been here before. And searches of a square mile might sound like diligent police work, but they're a time suck, and they'll kill this investigation. In my time working these cases, each abduction was a chance to do things a little bit better next time. Well, people, it's time to stop learning lessons! I'm sick of learning lessons. It's time to finally get it right and *catch* this bastard.'

Total silence.

Lomond took a long breath, and made eye contact with as many in the room as he could. 'Believe me when I tell you, you do not want to be standing in this room a year from now, going over the same details of yet another abduction. The clock's ticking, people.' He made a spinning motion with his hand. 'Let's get to work.'

DS McNair, standing next to DSU Boyle, let out a long puff, releasing all the tension he'd been holding in during Lomond's speech. He said, 'Ma'am, I thought DCI Lomond didn't know he was back on the case?'

'He didn't,' she replied.

'I didn't see him read from any notes. How long did he have to put together that briefing?'

'About five minutes.'

He shook his head in wonder. He would spend hours refining an eight o'clock briefing the night before. And there certainly wouldn't be any extra motivational part to it. Ross said under his breath, 'Freak.' Remembering who was standing next to him, he then corrected himself, 'All due respect, of course, ma'am.'

'No, you're right. He is without doubt a freak.' She smiled. 'You want to be good police, Ross?' She pointed at Lomond. 'That's what to aim for.'

Lomond joined Linda and Ross. 'Have you found me some guys, Linda?'

'Yeah,' she replied, turning to find them. 'Jason! Pardeep! Arses over here, please...' She kept hunting for another face among all the grey and navy suits, until she caught sight of a man in his late forties with a stern expression and short low-maintenance haircut that he cut with clippers at home once a month. Linda beckoned him over. 'Willie!'

Lomond looked pleased at the sight of him coming over.

DI Willie Sneddon might have looked on the slightly goofy side because of his small sticking-out ears, but he spoke with a broad Glasgow accent that suggested he shouldn't be messed with. He could converse with equal comfort with junkies and judges, and advocates and arseholes alike. He was just rough enough for the bams to take him seriously on the street, and by-the-book enough to keep the senior officers satisfied.

'Good to have you back, John,' DI Sneddon said, squeezing Lomond's hand.

Lomond shook it back warmly, immediately feeling like his new team was in safe hands. 'I'm just sorry that we're still on this.'

Sneddon had worked under Lomond on the original Sandman case, and had been one of the continuing officers when Lomond went on leave.

Linda laid her hand on Sneddon's shoulder. 'I'll leave you to it, Willie.'

As she retreated for consultation with the other detective sergeants, Willie handled the rest of the introductions. 'I gather you and DS McNair are already acquainted, John.'

Ross gave a firm nod.

Willie moved on swiftly to an Asian man in his mid-thirties who looked awkward in his suit, fidgeting with his lanyard that was tangled around his tie, which had been tied too big and loose, like a wedding guest starting to wind down the formality in his appearance once the dancing starts. He had a low hairline which he had tried to hide with a short buzzcut.

Lomond couldn't help noticing the Marks and Spencer label still stitched on the right cuff of the officer's suit. Pardeep didn't know that it wasn't meant to still be on there.

'This is Detective Constable Pardeep Varma,' Willie explained. 'He's not long come over from Pollokshields CID, where he's really excelled.'

'Sir,' Pardeep said to Lomond.

Lomond told him, 'I've known a lot of good officers who've come out of Pollokshields, Pardeep. I'm looking forward to working with another one.'

He maintained his formal stance, but allowed himself a hint of a smile.

Willie moved on to the other officer. 'And this is Detective Constable Jason Yang. He's worked with me and DS McNair for two years now. He's a bit of a Boy Scout, but we don't hold that against you, do we, Jason?' Willie flashed a crooked grin.

DC Yang seemed oblivious to the fact that anything remotely funny had been said.

First-generation Scots-Chinese, he was clean cut and had a powerful, muscular frame from a rigorous daily gym habit. Where Ross had more of a lean swimmer's build, Jason was a pure brick shithouse. He kept his hair cropped to a slightly fuzzy length, and dressed like every day was a job interview.

But despite his intimidating physical presence, he had a shy, nervy demeanour, as if a film director had told him "act like you're meeting your personal hero but you're scared stiff". He leaned forward eagerly to shake Lomond's hand, then launched into a series of near-run-on sentences in a thick west coast accent, with a tinge of Paisley about it. 'It's a pleasure to meet you, Detective Chief Inspector. I followed the Sandman case closely, and read everything I could about the investigation. I was working out of Paisley CID before I came here, but unfortunately I didn't get a chance to meet you. I'd really like to thank you for this opportunity. I can't tell you–'

Lomond felt like his only option was to interrupt, or they'd be standing there all day. 'Well, it was Willie who picked you, but thanks all the same.'

Jason nodded deeply. 'Of course, of course, sir.'

Willie rubbed his hands together. 'Okay, you two. You've both got fifty registration plates to start tracking. Get to work.'

Once they were safely away at their shared desk space, Lomond said, 'Bit of a sausage-fest here, Willie.'

'Aye, I know.'

'And I could do with another familiar face. I'm sure these two are good, but we're not exactly overloaded with getting-to-know-you time here.'

'Have you got someone in mind?'

Lomond took a beat. 'There's a constable working out of Mill Street that I want.'

'What's the name?'

'Donna Higgins. I need a hard worker. A safe pair of hands.'

Willie gestured at the twenty others in the room. 'This Helen Street MIT, John. These are all hard workers.'

Lomond smirked. 'Yeah. Not like this, they're not.'

CHAPTER SIXTEEN

As DC Donna Higgins launched into a foot chase, she puffed under her breath, 'Ye fuckin' junkie bastard...'

An old man, shuffling along with his walking stick and daily bag of groceries from Marks and Spencer, turned to follow the chase along the quiet halls of Braehead Shopping Centre. 'Go get 'em, hen!' he told her.

A constable should have been embarrassed at having a member of the public overhear what she'd muttered, but Donna Higgins had never been one for worrying about what people thought of her.

She was meant to have been done with this kind of work. Hoofing after bams who had decided to help themselves to a cheeky wee five-finger discount. She had passed her detective exam three weeks ago now, but an administrative error at Dalmarnock from an office temp had left her without a team to join. With shortages in staffing being what they were,

Donna had been roped into her old beat until it had been all ironed out.

Currently in her crosshairs was Tony McGoldrick. DC Higgins' assessment of him – foul-mouthed as it was – was entirely accurate. He was skinny. And he was most certainly a fuckin' junkie. On most days, though, Tony wouldn't be described as a bastard, exactly. He wasn't that mean. As far as junkie bams went, he was a good egg. If he saw an old lady heading for the lifts in the high flats that he called home at Gallowhill Court, he'd hold the button to keep the doors open. When he was done with last season's St Mirren home jersey, he donated it to charity. It just so happened that he was between jobs at the moment. The last job was several years ago, and the job had been stealing cars, but he was between jobs nonetheless.

Which is why he had been pinching Xbox games and Blu-rays from HMV at five past ten in the morning at Braehead Shopping Centre, and now had Donna haring after him through the mall.

The Braehead security staff couldn't get near her pace. The sedentary pace of work in the centre made them a bad fit for foot chases.

Tony's arms flailed about his head in a panic as he tried to manufacture more speed. Several of the stolen Blu-rays that he'd slipped into a Tesco bag-for-life spilled out onto the floor, destroying any pleas of innocence he might have claimed. Five separate CCTV cameras caught the moment.

He dropped the doctored bag, which was only going to slow him down. He had lined the bag with silver foil to stop the security barrier sensors at HMV's exit picking up the tagged items that Tony had slipped in there. Except the foil had fallen off on one side.

The call had come over the radio to the security guard moping about by the revolving doors at the main entrance. He could see Tony sprinting towards him from ages away, but that only gave him time to question his options. He wasn't allowed to physically restrain a shoplifter, but suddenly he felt the eyes of the security team watching in the camera suite on him, and he decided he was going to impress them.

Would he rugby tackle him? Turn in profile to offer a firm shoulder block? Or should he opt for the good old waist-high spear?

Before the guard could decide, Tony was bearing down on him, eyes wide and throbbing white like a man who was not cut out for jail time. The guard held his hands out like he was trying to catch a stray dog, then weakly grabbed at Tony's torso.

But Tony was carrying far too much speed, and sent the guard flying onto his back.

Tony kept going, careering into the revolving door pod, which was travelling much too slowly for him. With nowhere to go, he slammed side-on into one of the glass panels, the impact from which stopped the doors dead in their tracks.

Now he was stuck.

And DC Higgins was getting ever closer.

She yelled at the guard who was now sprawled on the floor, 'Stop him!'

Tony shoved the door panel through, heart racing as he heard DC Higgins' instructions getting ever louder behind. Now in the freedom of the outside, he hared off across the car park. His eyes were everywhere, searching for the best escape route. So much so, he didn't notice the white reversing lights of a car that pulled out in front of him. The driver hit the brakes, but caught enough of Tony to make him feel like he was stuck in a particularly shitty ping-pong machine. The impact knocked him to the ground, where he rolled over twice.

The driver threw her door open, gushing with worry, as Tony scrambled back to his feet.

All his years playing Grand Theft Auto, the idea of hauling someone out of their car and stealing it as a getaway vehicle seemed quite appealing when he had a two-lager-and-a-joint buzz on. In real life, there was no way he could throw someone to the ground and steal their car.

Back at the shopping centre, DC Higgins didn't waste time with the revolving door, which now had a panel hanging off its hinges. Instead, she saw a button twenty feet short of the doors that opened the disabled access doors. But they weren't opening quickly enough for her.

She turned in profile to fit through as best she could, but the gap was slightly too narrow. Her shoulder crashed into the metal frame. The force of the impact almost stopped her in her tracks.

Now she was really mad, and she wasn't about to let him

get away. She didn't mind the running. She didn't mind the physical exertion. Or the pain. What she minded was doing it all in a stiflingly humid morning, carrying a tonne weight of gear and wearing a stab vest that was bouncing up around her ears with each thrust of her arms.

Tony had opted for the cycle path, which was free of traffic and obstacles but was also a long straight drag where DC Higgins could tell how much closer she was getting.

In a way, she was impressed that Tony had kept going as long as he had. Most other junkie shoplifters would have given up half a mile back. He had won her grudging respect. That didn't mean that when she finally caught up to him that she wouldn't enjoy slapping the cuffs on him and dragging him back to the shopping centre.

At a certain point, passing the rear service entrance to Sainsbury's, Tony realised that DC Higgins quite simply wasn't going to stop. It was like being chased by the silver shape-shifting guy from *Terminator* 2. Normal human things like exhaustion, a pounding heart, and bloody incredible heat for such an early hour, didn't seem to affect her.

He couldn't do it anymore. It took him a dozen more strides to commit fully to stopping, but stop he did.

DC Higgins kept sprinting as if he was still on the move, and charged into the back of him, knocking him over like a tenpin.

'Right, bawheid,' she huffed, cuffing him. 'I should boot you out yer trainers for that! Luckily for you, I've got respect for the rule of law. And the fact that there are too many cameras around here for me to get away with dragging you into these trees and rearranging your face.' She took a moment to evaluate him. 'Although rearranging it might be an improvement.'

Gasping for breath, Tony whined, 'Haw, come oan, mate...I didnae even dae nuthin!'

'Come on.' She hauled him to his feet, grabbing a handful of his raggedy t-shirt around the shoulder, and was about to call in the catch when she received a call on her shoulder-mounted radio. She tilted her ear towards it, giving Tony a shake, whose rambling excuses were stopping her from making out the call. 'Sorry, say again...'

The operator said, 'The sarge wants you to call him. He says there's a DCI John Lomond asking after you.'

CHAPTER SEVENTEEN

BACK AT HELEN STREET, Lomond was getting into his suit jacket, even though it was the last thing he wanted to be doing given the temperature outside. Linda was knocking on her window up the stairs, but Lomond couldn't hear her and started towards the secure double doors.

Linda wrapped up her phone call, then ran to the top of the stairs. 'John!' she shouted.

Lomond waited.

She didn't say anything until she was standing right in front of him. 'Where are you going?'

Wondering what the rush was, Lomond said, 'I'm going out to Mill Street. There's a constable over there I've worked with that–'

'I've got Gartcosh on the line upstairs,' she said, looking for DI Sneddon and DS McNair. She called the pair of them over.

'What is it?' asked Lomond. 'The cuddly toy? The badger?'

Boyle nodded and led them all away from a shared desk space. 'They found a mark on one of the eyes.'

Linda didn't mean a stain or a blemish. She was using the technical forensic term for fingerprint.

'Is it someone we know?' asked Willie.

Linda stared at Lomond for a moment, hoping he was prepared for what she had to say. But she knew there was little chance of that happening.

Linda said, 'The mark belongs to Maggie Belmont.'

Willie's mouth hung open a little. 'Fuck me...'

Lomond let out a considered, long exhalation as he tried to work out how it was possible. Then he shook his head. 'That's impossible. That's...'

'It should be,' said Linda, 'but it's not.'

'There must be—'

She knew what he was going to say. 'They've checked. And no, it's not just some intern or student. This one went right to the top at Livescan. Believe me. Because the next call I have to make is to the Deputy Chief Constable.'

Ross couldn't understand what had spooked them all so much. 'Who's Maggie Belmont?' he asked.

Lomond said, 'An unsolved disappearance from twenty years ago.'

Willie said to Linda, 'I thought they closed it a few years ago.'

'Nope,' she replied. 'It's still open. Although, technically, it was closed for a while.'

All eyes turned to Lomond.

'Aye,' he said, his voice dropping an octave.

Ross could tell from the ensuing awkward silence that something had gone wrong with Lomond and the case. But what Linda had to say next was about to kick the Maggie Belmont news into the tall grass.

'That's not everything,' she said, focussing on Lomond. 'They found a DNA match in the carpet, John.'

Her dire tone was the only reason he wasn't excited at the news. 'Is it someone we know?'

She exhaled gruffly. 'It's Sandy Driscoll.'

Lomond shut his eyes, then looked towards the ceiling in dismay.

It was a name that even Ross had heard through the years. 'That rings a bell,' he said. 'Who was he again?'

Lomond put his hands on his hips, facing the others again. 'If you'd asked me that yesterday, I'd have given you a completely different answer. Right now? He's looking like the worst mistake of my career.'

CHAPTER EIGHTEEN

DI Sneddon and DS McNair leaned over the guardrail at the front deck of the Caledonian MacBrayne ferry – the MV Caledonian Isles – watching the island of Arran getting ever closer. With the sun beating down at the height of the school summer holidays, it had taken much longer than usual to get to Ardrossan from Glasgow because of crowds streaming to the west coastline for the beaches at Irvine, Troon, and Ayr – and Arran itself.

The queue for the ferry had been so long that the pair would never have made it on had DI Sneddon not demanded that the port staff let them jump the queue. It wasn't immediately obvious to the other passengers waiting that they were, in fact, police. With the temperature rising, so were tempers. Ross had held his badge out of the open window to mollify the complaints before things escalated.

There was a stiff breeze out on the Firth of Clyde, and the water was as calm as it would ever get. Willie had hooked his suit jacket over his shoulder, but now found himself putting it back on. Even at twenty-five degrees back on shore, out on the water the wind chill was knocking nearly ten off that number.

Ross kept his eyes fixed straight ahead on the peak of Goatfell that was at the centre of the island's mountains. From the right place and on a clear day, you could see the peaks from as far away as the west end of Glasgow.

Willie should have had plenty of time to explain the Maggie Belmont case in the car drive to Ross, but he had rambled on for so long, by the time they reached Ardrossan port, he still hadn't got to Lomond's part in the case.

Stuck on an hour-long ferry trip, Willie now had the time to fill in the blanks.

With her husband out on the water night-fishing, Maggie Belmont's mother Sharon had put her seven-year-old daughter Maggie to bed, then nipped out to the pub at Brodick for a quick drink on a Saturday night. But one drink turned into several, and before Sharon knew it, it was close to ten o'clock. When she got home, she found her back door flapping open, and her daughter gone.

At first, the local cops assumed it was a runaway job, as there were no signs of forced entry or a struggle. Maggie's bedcovers were rolled back neatly, much as any child would when getting up in the middle of the night. The next thought was that Maggie had got up and tried to find her mum, and when the search failed, she set out on foot to find her. But the Belmonts lived in a small cottage near the Glen Rosa hike trail and campsite. The only way that Maggie would possibly have gone was along a narrow B road towards Brodick. And there hadn't been sightings anywhere of a small child walking alone.

By midnight, the local police were locked into a full-scale search of the area. Local residents set off in groups carrying torches. Maggie's name rang out long into the night.

Come morning, she still hadn't been found.

By the time that back-up arrived from Glasgow, the entire island was on high alert. Being late July, there were plenty of tourists around, and the gossip became that some sordid mainlander had stolen Maggie. Every vehicle taking the ferry at the main port at Brodick and the smaller one north at Lochranza had been stopped and verified. The police were satisfied that Maggie was definitely still on the island.

They couldn't find her anywhere.

Around lunchtime, a couple hiking through Glen Rosa thought they had stumbled across a dead fawn next to the river. It was only when they took a closer look that they realised they were looking at a crumpled pile of clothes and a wool blanket covered in blood. Forensics later confirmed it as Maggie Belmont's, but there wasn't enough blood present to say conclusively that Maggie had been murdered.

Hours turned into days. Days into weeks, and no further evidence was found.

The case remained open for two years until an arrest was made.

'That's where John comes in,' Willie explained.

Ross asked, 'Did he catch the guy?'

'No, he wasn't involved like that. This was twenty years ago. John wasn't long a DC. Like everyone working out of Glasgow – and most of the country at the time – he'd heard of the case, but was never involved with the investigation directly. The MIT found a local boy they liked for the disappearance.'

'Sandy Driscoll?'

'Aye. On paper it made sense. He was in his twenties. A loner. A bit of a weirdo, you know. Just no' quite right. No' the full banana. Was always talking to himself when he was about the high street. There were rumours that he'd been seen prowling the Belmonts' back garden earlier in the day. He didn't have an alibi for when Maggie was taken, and he'd been spoken to by the local polis about talking to weans on the beach. So he was brought in for questioning. The guy cracked wide open after about an hour. He signed a confession that he'd taken her, but wouldn't admit to killing her. MIT worked him over for days until they finally got it out of him. Yes, he said. He had killed Maggie Belmont.'

'What about the body?' asked Ross.

'He couldn't tell them. Said he couldn't remember.'

'That doesn't sound right.'

'Of course it doesn't. But if he didn't kill her, why did he confess to it? Also, normally, the procurator fiscal needs either eyewitness statements, fingerprint evidence, or other forensic or scientific evidence. Apart from the confession, all they really had on Sandy Driscoll was circumstantial. But it went to trial and suddenly Driscoll told his lawyer he wanted to change his plea to not guilty. It didn't change anything, and he was convicted. That's where John comes in.'

'What happened?'

'I only heard the rest second-hand. John found an eyewitness who claimed that Sandy Driscoll was nowhere near Arran when Maggie Belmont was snatched. John spent a week going through old CCTV files until he found Sandy Driscoll, right enough, a hundred miles away. An appeal judge quashed the original verdict and Driscoll was set free. The papers gave the force a kicking over it for weeks. To top it off, Driscoll was given a new identity and shipped off somewhere secret for his own protection.'

'Bloody hell,' said Ross. 'John can't have been popular after that.'

Willie snorted. 'Are you kidding? He singlehandedly dismantled a solved case that had involved thousands of man hours and sent the enquiry right back to day one all over again.' He turned his palms up as if that was the end of it. 'It's been a cold case ever since.'

'Maybe not for much longer.'

'What do you mean?'

'Maybe Sandy Driscoll's been operating for far longer than anyone ever thought. Maggie Belmont could be where this all started. And if Driscoll's calling attention to that now...'

Willie could see where Ross was going. 'Then Jack Ferguson might be where this all ends.'

CHAPTER NINETEEN

L OMOND FOUND himself catching the dregs of rush-hour and the start of the regular work-day traffic – all those white vans and delivery drivers, speeding like rally drivers and parking like they had dying passengers inside. He wound his way through the Southside onto the M74, past an endless series of storage facilities, plant hire firms, trade wholesalers, and industrial warehouses, all made of the same corrugated steel frames in similar shades of grey. It was a thoroughly depressing sight. Lomond couldn't help but think, *They cleared the Highlands...for this? This grey shite?*

The bleak surroundings, and the fact that being called to Police Scotland headquarters at Clyde Gateway in Dalmarnock often meant getting a roasting from a senior official, had led to its nickname of Mordor – named after the dark lord Sauron's lair in *The Lord of the Rings*.

The glass building on the banks of the Clyde was easy to spot coming across Rutherglen Bridge, but Lomond was damned if he could find the actual street to access the car park. It had happened each time he'd gone there. Pedestrianised walkways and cycle paths taunted him from the busy road. Each time he tried a different roundabout exit, his sat nav reloaded, the robotic voice informing him that 'the route is being calculated'. Lomond shouted in frustration, 'Just tell me where to go! You've got one bloody job to do, lady!'

Finally, he found a way in.

The hierarchy in the car park was easy to spot. Bunched together at one end were all the mid-price family saloons, followed by the Range Rover and Porsche SUVs of the executives and senior management. A lot of people that had never walked a beat in their life. Parachuted in through direct entry schemes that meant someone could go from civilian to superintendent without any operational experience. They weren't really police officers, as far as Lomond was concerned. They weren't helping cut crime or keep people safe. They were little more than accountants and managers.

'God help me,' Lomond muttered to himself as he headed for the main entrance.

Reception was like a budget airline's departure lounge, with the usual Scandi-knock-off furniture so beloved by architects and interior designers, but not anyone who had ever had to actually sit down on it.

What had been pitched to Lomond as being seen "shortly" turned into fifteen minutes. Which turned into half an hour.

He sat there, shifting and adjusting his position, trying to get comfortable. It pissed him off knowing that Reekie was likely up the stairs doing naff all. He would have just liked the idea of keeping Lomond waiting.

In fairness, it wasn't the worst thing for him in the circumstances. Traffic had been too busy on the way over to get any decent thinking done. Now that he was alone with his thoughts, his mind was racing at what the forensics at Gartcosh had identified.

If someone had been given free rein to come up with a scenario designed purely to detonate Lomond's career, having Sandy Driscoll's DNA discovered in the Fergusons' bedroom would have been it. If his police work that had contributed to freeing Driscoll in the Maggie Belmont case had made Lomond a pariah back then, he would be facing the policing equivalent of a Siberian gulag after this.

———

WHEN HE WAS FINALLY CALLED for, Lomond found Chief Superintendent Alasdair Reekie removing his glasses with a sharp grimace. 'John,' he said. 'What...the actual...' His face reddened, desperate to swear, but something inside held him back.

Lomond took it on the chin. 'I know, sir.'

'Please tell me how the hell this is all possible.'

'I know that there's going to be some blowback on this, but the fact remains that we have a significant lead in this Jack Ferguson investigation.'

'Yes,' said Reekie, failing to see the up side. 'Just a pity that it will be at the expense of making this force look like the Keystone Cops. If this gets out there...'

Lomond tilted his head, unsure if he'd heard correctly. 'Sir...this *is* going to come out. It's impossible for it not to. The Colin Mowatts of this world have got their sources in Gartcosh. We can't keep it secret for long.'

Reekie pushed his chair back from his desk. He retreated to his window, taking in the view to the trees and pond at Richmond Park across the River Clyde. 'What about this Maggie Belmont connection?'

'We're working on possible explanations, sir. I've sent Willie Sneddon and Ross McNair to Arran to do some digging.'

'Do you think this Belmont case could have been a Sandman-type situation?'

'I'm not ruling anything out yet. After we found Leanne Donnelly and it was clear we had a serial killer on our hands, we had teams that combed through old case files to be sure we weren't missing anything. Nothing ever flagged with Maggie Belmont.'

'We're going to have to dig into this. Properly this time.'

'With respect, sir. If Jack Ferguson has been taken by the killer we know as Sandman, then we have four days left. Assigning other charges to a murderer we haven't caught yet doesn't get Jack back to his parents. We can find all the other charges we want at the end of the week.'

Reekie closed his eyes and rocked on his heels. 'How did we miss this?'

'Sir, we had nothing else to go on. In the time between

the other abductions, yes, we looked at the Maggie Belmont case, as we did hundreds of others. But we couldn't assign every unexplained disappearance of a minor in the last twenty years to the Sandman. There was no sand left in her bed. We didn't even have a body.'

Reekie took his time to consider this, then returned to his chair. 'Publicly, you'll have the full support of the Executive Team, John.'

'Thank you, sir. I–' Lomond was too quick with his gratitude.

'Only because to do otherwise will hurt the force. Not backing you is the same as admitting we screwed up. There are political implications here, too. I mean, what if we haul Sandy Driscoll in and it turns out he's innocent? Again!'

'Sir, the chances of it not being Driscoll that was hiding under that bed, expressed as a probability accepted by our own forensic scientists is so low, they'd class it as zero. Zero, sir! It was him. He took Jack Ferguson. We know that now. What remains unknown is whether Driscoll also took Maggie Belmont, and if he's been the Sandman this whole time.'

Reekie puffed. 'What do you need from me?'

'When Driscoll's conviction was quashed, he was given a new identity under MAPPA as an offender under risk of serious harm. I need inside his MAPPA file to see his last-known address.'

Reekie leaned forward on his desk, hands clasped together. 'You know I can't tell you where he is. When some-one's granted a new identity the only people who know their new name and location are a senior official in the Public Protection Unit, and the assistant chief constable for the area in which the criminal is moved to.'

'He's still in the West Command somewhere, isn't he? The assistant chief constable must know where he is.'

Reekie smiled nervously. 'He would personally kill us both if he knew what was being discussed here.'

'I've got four days to correct this, sir. You've got every right to not respect me, dislike me, whatever it might be. But don't do that to Jack Ferguson. I beg you.' Lomond's face tightened. 'When this is over, feel free to can me. But I need to know where Sandy Driscoll is.'

'The Assistant Chief Constable is not going to make that call, John.'

'No, but you can. All I need is the last location we had for him.'

Reekie paused.

'If I'm right,' said Lomond, 'we catch the Sandman once and for all, and we save Jack Ferguson. Have you thought about the political implications of *that*?'

Reekie took a moment, then he scribbled something down on a piece of paper and handed it to Lomond. Before he could take it, Reekie retracted it. 'I hope you're prepared, John. You're about to become the most infamous police officer in the country.'

Lomond reached out for the paper, snatching it out of Reekie's hand. 'I lived with it once,' he said. 'I can live with it again.'

CHAPTER TWENTY

WILLIE AND Ross nearly drove past the police station in the tiny village of Lamlash, three miles south of the Brodick ferry port. Once they had doubled back on a quiet residential street, Ross couldn't believe that they had really found the right place. He alternated between the maps street view on his phone and the view out of the car window.

Willie laughed. 'Jesus. It's Bala-fucking-mory.'

The 'station' was little more than a modified bungalow with a police sign outside it, and a Ford Transit police van parked in the driveway. The thin plywood door and A4 printouts stuck to the inside of the window made it look like the extension to a rather small church hall.

The sergeant manning the front desk – covering two other roles within the station because of sickness and holiday time – put down his cup of tea when he saw the two city detectives rolling in. He was in his late fifties and looked so natural behind the desk that he could have been part of the furniture. 'Morning, gents,' he said, spotting their Police Scotland staff lanyards. 'I'm Sergeant Davie Muir. What can I do you for?'

Willie introduced them, then got straight down to business. 'Are you the senior on-site today, sergeant?'

Davie gestured at the cramped reception area, which was just a wooden desk in a hallway. He chuckled. 'I've got five constables for the entire island, detective inspector. I'm everyone today.'

'Davie, I'll tell you what it is, right. We're investigating the Maggie Belmont case.'

'Oh, aye,' he said darkly.

'Were you here at the time?'

'Aye. Been here twenty-three year. I helped with the search the first night...'

The sergeant wasn't just remembering it. He was reliving it. 'I used to see her cycling around the path beside the golf course. Always seemed a happy wee lassie...It was hard to imagine something like that happening here. The worst we normally have to deal wi' is speeding, and tourists parking illegally near the ferry terminal. Stuff like wee kiddies being taken out their beds isnae meant to happen in a place like this. It wisnae the same for a long time after that. Especially when the Driscoll boy's conviction was overturned.'

Willie said, 'I think that took everyone by surprise.'

'Horrible,' said Davie. 'Awful. Everyone around here knew there was something no' right with the lad. A little bit slow. Kept to himself. He used to chat to the kiddies on the beach. I spoke to him about it more than once. The parents didnae like him. I mean, I think he liked the kids because they were closer tae his level than the adults. Mind, no one ever thought he was capable of that.'

Ross was confused. 'His conviction was overturned.'

'I know. But the people round here lost a lot of faith in the police after that. I could have done without it, personally.'

Ross couldn't resist pushing him a little further. 'Do people here still think he did it?'

'Aye. And I'm one of them.'

Willie couldn't help but step in to defend Lomond. 'You know, DCI Lomond risked his career to make sure justice was served, and the right man was put behind bars. We'd do well to remember that.' Before he lost all sense of coopera-tion, Willie asked, 'Do you have an address for Sharon Belmont, Davie?'

He didn't need to look it up. 'She's still in that same cottage up by Glen Rosa. The white one on the side of the hill before the campsite. You can't miss it.'

After saying thanks, Willie and Ross turned to leave, when the sergeant stopped them.

'She'll no' be there, mind. Not today.'

'Where will she be?' asked Willie.

'Where she is this time every year. The Glen Rosa trail. Where we found the blanket and Maggie's clothes.' The sergeant said it like it was obvious. 'She kips out there on the anniversary.'

Willie and Ross didn't say anything further about it until

they were outside and could check the map that Sergeant Muir marked up for them.

Getting back in the car, Ross said, 'I thought we had officers going through the case files this morning.'

'Apparently.' Willie sniped. 'How much longer before someone told us Maggie Belmont was abducted on the same day of the year as Jack Ferguson?'

'First Sandman abduction in five years, and it happens to link to this same case. That can't be a coincidence.'

As Willie started up the engine, he told Ross, 'If you want to dally with coincidence, go to a psychic. We deal with police work in MIT, son.'

CHAPTER TWENTY-ONE

WILLIE AND ROSS drew more than a few strange looks from passing hikers on the loose and rocky Glen Rosa trail path that ran alongside the river. While everyone else was cutting about in short-sleeved sweat-wicking t-shirts and walking shorts and boots, the two detectives were carrying their suit jackets, baking under the lunchtime sun. Willie particularly was suffering. He had never had the complexion for sunbathing, and without the aid of suntan lotion – which he had neglected to put on that morning – he was rapidly turning the colour of a lobster.

Ross, meanwhile, looked just as out of place but far more comfortable than Willie, exchanging courteous nods with each passing hiker, who wondered where on earth the two men in shirts and ties and dress shoes could be going.

Half a mile along the trail, they saw a tent next to the river, along with burned-down candles and a standing framed photo of a young girl. A stiff breeze was rolling down through the glen, blowing the plastic wrap on a bunch of flowers Sharon Belmont had bought in the Co-Op the day before. She had put them into an empty own-brand cola bottle, fashioning it into a vase by cutting the bottle across the middle.

Sharon was sitting in a foldable picnic chair, smoking a cigarette and holding a can of Tennent's. She paid no mind to the two detectives until they were so near to her that she could no longer ignore their presence.

'Mrs Belmont,' Willie began, shuffling his arms reluctantly back into his suit jacket. 'I'm Detective Inspector Willie Sneddon. I'm from Glasgow.'

'Good for you,' Sharon replied, not making eye contact. She sounded half-cut, with the merest hint of a slur.

Willie gestured at Ross, introducing him as well. 'I was wondering if we could maybe ask you a few questions.'

She finished a long drag on her cigarette. 'Twenty years,' she said. She turned to look at them. 'That's her gone twenty years. Now you want to ask me some questions?'

Willie hadn't expected the hostility, and wasn't sure how best to proceed.

Ross stepped forward. 'Mrs Belmont, I'm very sorry for your loss on your daughter's anniversary. I know this must be a difficult time for you. I don't know if you've seen the news...'

'I heard it on the radio. What's it to do with me and my Maggie?'

'Maybe we could go somewhere and discuss it.'

'This isn't private enough for you? All these cameras and

massive crowds. Who's listening in? The deer or the fish?' She snorted to herself.

'We were wanting to talk to you about this.' From a leather-bound ledger, Ross took out the photo of the toy badger found in Jack Ferguson's bedroom.

Sharon put out her cigarette by dunking it into the can of Tennent's then got to her feet. 'I was about to pack up anyway. I've had enough for another year.'

WILLIE AND Ross had helped her pack up her tent, and walked her home to her cottage just over a mile away.

While the men waited patiently and silently in the living room, Sharon stood pensively in the kitchen, watching the kettle boil. Her mind was racing at the sight of the toy badger. Had they found someone? Was the photo their way of trying to soften the blow? Had they found Maggie's body finally? Twenty years of questions swirled around at once.

Before she crossed from the kitchen into the living room, she took a steadying breath. She put down a tray on the table: two builder's teas for the police; a cold can of Tennent's for her.

She was about to light a cigarette, when she stopped the lighter at the tip. 'Do you mind if I...?'

The two men were all polite deferential gestures. A little second-hand smoke was an occupational hazard – and often one worth paying the price for.

'I know I shouldn't,' she croaked, 'but I don't really care.

You get like that after...' Her hands were trembling. A nervous condition that she kept at bay by picking at the skin around the base of her fingernails. They were red raw. 'Do you ever meet people that know they're bad?'

'How do you mean?' asked Willie.

'No one does the right thing anymore, do they. Always trying to get away with something. Lying. Cheating. Stealing.'

'We certainly see plenty of that,' said Ross.

She took a long drink of lager. 'That's why I drink. I'm not worth a damn. I deserve it. To hurt myself.'

Ross slid forward to the edge of the couch. 'You of all people, Mrs Belmont, don't deserve to be punished. What happened was—'

'It was my fault,' she interrupted. 'Everyone around here knows it. They were too polite to say it to my face. I could see it when we were all out searching. Stretched out in a long line, arms linked, staring at the ground looking for any sign of her. They all blamed me. And they were right. I went out when I shouldn't have. If I'd stayed in, Maggie would still be here. You shouldn't be allowed to get away with it. To cause harm to come to your child. But the way I see it, killing myself would be cheating. I deserve punishment for what I did.' She took another drink and a puff of the cigarette. She exhaled a thick cloud of grey smoke. 'And when it's all done, I've still got hell to look forward to.'

Ross didn't know what to say, so he looked to Willie to take the lead.

'Mrs Belmont, I was hoping we could have a chat about

some evidence that's come into our possession. As you know, there was a young boy taken from his home in Glasgow last night.'

Before he could get any further, Sharon butted in. 'Some rich family. That's the only reason you care about Maggie again.' She put her arms out wide. 'Where's the search party these days? Who's still looking for Maggie? Who cares?'

'We care very much,' replied Ross. 'That's why it's so important we talk about this.' He laid the photo down on the table. 'Do you recognise that?'

'It's Maggie's badger. She called it Billy.' She squinted. 'How come you've got a photo of that?'

Ross rummaged through the other photos he had, finding one from the original case file on Maggie's disappearance. It showed an angle of Maggie's bedroom, capturing a few cuddly toys sitting at the foot of her bed. One of which was Billy the Badger. 'This cuddly toy wasn't mentioned in the original report. Was it always here?'

'It's still here right now,' she said.

The two men paused.

Willie asked, 'When did you last see that toy, Mrs Belmont?'

'Last week.'

The surprise – and disbelief – on the men's faces was obvious.

Feeling bolshy from the lager, she snapped, 'Is one of you going to tell me what's going on?'

'Am I correct in saying that the cuddly toy in this picture,' Ross showed the Jack Ferguson forensic photo again, 'was Maggie's? Not just the same type, but the same exact one.'

She took a close look. 'Aye. Its left leg is all frayed. Maggie used to hold it in her sleep. It got worn away.'

Willie said, 'Mrs Belmont, last night that toy was found at the crime scene involving the Ferguson boy.'

'It can't be,' she maintained, getting to her feet. She stomped off towards the bedroom.

The two detectives followed.

When they reached Maggie's old bedroom, Sharon had frozen.

'It's gone,' she said quietly. 'It was here. Last week. I looked right at it!'

'You're sure?' asked Willie.

'I don't like coming in here. Everything's just like it was the day she was taken. All I do is a bit of a dusting now and then.'

Ross asked, 'Have you heard any suspicious noises in the last week? Like a window or a lock being tried?'

'Are you saying someone's broken in and stolen Maggie's badger?' Panic descended on her face. 'They're saying online that the boy in Glasgow...it's the Sandman killer again.' She started to cry. 'Does that mean she's...is she really...'

'Right now, we don't know what it means,' Willie said.

She wiped a tear from her eye. 'I kept saying to myself, as long as they don't find the body there's still hope. She might be okay. But if he's taken her...'

Ross took a slow look around the room for any signs of disturbance. 'Mrs Belmont, standing here right now, without rummaging around the place, is there anything that looks out of place? Anything else that's not as you remember it from last week?'

Her head flitted about frantically, unable to think clearly. 'I don't know...I don't think so...' Then she looked at the duvet, her eyes narrowing. 'Hang on...' She pointed. 'That's upside down.'

The geometric pattern looked to be the same regardless of orientation at first glance. But Sharon knew it inch by inch.

She reached out for the upper corner near the pillow.

Ross put his hands out to stop her. 'No, no, no! Touch nothing.'

She stepped back.

Ross took out a disposable glove from his trouser pocket. Then he lifted the duvet up and back.

Slowly.

He held his breath.

As did Willie and Sharon.

Ross knew what was coming. It seemed inevitable once it was established that the cuddly toy had been taken from the room.

Ross stared at the small pile of sand sitting on the bed sheet, flattened slightly from the weight of the duvet that had been on top of it.

Sharon was horrified. 'That wasn't there last week.'

'I'm sure it wasn't,' said Ross. 'Mrs Belmont, we need to leave this room right now. We need to do some further inspections here.'

Out in the hall, Willie was on the phone. 'Where are you?'

Lomond was on speakerphone in his car. 'Just leaving Mordor. What have you got?'

'I need forensics over to Arran. He was here, John. He was here in the last week.'

CHAPTER TWENTY-TWO

ONCE REEKIE HAD SECURED permission from the Assistant Chief Constable to open Driscoll's file, Lomond was given a windowless secure office to access the Public Protection Unit records. He had a code that would open Driscoll's file, and only Driscoll's. There were tabloid journalists that would have paid a lot of money for half an hour scrolling through the unit's files. A lot of notorious criminals had been spirited away under new identities, given new addresses, new lives – while the victims of their crimes had to make do with their old lives. The ones they'd had shattered. Stolen from them. All it would take would be one tweet with an address, and a vigilante mob would assemble in no time.

Lomond couldn't access them, but there was a list of the offenders' names on a main register. Seeing them all grouped together, it was a who's who of human scum. Child killers. Serial murderers and rapists. Paedophiles. Gangsters. Drug dealers. Names that had hung onto the front pages of newspapers like mould around a window frame. Festering and only getting more toxic as time went on.

It boiled his blood to think of them just walking around a supermarket. Now looking completely different after their multiple decades locked away. So long that they couldn't even be recognised. Men who had murdered school children, now mixing mere feet away from playful children with their parents at the yoghurt aisle in Tesco. The parents with no idea how close their wee one had just been standing to a murderer.

Lomond scrolled to Driscoll's name and input the six-digit code.

There was a pause. Then a pop-up notification.

"NO ENTRY FOUND".

Lomond did a double-take. Then he entered it again.

Same result.

He called Reekie to double-check the code. He had the right one, it seemed.

This disturbed Reekie so much that he came down to check it himself.

When he got the same result as Lomond, he swore under his breath and covered his mouth while he thought through what had happened.

'It doesn't make any sense,' Reekie said. 'There's only one way this can happen.' He ran a hand over his thin hair. 'The file's been deleted.'

'Deleted?' exclaimed Lomond. 'How could that happen?'

'The only way is if someone with authorisation has gone in and deleted it manually.'

'Who has the authority to do that?'

'Only me, and—' He didn't want to finish his sentence.

'Who?' asked Lomond. He then insisted, 'Sir, who else has access to this file? You and the Assistant Chief Constable, right? I want to speak to him.'

Reekie backed away, raising his hands defensively. 'Let's not get too hasty. You can still access the physical file back at Helen Street.'

'Sir, that could take hours. In any case, the Assistant Chief needs to know, surely.'

'Best leave that to me,' said Reekie, puffing out his chest and heading towards the door, eager to draw the conversation to a close. 'I'm sorry, John. I'll look into it.'

Lomond packed up his things with a grumble once Reekie was gone.

In their long, antagonistic relationship, Reekie had never once apologised to Lomond. For anything. Lomond's polis senses were tingling. The same way when a criminal starts to panic during an interview, and can't remember what lies they told an hour ago. Reekie's eyes had the same panicked look to them.

The question was: why would someone go to such lengths to protect the location of Sandy Driscoll?

CHAPTER TWENTY-THREE

LOMOND HIGHTAILED it back to Govan with Reekie's weaselly words still echoing in his head – 'Publicly, you'll have the full support of the Executive Team, John...' – as he approached the entrance to Helen Street. He then saw what he recognised as DS Ross McNair's purple Ford hatchback. A boy racer car if ever there was one. An enlarged-cock-on-four-wheels. And exactly the kind that his idols on the Organised Crime squad cut about in.

But Ross didn't recognise Lomond's much plainer, anonymous saloon. He gunned the accelerator, cutting off Lomond so hard he had to slam the brakes on.

All Lomond saw was DI Sneddon pushed back in the passenger seat looking terrified, as he was the one in the firing line in a side-on collision.

Lomond didn't even have time to blast the horn, which made him doubly angry, because he wanted Ross to know that he was raging at him. And how better to demonstrate that than leaning on the horn for a good ten seconds?

Ross parked up, his heart pounding. He knew what he'd done. And Willie had now informed him who he'd done it to.

He glanced at Willie hopefully. 'Was that as bad as–'

'Aye,' he interrupted. As he struggled out of the cramped seat, he said, 'Cock socket. I'm driving next time.'

Lomond abandoned his car across two spaces in a blind rage, then stormed across the car park, shouting at Ross from a distance. 'Ho! Love Island. Cut me up like that again and I'll change your life.'

Ross held his hands up. 'Sorry, sir. Rush of blood and all that. My bad.'

Lomond corrected him, 'No, it was your fault. Not your "bad". "My bad" is a fucking meaningless combination of words used only by Yanks and total rockets. Which makes sense, clearly,' he gestured at Ross, 'as you are obviously a fucking rocket.' He pointed towards the staff entrance. 'Come on. We've got work to do.'

Out of earshot, Willie muttered to Ross, 'He's under a lot of pressure.'

'I noticed,' replied Ross. 'He was just applying it directly to my balls.'

'He likes the ones he shouts at. If he didn't like you, he'd just ignore you.'

Sounds ideal, thought Ross. And less scary.

Once his team had assembled in a conference room, Lomond steamed inside, kicking the door shut with his heel on the way past. 'Where are we?' he asked. 'Willie. Ross. Arran.'

Judging by Lomond's tone, Pardeep and Jason resigned themselves to a bollocking, knowing that they had little in the way of good news.

Willie said, 'Well, we left forensics at Sharon Belmont's house like you asked. They're checking everything, of course. Personally, I'd be amazed if they pull a mark that's worth anything.'

'I think,' Ross ventured, 'we can safely say that whoever abducted Jack Ferguson was in Sharon Belmont's house and stole the cuddly toy.'

Pardeep, flicking his pen fluidly up and down his knuckles, said, 'The question then is why? Why the need to now claim Maggie Belmont as one of his?'

'Posturing,' said Jason. 'He wants the credit. And taking Jack Ferguson is his chance to do that.'

Lomond raised his hands to stop them. 'Folks, I don't care. Does Maggie Belmont look like it was a Sandman case now? Probably. Does figuring that out help us find Sandy Driscoll in the next twenty-four hours? No. Now, Driscoll was given a new identity when he was released from prison, which was protected under the Public Protection arrangements, as it was felt he would still be a target for the public who were disinclined to believe his innocence. If only I'd been one of them, Jack Ferguson would be with his parents right now, along with five other wee souls...'

He wanted the ground to swallow him up at having to say it all in front of officers he barely knew. He felt their eyes on him. *"You did this, genius. You're the reason he was out walking the streets."*

Lomond concluded, 'But that's on me. I don't know how, but there must have been a flaw in the evidence that freed Driscoll last time. And I'll have to find a way to live with that. Right now, I need all of your attention on finding the hard copy of Driscoll's file.'

'What about the digital copy?' asked Willie.

'It's been deleted. And yes, that stinks in a way that I can barely process. But people, we have got to keep our focus on the task: find Sandy Driscoll. If we do that, I'm sure we'll find Jack Ferguson.'

There was a knock at the door that made everyone turn towards it.

It wasn't a meek knock of someone embarrassed at being late. It was an open-this-door-before-I-kick-it-in smack. Then DC Donna Higgins appeared.

'Sorry, sir,' she said, already marching towards a free seat. 'I got held up trying to get this.' She showed Lomond her lanyard. 'The Det Sup told me to come through.'

'You're just in time, Donna,' said Lomond.

He led them down to the basement, where the remaining hard copy files had been banished to. Row after row of metal filing cabinets stretched along a chilly concrete corridor, lit by harsh white lights of the buzzing and flickering variety.

'Welcome to your office for the next,' Lomond checked his watch, 'however bloody long it takes.'

Pardeep craned his neck, trying to see how far it went. 'There must be thousands of files here, sir.'

'Correct, Pardeep. And we're going to check every last one until we find Sandy Driscoll's.'

There was a lot of shuffling of feet and restrained complaints. Lomond knew what everyone was thinking.

He said, 'Guys, this is ten years of MAPPA records, right up until digitisation hit. All of them are sealed. We only have permission to open Driscoll's. And I might remind you all that opening a MAPPA record without senior permission is a crime. When you find Driscoll's file, you take it straight to either me or Willie.'

Jason raised his hand.

Willie said, 'You don't have to put your hand up, Jason. You're not in school.'

'Though it's not the worst idea in the world,' Lomond added.

Jason peeled one of the files out of a drawer. 'Sir, how will we know which one is his? There are no names on these.'

Donna, Ross, and Pardeep crowded around, hoping to hell that Jason was mistaken.

Overly bright, Lomond said, 'Correct, DC Yang. The file's six-character code is a mixture of letters and numbers, so remember it. God help you, if anyone has the file in their hands but passes over it because you lost concentration. Because believe me, people, we don't leave this corridor until we find the file.'

Ross looked at a few examples, then he looked ahead at

how many cabinets there were. His shoulders slumped at the scale of the task awaiting them.

Turning away from Lomond, Pardeep exhaled, then mouthed at Donna, 'Fuuuuck.'

Donna replied, 'That's what I was thinking.'

Lomond wondered why the beleaguered crew were standing still. 'Are you waiting for a starting pistol or something?' He clapped his hands. 'Let's go, people.'

From the warmer light of upstairs, one of the DSs from the bullpen crouched down to see the group. 'DCI Lomond? There's someone at reception asking for you.'

Ross flashed his eyebrows up at Donna, looking for an ally in the misery. 'Convenient.'

Standing next to them, eagerly beavering away already, Jason announced cheerily, 'At least it's nice and cool down here, guys!'

Not in the mood for levity, Ross directed Jason to the cabinets on the opposite side of the corridor. 'How about we make this a quiet job, eh, Jason.'

Everyone struggled to remember the code, stopping every second file to check it again. Except for Jason, who was the only one pleased at the task. It was a challenge mentally as well as physically, requiring the dextrous fingers of a pianist (which he was) and the numerical mind of a savant (which he also had).

After the first hour, the file code would be imprinted on all their brains like a red-hot iron brand. They'd be hearing it and seeing it and mouthing it in their sleep for days.

THE DETECTIVE SERGEANT waited for Lomond to emerge from the concrete stairwell.

'What's their name?' asked Lomond.

The DS answered, 'Campbell Fotheringham.'

He knew who it was. As did Lomond. As did almost every cop with a pulse.

Lawyer to the scum of the earth.

If Chief Superintendent Reekie was an arsehole, then Fotheringham was just a bastard. A lot of people used such swear words interchangeably. But to Lomond's mind, there was a clear distinction between the two. Arseholes were idiots who didn't know they were idiots. But bastards? They knew exactly what they were.

If a bastard like Campbell Fotheringham was making personal calls into Helen Street police station, then it had to be for a good reason.

And nothing could have prepared Lomond for what he had to say.

CHAPTER TWENTY-FOUR

SITTING in the cramped interview room, Campbell Fotheringham looked like a Tiffany diamond that had been left in a pound-shop. His suit cost more than most of the cars in the car park, and it wasn't even one of his better ones. He examined his recent manicure with a dissatisfied tut, then crossed his legs, carefully arranging the fabric on his trousers to limit creasing.

The windowless room was grim and stuffy. The walls marked and scratched when interviewees had kicked off, or the occasional chair had been thrown. There was a lot of good faith being demonstrated in the layout of the room: the furniture wasn't bolted to the floor as if Govan was hosting Hannibal Lecter. It was just a plain wooden table, and four plastic chairs that you would find in any secondary school up and down the country.

Campbell Fotheringham couldn't have looked more out of place.

He was getting into his sixties now, and had accrued more money from his career, along with a series of shrewd investments through the years, than he knew what to do with. It wasn't about the money now. He just liked screwing with police. And winning. Which he did, more than anyone else Lomond had encountered in the legal profession. It wasn't luck. Fotheringham was the best.

'Chief Inspector Lomond,' he cooed, keeping his legs crossed.

'Oh aye,' said Lomond, 'no need to get up on my account. What do you want, Mr Fotheringham?'

He smiled. So far Lomond was exactly as he had remembered from those Sandman-era press conferences. 'I'm here on behalf of my client, Frank Gormley.'

He didn't have to check with Lomond that he knew who he was.

After a dozen true crime books that were always serialised in the *Glasgow Express*, an endless fascination from Glaswegians about his crimes, and a pretty shite low-budget movie, everyone in Glasgow knew who Frank Gormley was.

Gangster number one. Son of Arthur Gormley, inheritor of the biggest drug empire in Scotland. And who was currently serving a ten-year stretch for money laundering and fraud. It amused Gormley no end that for a man who had personally murdered over a dozen people – even he couldn't remember exactly – Police Scotland had only ever been able to put him away by the same method that nailed Al Capone: the bloody paperwork.

Fotheringham went on, 'There isn't any need to beat

about the bush, Chief Inspector. Mr Gormley wishes to inform you that he has certain information that could be valuable to your current enquiry involving Sandy Driscoll.'

Lomond leaned forward aggressively in his chair. 'We haven't released that name to the press. My team's airtight. We don't leak around here. Everyone knows it would be their arse if they did. How does Gormley know who we're looking for?'

Fotheringham shrugged. 'I am merely here to communicate a message of cooperation from my client on a deeply important enquiry.'

Lomond said, '"Certain information" sounds about as vague as whatever the offside rule is these days. Why don't you just tell me what he knows right now?'

'My client isn't prepared to do that at this moment. He has a long history of being let down by this station, your officers, and Police Scotland when it comes to keeping promises.'

Lomond chuckled. 'Your client has a long history of drug trafficking and murder.' Before Fotheringham could open his mouth, Lomond amended it to say, 'Alleged.'

'He's operating on good faith, Chief Inspector. He could have gone to the press with the information. And believe me, when you hear what he has to say, you'll be mightily relieved that he chose to do the honourable thing, rather than the profitable one. The *Glasgow Express* would have paid handsomely for what he has.'

'The honourable thing?' Lomond waited for the punchline. 'Are you taking the piss? I mean, seriously, are you attempting to extract urine right out of me?' He began to stand up. 'Let me guess. He's looking to cut his sentence. Nothing more. This conversation is over.'

Fotheringham cut in. 'I should tell you that my next appointment is with Colin Mowatt.'

Lomond stopped.

'Chief Inspector, I can assure you. I have reviewed my client's information personally. Mowatt and the *Express* will have a field day with this one. Mr Gormley is committed to doing the right thing here. But there has to be some *quid pro quo*. He's very serious.'

'And so am I when it comes to abducted children,' Lomond retorted. 'I'm amazed it's taken cretins like him as long as this to exploit a tragedy. I don't know how he found out that Sandy Driscoll is a person of interest, but—'

'Mr Gormley would like to see the man responsible arrested and put in prison. And in return, he would like his part in that adequately acknowledged.'

Lomond paused. 'I'm in the middle of a child abduction enquiry. I don't have hours to waste galavanting over to Barlinnie to hear fairy tales. I can send uniform, and that's it. If his information checks out, we can discuss it.'

'Oh, no,' Fotheringham scowled. 'Mr Gormley will only provide the information in person. To you. And you alone, once the sentence reduction has been confirmed in writing to me.'

Lomond breathed in heavily, then huffed it back out.

'I'm not authorised to unilaterally reduce a prisoner's sentence, and run roughshod over the entire Scottish legal system, as you well know.'

He flashed an unfriendly smile. 'Quite. Alas, Mr Gormley isn't entirely sympathetic when it comes to agreeing to his terms in business arrangements. But I'm sure I could convince him with a personal assurance by you should the information work out.'

Lomond leaned on the back of the chair, looming over the table like an angry cloud. The fact was, Gormley was sitting on something potentially explosive. He asked himself if he was seriously ready to risk Jack Ferguson's life over the matter. Gormley could have a location for him, for all Lomond knew.

He didn't see any other way out.

'Fine,' Lomond relented. 'But Fotheringham...if my time is being wasted while a small child is missing, tell Gormley that I'll unleash the most poisonous vendetta seen against a prisoner since *The Shawshank Redemption*. It'll make *Papillon* look like a weekend at Butlins–'

Fotheringham had heard it all before. He nodded with an expression of boredom that only the truly rich and powerful can pull off. 'I get the point, Chief Inspector.' He stood up, picking up his briefcase. 'Make your calls.' He offered Lomond a hand to shake.

Lomond drew his eyes off it. Then reluctantly shook it. 'Like I said. There's nothing I won't do to get back Jack Ferguson. Even if it means shaking hands with the devil.'

Fotheringham smirked. 'I'm not the devil, Chief Inspector.'

'No, you're right,' said Lomond. 'You're just the guy who keeps the heat running in hell.'

CHAPTER TWENTY-FIVE

THE TEAM HAD BEEN COMBING through the cabinets for an hour. The only sounds were the rustling of manila folders, and the occasional metallic *thunk* of a cabinet drawer being closed and another one opened. Occasionally you would hear a mumbled complaint of, 'Fuck's sake...' – usually from Pardeep.

When Willie was called upstairs to talk to the forensics team on Arran, Ross took the opportunity for some much-needed conversational relief. Anything but that bloody file code.

'So, Donna,' he began. 'You've known the gaffer the longest. What's he really like?'

'You've seen what he's really like,' she replied.

'You know what I mean.'

'I really don't.'

'He could have drafted in anyone to this team, and he chose you. He must have told you something?'

'We worked CID together, Ross. I made a couple of nice arrests and he remembered. That's it. He needed someone to do shit like this. It's not like we're Hillary and Norgay.'

Ross didn't respond. He looked in Jason's direction.

'The first two to climb Everest,' Jason answered.

'I'm a safe pair of hands,' said Donna. 'This isn't some muse situation, or where he tells me his innermost thoughts. I don't even know where he lives.'

Ross kept on, 'You must know a little something about what happened.'

Pardeep had had enough of the euphemisms. And the distractions. 'Donna, he wants to know why he left the original Sandman enquiry.'

Jason added, 'I heard he was closer than anyone to catching him.'

Donna said, 'If he wants to tell you, then you can hear it from him.'

Ross wasn't quite ready to give up yet. He was standing there doing the most boring job imaginable. He was at least going to get some gossip, rumour, or innuendo out of her. 'I kind of got the feeling that I put my foot in it last night when we were out in the car.'

'Oh yeah?' said Donna distantly, carrying on with her work.

'I was telling him about the wee fella at home, and so I asked if he had any kids.'

'Jesus,' Donna replied. 'Of all the things to ask him, not that...'

Ross stopped searching. 'What? Why?'

If for nothing else than carrying on her work in peace, Donna decided to throw them all a bone. Everyone was working at fifty per cent capacity with half-averted eyes and ears anyway.

'You really did put your foot in it,' she said. She glanced back towards the concrete stairs, seeing no sign of Willie returning yet. 'This is just what I heard. I can tell you, but you have to swear yourselves to secrecy.'

CHAPTER TWENTY-SIX

LOMOND HAD SPENT another crushing day at Helen Street station, ploughing through yet more criminal records of paedophiles and degenerates, desperately trying to capture that one connection that would unlock the Sandman case for good.

The fifth victim, Taylor Clark, was only a few weeks in her grave, and Lomond wasn't going to hang around waiting for another abduction before kicking into top gear again.

He was impatient and snapping at his team. And if anyone made the mistake of suggesting – barely even hinting – that they might make tracks home after a tenth fourteen-hour shift in a row, Lomond would lose his rag at the entire team, questioning their commitment, which he would inevitably apologise for once he'd cooled down ten minutes later.

It wasn't just the stress of leading the enquiry into one of the country's most baffling serial murderers. Lomond was worried sick about his wife Eilidh, who was nine months pregnant with their first child.

Lomond would work himself raw, but as soon as he walked in the front door and found Eilidh bouncing on her birthing ball in the living room, bobbing along to Nirvana's 'Lithium', reliving her teenage rebel-rock years, he managed to forget about work for a little while. It made him guilty to feel any kind of happiness, when five families were out there grieving for the loss of their wee ones.

Lomond grimaced at the volume of the music. 'Is that really a good idea? The wee dude's going to be born with tinnitus.'

She kept bobbing along in time to the music, then nodded in a gentle and very cautious headbang when the chorus kicked in. 'This could be our last chance to listen to something loud for quite a while!'

Lomond couldn't resist. While she headbanged, he recorded a brief video clip of her on his phone.

When she heard him chuckling, she looked over and waved at him to stop. Her face was glowing.

He had never seen her so happy before.

Then, suddenly, the happiness disappeared. Shifting instead to intrigue. Then concern. Then a sharp intake of breath.

Lomond rushed over to her side.

'Yep,' she said, trying to stay calm. 'Okay, that feels like a surge.'

He helped her gently off the birthing ball. 'Are you sure?'

She quipped, 'Well, I have had all those other babies in the past to compare it to...'

'No, right,' he replied. 'Sorry.' He turned circles, like a dog chasing its tail.

'The bag is in the–'

'In the hall, of course. Right.' Cue more frantic spinning.

Eilidh cradled her bump, shutting her eyes and reacting with a variety of different faces each time she felt a different pang in her uterus. 'Yeah, we need to start counting these.'

Later in the car, Lomond held her hand, counting off breaths as they went. He had practised the drive to the hospital so many times he could have done it with his eyes closed. He had mapped three alternative routes in case of road closures or heavy traffic. In the end, Eilidh had gone into labour at the perfect time for the roads to be clear: nine at night.

Lomond had remembered to cue up their Spotify playlist of happy songs to listen to for distraction in the car journey over. *The Beatles* 'Golden Slumbers' came on, and Lomond felt the first pang of what was about to happen: he was going to become a dad.

As another surge faded, Eilidh opened her eyes and loosened her grip on Lomond's hand. At a red light, they had a moment to look at each other without saying anything. Just listening to the song.

'I love you,' Lomond said, re-gripping her hand.

'I love you too,' she replied. She looked over her shoulder and smiled. 'You remembered, then?'

Lomond looked back at the car seat installed behind

Eilidh's seat. 'Yeah. Only took about an hour, and eight YouTube videos to get it right. I honestly don't know how men like me got anything built before YouTube.'

———

THE LABOUR WENT AS SMOOTHLY as a first labour could be expected to go. As they had requested in their birth plan, the two young midwives present in the private room had kept the room calm as a mega three-hour playlist of their favourite songs played on a bluetooth speaker.

Eilidh was only slight, but Lomond had never seen her so forceful or determined. Labour had progressed to the point that the time for visualising of breaths and meditative stuff was over. Now it was time to push and get the baby out.

It was more physical and visceral than Lomond had prepared for. The baby's head had crowned, but Eilidh couldn't quite get it over the line.

'You just need one more massive push,' the midwife told her.

Yeah, she thought. Like I haven't been doing that for the last hour.

The longer the pushing went on, the more concerned Eilidh got about the baby's stress levels. She and John had wanted to avoid any interventions, and he was getting the feeling that they might not be far away from that.

Eilidh pushed until the veins in her temples throbbed, continuing to push after the midwives had stopped their countdown. She simply couldn't hear them from the effort.

She was almost in tears from the exhaustion and effort. She was so desperate to keep the baby out of distress at being stuck, she was willing to hurt herself to previously unimagined degrees in order to make it happen. It was the purest expression of love that Lomond had ever seen.

All the while, in the background of his mind, he heard 'Golden Slumbers' by The Beatles.

Then, when everyone seemed to be gearing up for an intervention, another push proved to be enough, and a baby boy entered the world.

Their birth plan had requested that the midwives hold the baby up so that Lomond could tell Eilidh whether it was a boy or a girl. But they weren't holding the baby up. In fact, Lomond couldn't see what was happening over the tangle of blue sheets between Eilidh's legs that were covered in blood.

And there was no crying.

One of the midwives lunged for the red crash button on the wall, sounding an alarm outside.

Before Lomond could get an answer to his questions of what was going on, two doctors and a consultant came running into the room and took control of the scene. The baby was whipped aside to a separate table.

A midwife was trying to explain to Lomond what was happening, but he couldn't understand the words. He was still holding Eilidh's hand.

He gave it a shake, to let her know that he was sure the baby would be okay. The baby would be okay. He was sure of it.

Then, he finally got another look at the blue sheets that a

midwife had piled up between Eilidh's legs. They were now all completely red. Fresh surges of blood kept coming in an endless wave. The midwife couldn't find enough sheets to stem it.

She asked for help. And for the first time in several hours, the midwife, who had been unshakeably calm before, now looked properly scared for Eilidh.

Lomond looked at his wife, who couldn't see anything. Her position tilted far back on the bed. He tried to get a better look at the baby, but the medical team had it surrounded.

The consultant took Lomond by the shoulders and moved him away. 'Mr Lomond, I need you to step back. We're having a bit of trouble with the baby's breathing...'

'Is he going to be okay?'

Eilidh called out, 'John? What's happening?'

'I–I–I don't know, honey. Hang on...'

The consultant had seen plenty of episodes like this. 'The best thing to do right now is stay calm.' He took Eilidh's hand and put it back in Lomond's.

The consultant explained, 'Mrs Lomond, we're having some trouble with the baby's airway. But you've also got some bleeding that we need to take care of, okay? The doctors are doing everything they can. Just stay sitting back for me...'

Lomond looked on helplessly. One by one, more doctors came in. The serious-looking ones with different-coloured scrubs to each other. There were paediatricians, anaesthetists, consultants...all of them telling Lomond as soon as they arrived not to worry.

He kept waiting for one of them to be the one who told him that it was all fine now. It was over. But that didn't happen. It kept escalating with each new uniform that entered the room.

He couldn't tell if they were to be trusted, or if they were lying to him to stop him going totally postal with worry. The more doctors that told him it was going to be okay, the less he believed them.

'You all keep saying that, but I still haven't heard the baby, and there's now five of you in here working on Eilidh.'

She had suffered a bad tear from the baby's final movement, and the doctors couldn't get the bleeding to stop. They had stitched the wound, but they couldn't see it properly from all the blood. Three separate doctors had a go. Still, she kept bleeding.

But Eilidh and John weren't thinking about that. They were too busy staring at the doctors who were now performing CPR on the baby.

Eilidh looked away, in agony of her own, and started to cry.

Lomond couldn't move. He was paralysed with fear. He held Eilidh's hand and told her it was alright, it was going to be okay. But he didn't believe it. He had no idea what was going on.

The pair looked on in horror as the doctors finally relented and stepped back from the baby.

It fell to the senior paediatrician to give the news.

The baby hadn't made it. After nine months, he had been ten centimetres from safe passage into the world.

Lomond covered his mouth. He reached for Eilidh, whose hand had gone limp. Though it wasn't from grief.

Her head had tilted to one side and her eyes had closed.

The doctor working between her legs stood up with more than a hint of alarm. 'I need some help over here!'

Lomond tapped Eilidh's hand frantically, saying her name over and over again. He got no response. 'Eilidh? Eilidh? Please. What's happening? What on earth is happening?'

He couldn't breathe. His brain had been flooded with every emotion imaginable, and now that was giving up, too. His vision was turning foggy.

The doctor who had taken over, swiftly stood up too. 'We need to get her to theatre,' she told her colleagues. 'Now!'

In a matter of seconds, Eilidh's bed was on wheels and on the move.

A doctor tried to explain to Lomond as they went. 'We're having trouble getting the bleeding to stop, Mr Lomond. She's haemorrhaging, and her body has gone into shock from blood loss. We need to stop the blood loss before she has organ failure.'

He looked back at the midwives who were standing over the baby on the table, finishing wrapping him in blankets.

Lomond didn't even have time to dwell on the death of his and Eilidh's baby. Now all that was left was to try and save his wife.

WHEN IT WAS all over five hours later, the sun was already up.

Lomond left the Maternity unit, carrying his wife's overnight holdall, full of an exhaustive collection of ointments, special clothes, a mood board pinned with photos of happy memories and inspirational quotes to help Eilidh through labour.

Lomond stared blankly at the pavement as he walked towards the car. Numb. His head a shambles. He kept thinking about Eilidh's things, and what would he do with it all. He had never had to think about such practical concerns when someone dies in hospital, like "what happens to all their things?"

The answer was simple: someone has to take them away. They won't just bin it all for you. There's no all-inclusive mop-up service other than for medical waste and mopping up blood. Everything else would have to be carried home.

In the end, he was glad they hadn't let him into theatre. That would only have made things worse.

When he got into the car, he noticed a smear of blood on the side of his face from when he had said goodbye to Eilidh on the operating table.

Over the course of forty-five minutes, he had gone from expectant father, to new father, to grieving father, and finally to widower.

It was the car seat in the back that set him off properly. He had kept it together up till then. Unable to cry. Now he cracked. Fully. He rested his head on the steering wheel, and cried his guts out.

There were only two things he wanted to hear.

His wife's voice.

And his baby son crying.

CHAPTER TWENTY-SEVEN

It had a lot of names.

The Big Hoose. Bar. Bar-L. Bar-L Hell.

HM Prison Barlinnie in the middle of Riddrie, surrounded by terraces and low flats and suburban streets. The biggest prison in Scotland.

The exterior had been somewhat modernised over the years, but the prison's foundation, its internal architecture was Victorian. It gave the place a haunted, time-out-of-place sensibility. It had been decided in 2018 to sell the place off and turn it into a museum, while a new superjail would be built over fifty acres opposite the Provan Gas Works site beside the M8.

DSU Boyle had called ahead to the governor to request special dispensation for Lomond to visit Gormley. An inmate that the governor wasn't exactly inclined to want to do favours for. Since his incarceration began, Gormley had been nothing but a thorn in the prison's side. He brought with him an entire industry in tiny mobile phones (the most sought-after item in prison), and of course the ever-present class-A drugs and cigarettes.

Getting the stuff in was the easy part. You could 'bank' all sorts of things before coming in. If you could stuff it up your arse, then there was decent money to be made from it inside. A tiny phone that cost twenty quid on eBay could fetch over five hundred inside. There were even inmates at Bar-L who had intentionally put themselves there for the sole purpose of trading illegal goods. Offenders on Home Detention Curfews were supposed to wear an ankle tag everywhere they went. A few days out, they would breach their curfews, which got them sent straight back in. Only this time, they'd be banking.

The man at the end of that very unpleasant rainbow was Frank Gormley. Everyone made sure he was given his due on everything that came through there. He had people everywhere. Eyes, ears. Nothing was missed. Ever. Even the screws were in his pocket, letting him know the moment someone grassed.

The term 'prison' was a joke to someone like Frank Gormley. He wasn't going to do a day of actual time in his entire sentence. It was a walk in the park. Short of a nice holiday or a car to drive around, there was little that he couldn't get his hands on.

Lomond was taken by two prison officers to an interview room, surrounded by shatterproof windows so the officers could monitor anything being passed to an inmate by a visitor.

In Gormley's case, no one was going to stop him.

Lomond was first to arrive. A detail that Gormley had insisted on. He wasn't going to just sit there and wait for the polis.

When he arrived, he looked well rested. He even had a suntan from sitting out in the yard during the heatwave.

He might have had on the usual prison uniform of a red polo shirt, but he wore it with so much more flair than anyone else. Lomond was reminded of how much larger than life he seemed. He had small eyes but saw everything, and he had a face like a hundred miles of bad road.

Compared to other tough guys in Barlinnie, they were scary like they were deciding whether or not to kill somebody. But Gormley looked like he was already deciding where to dump the body.

Gormley didn't just rely on the help when it came to tidying up business on the street. He had always been willing to get his hands dirty. Rumour had it that he was personally responsible for a number of hits on gangster rivals across the city since the nineties, which was almost unheard of. That kind of trigger work and blade-happy slashing was normally the preserve of the expendable youngsters. Not so Gormley. The rough stuff was part of the fun.

'How we doing, John?' Gormley asked like a long-lost pal.

'I'm alright, Frank. How's yourself?' he asked.

'I understand Campbell spoke to you.'

'He did.'

'And?'

'I'm a little confused, Frank. You see, we haven't made Sandy Driscoll's name public yet. Do we have a leak I need to know about?'

'There's no leak, John. I promise you that. I don't want you getting your team into bother. Naw, I'm just a connected man. I know things. I hear things.'

'Thing is,' said Lomond. 'The man you've named is a person of interest in a child abduction case.'

'Really?' Gormley said with a total lack of fascination.

'You seem to be aware of that already.'

'Sounds to me like what I have to say is worth something.'

'I need something first. Before I can do a thing for you, I need to know everything you have about Sandy Driscoll. And you know that. Because you're not an idiot.'

Gormley nodded his head gently. It had been a while since anyone had dared to speak to him like that. He ran his hand through his short, wiry grey hair and then his trimmed beard. When he looked at you, his eyes turned into slits. Assessing you. Sentencing you with a glance. 'What am I, then, Chief Inspector?'

'You're a family man,' replied Lomond. 'Three weans at home at that massive pad in Newton Mearns. If you've got information that could save wee Jack Ferguson, I think you'd give me it.' He added, 'Unless you're full of shit, and this is all just a wee game. But I don't think it is. You're not short on amusements in this place. You don't need this. Which means you must be doing it for a reason.'

Gormley smiled, then broke into a laugh, wagging his finger. 'Campbell warned me about you.'

'I find it easier to speak plainly, Frank. So's we both know where we are.'

'Awright, then,' he said. He spoke with a nasally twang – a product of growing up on the streets – whose sharper edges were sometimes softened from years spent at expensive resorts and hotels, hobnobbing with footballers and business people and titans of industry in retail and hospitality. On the street, Gormley needed to be one thing. But in those other places, he couldn't just be Frank Gormley. He had to be the smartest version of Frank Gormley.

The real him would always be the guy whose "didn'ts" and "wasn'ts" turned into didnaes and wisnaes.

Gormley said, 'Fifteen years ago, I was approached about chibbing Sandy Driscoll when he was up in here for that Maggie Belmont case. You see, somebody got wind that Driscoll was going to walk soon, and they didnae want him back on the streets. I knew someone in here at the time for the job, and you know me, business is business, and the prick had done in a wee lassie. Didn't I feel like the prick when the judge released him the next week. Innocent, he says. So I never got round to doing it.'

Lomond shook his head. 'That's it? That's your big story? The one that your arsehole lawyer said the *Glasgow Express* would hold the front page for?'

'Hang on,' said Gormley. 'I'm not done yet. You never asked about the guy who paid me to do it.'

'Who was it?' asked Lomond.

'Martin Scullion.'

Lomond didn't take his eyes off Gormley, trying to work out if he was bullshitting or not.

Gormley said, 'You know the name, then?'

'Of course I do.'

'Bad rep. Even for polis.'

'I was going to say he was probably the sleaziest, dirtiest cop the force has ever seen. But yeah. Bad rep about covers it. What's this got to do with Sandy Driscoll now?'

'You think it's just coincidence that right before you found evidence that proved Driscoll was innocent of snatching, and possibly killing, Maggie Belmont, one of your fellow cops was putting a hit out on him? One of my boys on the street heard he was up to his neck in something. Hasn't been seen for a while.'

Lomond sighed. 'I agree. It warrants investigation, but I don't see–'

'Scullion's fitting the boy up for this one as well.'

'Martin Scullion was fired in disgrace a decade ago. I don't even know that he still lives around here.'

'Well, I'd be checking it out,' insisted Gormley. 'If you want to know about Sandy Driscoll, Scullion's your man.'

Lomond smirked. 'Of course. A cop. Do you want to just tell me why you want revenge on him, or are you going to make me jump through the hoops of having to look it up myself.'

'I've got no history with Scullion, John. I swear.' He nodded once in Lomond's direction. 'I've heard about you. That you're decent. Fair. And if Sandy Driscoll's innocent

THE BONNIE DEAD 189

again, it's going to be you on the front pages. Not Martin Scullion.'

'And all you want in return for this name – this selfless act of yours – is, what, five years off?'

'Five years?' he exclaimed. 'I want sent home.' He stabbed a finger down on the tabletop. 'Pronto.'

Being honest with himself, Lomond knew that it didn't make a blind bit of difference whether Frank Gormley was locked up or not. Behind bars or not, he was still very much running the show in Glasgow's gang wars.

'Trust me,' said Gormley. 'You find Martin Scullion, you'll find Sandy Driscoll.'

Lomond stood up, eager to get cracking. Either it was a waste of time, and he wanted to find out as soon as possible. Or Gormley really was onto something.

'I suppose a handshake in the circumstances...' said Lomond.

Gormley did a one-eighty through the windows, assessing the guards watching him. 'I appreciate that. But I've got a reputation to think of.'

'Fair enough,' Lomond replied. 'My people will contact your people, etcetera.'

CHAPTER TWENTY-EIGHT

DONNA HAD NOW READ back the code on a file five times to check it wasn't the right one. She slammed the file down on top of the others and stretched her neck out. This is ridiculous, she thought. They were going to be there for days. Jack Ferguson's body was going to be found at Govan docks, or wash up in the Clyde outside Braehead by the time they found Driscoll's file.

It got her thinking – what mattered was finding addresses associated with Driscoll.

She shunted the filing cabinet drawer closed with her hip, then headed upstairs. On her way past, Willie asked, 'Do you get to pick and choose what jobs you do while everyone cracks on with the mundane ones? We're trying to find Driscoll in here.'

'No,' she replied. 'We're trying to find out where he was fifteen years ago. There's no guarantee there will be any credible information on where Driscoll is now in any file we happen to find down here.'

'You clearly have a better idea than the gaffer, then.'

'I'm going to run through the Maggie Belmont files again.' She started towards the stairs again.

'You've been reading too much crime fiction,' said Willie. 'Mavericks don't actually do very well in this force. Team players who think to buy their colleagues a steak bake and a cookie from Greggs are the ones that get on.'

What Willie didn't realise was that he had made the cardinal mistake of telling a maverick to not be a maverick. It was the policing equivalent of 'do not press this button'.

So Donna did the thing any maverick who wants to survive must do: prove herself right.

Back in the bullpen, she slipped onto the nearest computer and booted up HOLMES to find the Maggie Belmont case files online. She scrolled quickly through the endless witness statements and records of car searches at the ports on Arran, finding instead the section on Driscoll.

This was the magic of searchable digital files instead of thumbing through hard copies for hours at a time. She entered "Driscoll" and "address" in the search terms, but nothing came up.

What she did find, though, was reference to a flat in Paisley that Driscoll's dad had once rented out.

Curious, she then opened up Scotland's Land Information Service webpage, entering the postcode, then selecting the address. The result showed the entire purchase history of the address. How much it had ever sold for and when. You couldn't see the name of the owners, but all Donna needed was to see whether it had been sold recently or not.

It hadn't. It was with the same owner as twenty years ago.

She rapped her knuckles on the desktop.

She raced to the stairs and told Willie she had a lead. But he refused to give her backup to check, telling her that Lomond wanted all manpower on the file search. She would have to wait.

Like any maverick worth their salt, Donna wasn't going to wait.

She slipped out of the bullpen, then swiped her lanyard at the station exit.

She couldn't wait to see Willie's face when she brought in Sandy Driscoll on her own.

BACK DOWN IN THE BASEMENT, no one had any idea that the sun had set, beckoning in yet another sticky, hot night.

Pardeep was staring at a file, re-reading it again and again. Eventually, he passed it to Jason to confirm it.

'That's it, right?' asked Pardeep. 'I'm not imagining it?'

'That's the one,' Jason said.

Pardeep held it aloft. 'Willie! I've found it.'

Willie took the file upstairs to Linda's office because Lomond was out of the building. After they had opened the file and found the last-know address for Driscoll after he's been released from jail, Willie hot-stepped it down the stairs to the bullpen.

He called out to the team below, 'Pardeep and Jason, you're in car one. Ross, you're with me.'

Expecting to be told that Willie was driving this time, Willie instead told him, 'Get your keys, son. I want you to drive like a boy racer this time.'

CHAPTER TWENTY-NINE

AFTER HOURS of negotiation and conversation and arguments in the prison governor's office with Lomond, and Reekie on speaker, Lomond emerged into Barlinnie's car park. His shadow stretched out for nearly twenty metres along the ground, as the final shafts of sunlight disappeared below the horizon.

On the way to his car, Lomond was on the phone to DSU Boyle. 'I don't know what I was expecting to hear in there, but it wasn't Martin Scullion's name.'

'What's your gut reaction?' she asked.

He stopped by his car and rubbed his face in anguish. 'I don't know...I mean, even if this story about being paid to have Driscoll killed in jail is true, why would Scullion still have a connection to Driscoll all these years later? Now I need to burn an hour finding this creep.'

'It's a lead, John,' said Linda. 'Take it. There's been a bit of action over here too since you've been gone. The guys found an address for Driscoll in Paisley. They're on their way now.'

Lomond made a celebratory fist. 'That's brilliant, Linda. Can you get me that address?'

'No,' she said. 'Check out this Scullion thing. It has the potential to do a lot of damage.'

'What do you mean?' asked Lomond.

'Gormley's threatening to go to the press, John. Do you really want to call his bluff on that? We can weather the storm of Driscoll making headlines again, but not a corrupt perv of a cop trying to have him killed in jail. It'll set back public relations with the police by decades if it gets out.'

'It doesn't make sense,' Lomond said. 'If Driscoll really was innocent of snatching Maggie Belmont, but it looks like he's behind Jack Ferguson's abduction, why all these links to Maggie?'

'Maybe Scullion has got the answers to that,' replied Linda.

He slapped the roof of his car affirmatively – the decision made. As he swooped into the driver's seat, he said, 'Right. Find me an address on him.'

'Will do. Oh, by the way. Your star pupil has done a bunk already. That's got to be an MIT record.'

'What are you talking about?'

'Donna Higgins. She's gone off on her own somewhere. Willie's raging, John.'

'Willie is? *I'm* raging.' Lomond grumbled, 'Shite. Okay.

I'll have a word when she gets back. It'll need to wait. I'm pulling out of Barlinnie now. Where am I going?'

Linda paused, while she pulled up an address for Martin Scullion.

CHAPTER THIRTY

DONNA WAS HARING it down the M8 towards Paisley, still inputting the target address on the sat nav for Foxbar in Paisley.

She knew that she was taking a risk running out on the team. In her maverick brain, she could simply gun it to Paisley, bang on the door, and haul Sandy Driscoll back to the station after finding Jack Ferguson safe in a bedroom, unharmed. To any other officer, what DC Higgins was doing virtually guaranteed disciplinary action, even if it was just a verbal warning. Donna didn't see herself as any other officer, though. That was why they failed to make the big collars. She had decided a long time ago that she was going to do some good in this world. To make a demonstrable difference. She wasn't going to watch violence tear families apart, and innocent people fall victim to the callous and the cruel.

There was also a bit of her that wanted the glory. Which was why she was touching eighty miles an hour by the time she reached the long straight past Hillington, and the high-flats in Gallowhill came into view. If she brought in Sandy Driscoll – the Sandman – and saved Jack Ferguson, on her own, through only her own intuition and solid police work, she would be on a fast-track to DS and a permanent spot on any MIT she wanted. If she had to share the win with four other officers, all of that went on hold.

Her phone rang as she snaked from lane to lane to get past the sluggish drivers who didn't understand what a fast-lane was really for.

She put them on speaker. 'This is Donna Higgins.'

'Donna? It's Pardeep.' His voice was distant and had an echo.

'Pardeep? What's going on, I can barely hear you?'

'I'm in the car with Jason. Willie and Ross are in the car ahead. We've got an address for Driscoll.'

Donna turned her head away and mouthed, '*Shite!*' She knew she had to play dumb. 'Where are you going?'

'Foxbar in Paisley.'

'Oh, aye?' She did a poor job of masking her disappointment.

'How come you're out on the road?'

She paused.

How did he know?

She said, 'Sorry?'

'Your GPS. DI Sneddon said you were last logged on the M8 westbound. Are you going to Paisley too?'

She couldn't think of another way out. She couldn't just drive around while they took in Driscoll. She had to think fast. 'Yeah, I called the incident room and they said where you were going.'

'Oh,' said Pardeep, with surprise. 'It's just...you took off without telling the gaffer. He seemed to think you were bunking off or something.'

'No, no,' she said. She needed to bide some time to think of a better excuse. 'Look, you're breaking up a bit, but I'll be there in about nine minutes according to the sat nav. If I get there first, I'll wait for you outside the address.'

'Aye, alright,' he said. 'Sounds like you'll be there first. See you shortly.'

Donna shook her head. She had missed her chance of making the arrest herself.

When she hung up, she waited a moment, then punched the steering wheel with the side of her fist. 'Bastard!'

———

WILLIE AND ROSS were first to the Crowfoot Avenue address, parking up a few houses short of Driscoll's residence. The sun was fully gone now. The orange streetlights taking over.

The street was a grey block of 'low flats', three floors high, operating with a shared close much like a west end tenement, but without any of the style or history. They had tiny square windows that let in hardly any light. Not that there was much around the area.

The streets were covered in litter and dog shit and the grass verges were overgrown. The front gardens of the low flats varied wildly in condition. Some immaculate. Some totally wild with weeds and nettles. Small children were running around playing with footballs, up way later than they should have been, even accounting for it being the summer holidays. There didn't seem to be any adults around, other than a few neds hanging around outside the newsagent.

The area felt feral.

Willie got out of the car but stayed on the pavement. This would be Ross's op.

Ross directed Pardeep and Jason as soon as they pulled up behind his car. He peered around from side to side. 'Where's Donna?'

Pardeep answered, 'She said she was on the way.' He checked his watch. 'She should be here by now. She said she was nine minutes out.'

'We're not waiting,' Ross said.

His team briefing made clear that although there was no known violence in Sandy Driscoll's past, given the crime he was suspected of, they weren't taking any chances. It was stab vests all round, and Jason would be armed with a taser. With an abducted child possibly in the property, Ross wasn't sure whether to expect much resistance or not.

As the team crept quietly towards the close door of Driscoll's building, Jason said quietly to Pardeep – enjoying having an unofficial partner for the day – 'Surely he won't fight when he realises we've got him?'

Pardeep replied, 'Mate, don't ever expect a suspect to act in their own best interests or what's sensible.'

Once Ross had the close door open from buzzing a neighbour, he stopped everyone, jamming his foot in the doorway to stop it closing again. 'Remember,' he said. 'Once we've chapped the door, I'm giving minimal time for him to answer or acknowledge. If he's in there, there's no telling what he'll try to do before he gets cuffs on him. The Det Sup will be alright with a bill for a new door, I'm sure.' He looked them over one by one, suddenly feeling quite young to be leading the charge. 'We ready?'

They each nodded.

Back at the car, Willie relayed the action to Linda Boyle back at the station.

They filed up the stairs. A strong smell of bleach emanating from the concrete steps. It hadn't so much been cleaned, as just having had chemicals poured all over them.

The close lights came on, filling the stairwell with white light.

There was various gang insignia and graffiti for the local 'young team' scrawled on the walls, as well as threats against specific people:

"DANNY F IS A GRASS"

Once your name was out on the street as a grass, especially in the rough side of Foxbar, it was almost impossible to change anyone's mind. It was like trying to unknit a sweater.

Ross held a finger to his lips as they passed a middle-aged woman on the first-floor landing.

She froze, pressing her back against the wall.

Ross pointed upwards. 'Three two?'

The woman pursed her lips. 'There's naebody in that.'

Ross pressed on anyway. Someone like Driscoll would have kept a low profile. Made little noise. In such a building, it was possible to go months without seeing your neighbours.

When Ross reached the front door of flat 3/2, he announced that he was the police, and that Driscoll was to open up.

No answer.

After a few more heavy thumps on the door, Ross waved Pardeep forward, who was carrying the red Enforcer battering ram. The paint on it was well chipped now. It had seen plenty of action over the years on many stubborn, reinforced doors.

Ross gave the signal.

Pardeep called out, 'Police!' Then swung the ram against the door at the lock.

It collapsed and came flying off the hinges. It couldn't have been made from anything stronger than plywood or chipboard.

The team streamed in. But Ross had a feeling just from the hallway that they were going to leave disappointed. The floor and the walls of the long hallway were bare. Not even a carpet laid.

Ross again shouted Driscoll's name and that they were the police. No response.

The doors along the hallway were all wide open, and it was stuffy like none of the windows had been opened for a very long time.

The team went room to room, calling each one clear.

Ross hunted through each room. Determined to find a cupboard or closed nooks.

But there was nothing to find.

There wasn't a lick of furniture anywhere. The living room fireplace had been stripped out, and the kitchen cupboards were bare and doorless. All the windows had cobwebs hanging in them.

The team reconvened in the hallway. 'Bust,' said Ross.

Pardeep concurred. 'There's been nobody here for a while.'

Ross's phone rang. He answered it, not recognising the number. The team was still so new he hadn't assigned caller IDs to anyone there.

'Ross McNair,' he answered.

'Ross, it's Donna,' she said, sounding confused. 'Where are you?'

'I was about to ask you the same thing. We're in the hallway at the front door. Driscoll's not here. He's not been here for a very long time, if he ever was.'

'Did you say you're in the hall?'

'Yeah, why?'

She paused. 'I just walked through there.'

'Don't be daft,' said Ross. 'We're all standing here.'

Jason and Pardeep moved closer, wondering what was going on.

Ross started to move from room to room. 'Where are you?'

Donna said it like she couldn't have been anywhere else. 'I'm in the main bedroom...'

Ross shook his head like she was mad, gesturing impotently at the main bedroom he was standing in.

Donna said, 'Ross? You still there?'

It took him a moment to figure out what might have happened. Then a terrible feeling came over him. 'Donna, where are you? What address?'

'One sixteen Crowfoot Avenue.'

He clicked his fingers at Pardeep, who was standing in the hall thinking all was well. Ross half-mouthed, half-spoke, 'I told you to check what address she was going to.'

Pardeep raised his palms in innocence. 'I was going to, but she said she was going to Crowfoot Avenue in Foxbar. That's where we are!'

Ross did his best not to curse his colleague. He retreated to the close, bounding down the stairs. It wasn't exactly rule number one – there was a lot of pretty important shit to get right first – but it was certainly in the top ten: don't assume anything. Ever.

Ross took the stairs two, three at a time, galloping down until he was back on the street. He did a quick recce of the neighbours to figure out which way the numbers ran.

Shite, he thought.

They were at seventy-two. She was at one hundred and sixteen.

'Stay where you are,' Ross told her, breaking into a run. Then a sprint. 'I'm coming.' His voice shook from his feet thudding the pavement.

Still waiting for an acknowledgment, he said, 'Donna?'

There was no answer.

CHAPTER THIRTY-ONE

DONNA WAS STANDING IN A DARK, furnished flat. It was spartan and tidy. Like an old person's flat. Functional but with outdated furniture.

There had been no reply to her requests to come in. The door was unlocked. Off the snib. As if the resident was expecting someone.

Donna was getting freaked out by the tone of concern in Ross's voice. Did he know something she didn't?

She had her wits about her, ready in case Driscoll pounced from around a doorway. She had to be ready for anything.

As she spoke to Ross on the phone, moving from room to room, she realised something was wrong. She had assumed she was bound for the same address in Foxbar that Pardeep referred to. But he never gave her the number.

That was when she took a second look at a door at the

end of the hall. It was closed. But the light was changing under the door. As if from a TV.

She hung up, not wanting to give herself a way. There was still a chance to make the arrest.

She crept further down the hallway, seeing the faint glow of the TV brightening. The sound was off. The TV seemed inordinately bright in the gathering gloom outside.

She held back at the doorway, then nudged it open the tiniest amount possible to see in.

There was a cup of tea sitting on a side table. Steam rising from it.

What she wasn't ready for was the creak of the floorboard behind, coming from the front door.

Before Donna could respond, she saw a long shadow on the floor between her feet. Someone was standing behind her.

She spun around to see who it was, then everything went black from the blow of something blunt and heavy on her head.

CHAPTER THIRTY-TWO

MARTIN SCULLION LIVED in the heart of Cessnock, on a street that even Lomond wasn't feeling great about being on after dark. The two shops on the corner of the T-junction were both shuttered, and looked like they'd been out of business for a while.

Scullion lived on the first floor of a run of tenements that were pockmarked with satellite dishes. The close doors had taken a battering, most of them with heavy scuffs around the height where a foot had landed in an attempt to kick it in.

All the front gardens were bare or concreted over. A lot of windows were bare, and the rooms behind them empty. There had been a lot of evictions on Scullion's street.

Lomond locked the car door, then turned around a few metres later to check it was definitely locked. All around him there were noises of aggression and violence. He wasn't buying the laughter and whooping from marauding youths in the neighbouring streets. There had been nothing light-hearted about that part of the city, especially at night.

Lomond struggled to work out if he had the right house number, as there were no names on the buzzer, and there was no house number attached to the building. He had to back out onto the street again and work it out based on what number the tenements on either side were.

He tried Scullion's buzzer but got no reply. When he buzzed the neighbours, informing them he was the police and needed entry to the building, it took three attempts to find someone to let him in.

Lomond had walked a beat through Govan for many a year early in his career. Over time, he'd found the place to be full of the loveliest salt-of-the-earth folk that Glasgow had to offer. But tonight, Lomond sensed something rotten in the air.

When he reached Scullion's door, he hesitated for a moment, wondering if it was a mistake to try and enter alone. There were all kinds of violent outbursts in Scullion's past, and that was when he was still with the polis. God only knew what he'd got himself into since then.

Lomond knocked on the door.

Nothing.

He held his ear close to the door, listening for a TV or some indication of someone being in there.

Then it came.

A soft creak. It wasn't near the door. It was farther back, but Lomond heard it.

He knocked again. More insistently this time.

'Open up, Mr Scullion. It's the police.'

A voice on the other side said, 'John?'

Lomond recognised the voice but couldn't quite place it. He straightened his back a little when the door opened, then when he saw who was standing there, his posture relaxed again.

'What the fuck are *you* doing in there?' Lomond asked.

Colin Mowatt shushed him, then beckoned him in with rapid circles of his hand. 'Keep your voice down,' he said.

'I will not keep my voice down, Frodo fucking Baggins. I'm working here.'

'So am I,' said Mowatt. 'Martin Scullion's not here.'

'Aye, well I can see that.' Lomond cast his eye about the place. It was a total midden. Not just messy and crammed with junk from floor to ceiling. But filthy. Lomond couldn't see them, but he could feel things crawling around between the large piles of ancient newspapers and dirty magazines. It was like he'd wandered into the cave in Indiana Jones and the Temple of Doom – the one filled with thousands of insects and beasties.

'How did you get in?' asked Lomond.

'The door was unlocked.' Mowatt continued doing what he'd been doing before Lomond had arrived. Taking pictures of the place on his phone.

'Just what the merry hell are you doing here?'

'I got a tip on the address.'

'Let me guess,' said Lomond. 'Frank Gormley.'

'I don't name my sources.'

Lomond couldn't understand why Gormley was so keen

to get the press involved. He'd threatened Lomond with it earlier, but had tipped off Mowatt anyway.

Mowatt explained, 'I was told there was a good story lurking behind Scullion's door.'

'The only story in here is who the hell could live in a place like this. It's bloody rank, so it is.' He started to look from room to room, and was surprised to find crucifixes hanging on every wall. Hardly what he expected from someone like Scullion.

Lomond asked, 'Any sign of someone at home?'

Mowatt pointed out the enormous pile of junk mail behind the front door. 'There's not been anyone here for years, I'd say.'

'And no dead bodies?'

'Nuh,' Mowatt replied, pocketing his phone. 'Must have been a bad tip.'

Lomond consulted the bureau. Or what had at one time been a bureau. Before it became a dumping ground for random crap like out of date Yellow Pages, takeaway menus, and clothes. He picked up a handwritten note that said:

"*BOTANICS. TUNNEL. THE BEAST. 10pm.*"

Lomond showed it to Mowatt, 'Or maybe we're in the wrong place.'

CHAPTER THIRTY-THREE

MOWATT WAS BUZZING around Lomond's side like a fly on livestock, firing all manner of questions at him about the Sandman enquiry as he followed Lomond over the fence into the Botanic Gardens at the crossroads of Byres Road and Great Western Road.

'Where the fuck do you think you're going?' asked Lomond.

'To find out what the Beast is.' Mowatt jumped down off the fence on the other side. 'What are you going to do? Arrest me, and miss the Beast at ten p.m.?'

Shite, Lomond thought. The wee Ed Sheeran-but-with-no-talent lookalike was right.

The park had long since shut to the public, but Lomond was determined to get to the bottom of the Martin Scullion conundrum before it was time to return to the station.

'So is Martin Scullion a suspect?' Mowatt asked. 'He

must be if you're running down his address in the first couple of days of another disappearance.'

'You can ask the question or answer it, Colin,' said Lomond, 'but when you do both, it's bloody irritating.'

'You really don't like me, do you.'

'What on earth gave you that impression?' Lomond said with mock-hurt.

'I've got good relationships with plenty of cops. You're the only one that never gives me anything. Not a phone call, a tip, a heads-up or anything.'

'Well, that's a particular ecosystem that I'm keen to see die out quickly. You pay us for leads, and we end up leaking something back to you. But see, I've got a better plan: how about we give you nothing, and you and your whole crooked profession behaves itself. Like not hacking the phones of grieving parents of dead children.'

Mowatt raised a warning finger. 'I never did that.'

'No, but it was a guy you shared a desk with, that you offered a character for at his trial. Didn't seem to help much, mind. Thank god the judge saw through your bullshit. I wonder what that says about how the world sees the great Colin Mowatt. You're like antimatter. Ginger antimatter. All living things just want to get the fuck away from you.'

'Has anyone ever told you that you've got anger issues that need dealing with?'

'Anger? Of course I've got fucking anger issues! I'm trying to catch a man who kills children. And I've got to do it while creeps like you are harassing victims' families and getting in the way.'

'It's the biggest story in Glasgow for decades, John. You want me to pretend it's not happening?'

Lomond stopped and turned around. 'It's an enquiry, Colin. A case. Not a story.'

'That depends on where you're standing.'

Lomond stopped at a small copse where a tall metal fence had been installed to stop the very thing he was about to do.

Mowatt said in horror, 'We're not climbing over that, are we?'

'I've no idea what *we* are doing, but *I'm* climbing over it.'

The fence was surrounding an enormous cavern that was overgrown with weeds and littered with rubbish. Fifty feet below had once been a train platform, now almost unrecognisable. Once you knew it had been a train platform, the architecture started to make sense. It was part of the underground tunnel network that was shut off in the sixties. They had been largely forgotten about. Boarded-up and fenced-off. The tunnel in the Botanics had a hidden entrance that required some perseverance and steady feet to get to, scrambling down through some heavy scrub which had been dried to a crisp in the last week.

Lomond took out a pocket torch to light the way, which was treacherous until he reached solid concrete ground. Despite the relentless sun in recent days, there was still stagnant water in patches where the heat and light hadn't penetrated.

Once at the platform level, Lomond pointed his torch left and then right. The tunnel ran for another two and a half miles to his right, all the way to Sandyford under Kelvingrove Park. At one point, there had been discussion of one of the city's major bar and pub owners building a drinking establishment down there, but no doubt the thought of clearing all the foliage and the very real prospect of digging up dead bodies of the homeless and wild animals was enough to put them off.

In all, there were ten tunnels in the west end, and six in the East. Most of them inaccessible from padlocked fencing, but a crowbar and a little imagination was often enough for urban explorers to circumvent them. The tunnels had gained a bit of a cult following on hillwalking forums for folk who wanted something truly off the beaten path. There were no maps for down there.

The tunnel at the Botanics was the most widely known, and had attracted the most 'visitors' over the years, leading to excessive rubbish dumping. But the other tunnels had been largely ignored or plain missed, which had left them devoid of rubbish or rats or even graffiti.

Even in a city as overbuilt and increasingly crowded as Glasgow was, there was still an entire forgotten city underground, a hidden-away wasteland right under the noses of tens of thousands of Glaswegians.

Struggling down behind Lomond, Mowatt puffed, 'Great. Now what?'

'You stay out my way,' Lomond said distantly, flashing his torchlight around. He caught more than a few rats scuttling around at his feet before rushing back into the sludgy water. 'You should feel right at home here,' he quipped to Mowatt, then checked the time.

Ten minutes to ten.

What could the Beast be? he wondered. There were plenty of beasties, but the note was more specific than that.

He walked for a full minute, getting deeper and deeper into uncharted territory. Not many people went down there, and even fewer ventured as far.

It was baffling how some of the rubbish had found its way into the tunnel in the first place given the effort required. There were long sheets of timber. Tins of paint. Burst footballs. A stack of paperback books. A pram. And, of course, several shopping trolleys. Further along was the one that really took the biscuit, however: the rotting corpse of a Ford Sierra Cosworth, completely rusted inside and out. The Glasgow equivalent of a ship in a bottle.

Lomond kept his torch trained on the curved brick wall, looking for clues in the graffiti. That was where he saw it.

A figure etched in white paint that looked much like Death in *The Seventh Seal*. A reaper-like figure in a cloak. Above it was the phrase, 'Meat for the Beast.'

Lomond pointed his torch around the ground below it. There was a pile of rags and a roll of old heavy carpet on top of something.

Further back, Mowatt was still struggling along, complaining under his breath. He had to use the torch on his phone to see where he was going.

Lomond crouched down for a closer look at the pile. He

put the back of his hand to his mouth. He knew that smell anywhere. It was unforgettable.

Death.

He pulled back the carpet, then a sheet of metal that was covering something underneath. When he shone the light on it, he jolted back in revulsion. He held his arm up. 'Colin, stay there! Don't come any closer.'

'What is it?' he called back. He wasn't too enthusiastic about finding out for himself.

'Dead body.'

'Is it Scullion?'

Lomond had to turn away. He gulped hard and shut his eyes firmly. 'It might have been at some time.' He had to go back for another look, because something had caught his eye when his torch had passed over the skull.

The skeleton itself was brown and grey, preserved abnormally in the damp conditions – the recent heatwave notwithstanding. The teeth were still prominent, crooked. The jawline had decomposed in such a way that made the body look like it was held in a scream pose.

'Shite,' said Lomond, holding the torchlight over the skull.

In the eyeholes were little piles of sand.

That was only the start of it, though. Next to the body was something Lomond had only seen a handful of times in his career – though once was already too many.

Mowatt had been creeping ever closer. This was all a little too real for him.

He clamped both hands over his mouth. 'Scullion?'

'Possibly,' replied Lomond. 'And someone else.' He shone the light on a pile of bones next to the body. The bones were small.

Again, in the eyeholes of the skull, more piles of sand.

CHAPTER THIRTY-FOUR

LOMOND MIGHT HAVE DISAPPROVED of Ross's slim-fit suit and penchant for the occasional sun bed, but an undeniable truth was that the boy could run. Thanks to his twice-weekly five-a-side football matches where he played winger, Ross was an explosive runner. He couldn't have kept up with a Donna Higgins for endurance. But on short hauls, Ross was the one you wanted in pursuit.

116 Crowfoot Avenue was up a slight incline. In a car, the long drag uphill would have been barely noticeable. But running? After ten seconds of maxed-out sprinting, Ross's thighs were on fire. He yelled into his radio, 'Pardeep, I've got the front, but I need cover at the back. Jump in the car and go around Spey Avenue...Tell Jason to stay where he is.'

He saw the sign for 116. There was no indication of activity in any of the windows, and he wasn't sure if that was a good or a bad thing.

His frantic pursuit came to a sudden stop at the close door. It wouldn't budge. Ross ran his hands up and down the buzzer buttons for the other flats, calling into the microphone behind the steel grill, 'Police! This is an emergency. I need access to the building. Now!'

Multiple terrified residents buzzed him in.

The second the close door gave way, Ross shoved his way through and bounded up the stairs. He had been on a few high-risk arrests in his brief career, but he had never felt adrenaline pumping through him the way it was now. It felt different because it was about coming to the aid of a colleague, a constable he felt responsible for as sergeant.

Pardeep radioed back that he and Willie were in the back lane.

'No sign of anyone,' Pardeep confirmed.

Ross threw the door open and found Donna sprawled face-down on the hallway floor. She was hurt, but moving.

She gingerly reached for her head, where the shooting pain was.

'You're alright,' Ross said, helping her up carefully. 'Somebody's given you a fair old whack.'

'He was here,' Donna croaked.

'Who? Driscoll?'

'It must have been.'

'Stay here,' Ross told her. He checked room by room, but there was no one in the property. 'It's all clear,' he said. He got back on the radio in the spare bedroom. 'Pardeep, do you have anything out there?' His shoulders had already slumped. If Pardeep had found someone, he would have told him by now.

'Sorry, nothing, Ross,' Pardeep replied. 'They must have run off already.'

Donna struggled to her feet. She blinked heavily, trying to readjust as the black edges faded from her vision. She blew out her cheeks as she made her way to the spare bedroom where Ross was standing.

'What's going on?' she groaned. 'Where were you all?'

'Us?' asked Ross. 'What are you doing *here*? Pardeep said you called the station and they told where we were going. Why did you come here?'

Busted, she thought. Lying would only make it worse.

She said. 'It was in the Maggie Belmont file as a possible location for Sandy Driscoll. I thought there was a chance he might still be using it.'

'We found his sealed file. His last known address was at seventy-two.'

'He gets given a new identity for his own protection, and he stays on the same street?'

Ross had his back to her. He had frozen.

'What is it?' he asked.

He turned to her. 'Have you seen this?'

When she joined him and saw a piece of torn fabric lying under the bed.

He had recognised it straight away because Fiona Ferguson had described the fabric to him and Lomond that first night.

Ross got on the radio again. 'Willie...Jack Ferguson was here.'

'What?' said Willie. 'How do you know?'

He crouched down for a closer look at a patch of fabric that had been torn off on the rough wooden bed frame. 'Because I'm looking at a piece of the pyjamas he was wearing last night. Someone must have grabbed him, and in a hurry.' He waited for Donna to draw the conclusion.

She said, 'Someone was making a quick getaway.'

BACK AT THE original address at 72 Crowfoot Avenue, Jason had been left on his own. He was glad to hear over the radio that Donna had been found and was safe, but he felt left out of the action. There he was, guarding an empty property. It didn't feel like the action and investigation that had made him want to apply for detective in the first place.

He took the opportunity to look around a little more, kicking his feet absentmindedly at the bare floorboards. If Sandy Driscoll had ever lived there after having his Maggie Belmont conviction quashed, then he had made sure to clear up thoroughly after himself.

He heard the close door click open then shut downstairs. Expecting the return of the others, Jason returned to the hallway to greet them. Then he paused.

It was too quiet. There was no conversation or radio chatter.

Still footsteps continued towards the flat.

Jason tilted his head slightly towards the door to try and hear better. He cracked the front door open just a smidge, but it let out a creak that echoed through the stairwell.

The footsteps stopped.

Both the mystery figure and Jason froze.

Jason decided to make the first move, throwing the front door open. On the landing between the third and second floor he saw a scared male, arms held out like he was playing musical statues.

He was wearing a button-up shirt that was tucked into a pair of blue jeans that were two inches too short for him, and a baseball cap. He was skin and bone, and stood hunched over in tension.

When he locked eyes with Jason, his eyes went wide with terror.

It was unmistakably Sandy Driscoll.

Jason yelled out, 'Stop! Police!'

But Driscoll was already off and running. He took the stairs side-on, moving in an un-athletic lumbering way. It was like watching an octopus fall out of a tree. His legs seemed to be disproportionately long for his body, and he wheezed with panic when he ran, wheezing and grunting in time with his strides.

Jason took off like a greyhound, grabbing the stairwell pillars to help sling himself around the corners. By the time he reached the ground floor, he could smell Driscoll he was so close.

Driscoll made a hash of opening the close door – pushing when he should have been pulling – then fumbled with the small snib handle. He made it outside but could sense Jason close behind. He knew he could never outrun the cop – still, he tried. His cap blew off his head as he gained speed, but against the speed of Jason he only made it to the end of the footpath to number 72, when he felt something tug at his waist.

Coming down the hill from 116, Ross and Donna could see the commotion taking place in front of the building, and started running towards it.

Pardeep, feeling a kinship with Jason after spending most of the day side by side in the records corridor, yelled out his name, then he set off in a sprint towards the fray, over-taking Ross and Donna in the process.

Willie was bringing the car back around to 116, despondent at not finding Jack or Driscoll. All he saw next was a hooded figure running out of the building, limbs flailing, then Jason pumping his arms to catch up.

Willie squinted. 'Is that who I think it is...'

Then, with a single committed leap, Jason caught Driscoll by the waist and rugby-tackled him to the ground. It was like watching a lion taking down a lamb.

He grabbed Driscoll's hands to cuff him just as Pardeep arrived to help.

Jason read Driscoll the statement governing arrest as laid out in Police Scotland's Standard Operating Procedure, word for word.

He was by far the calmest person at the scene.

Willie was last to jog over – all that he was capable of. 'Mother of god, where did he come out from?'

Ross slapped Jason's back. 'Well done, mate.' He pumped his head once in celebration as Driscoll was led away to Willie's car. 'Bloody caught him,' Ross said, exchanging low fives with Donna and Pardeep. 'Wait till the gaffer finds out.'

CHAPTER THIRTY-FIVE

THERE HADN'T BEEN as many people in the Botanics tunnel for decades. Forensics had erected a tent around the dead body to preserve what remained of the scene. It also kept the swarms of moths and flies at bay that had been attracted by the scene examination team's bright lights. It had been quite an operation getting all of their gear down, and assembling a team so late at night was always a big ask, but DSU Boyle had called in every favour she was owed to make it happen.

When Scene Examiner Moira McTaggart made her way over to Lomond and Linda, Lomond sighed. 'God help us,' he muttered.

Word of Moira's personality and unique manner had spread far and wide since her joining the Scottish Police Authority Forensic Services unit. Every MIT that encountered her left thinking that they had never met anyone quite like her before.

No one had ever seen her smile. She never seemed to

experience any significant highs or lows, or changes in the pitch of her voice, or enthusiasm of any kind. For anything. Apart from examining crime scenes.

It wasn't even that the grim reality of the job had robbed her of vitality. It was simply the way she had always been. She could find a movie hilarious and not make a peep the entire time.

Her apparent dour demeanour had led to the unfortunate nickname of Moira Dreich – which had been coined by Lomond, inspired by a Billy Connolly bit.

'John. Linda,' she said, looking through her notes, which amounted to a few pages, front and back.

'How is it looking, Moira?' Lomond asked.

'If you're looking for confirmation that Martin Scullion is lying over there, you'll have to wait a few more hours. Circumstantially, it's Scullion's wallet that's been left behind, and the dimensions do appear to match his physical description. But I'll need to wait for dental records to confirm.'

Lomond felt himself stifling a yawn just looking at her face.

'What about dating the body?' asked Linda.

'It's looking like roughly five years, give or take.'

'Give or take what?' asked Lomond. 'A year?'

'No. Months. Allowing for exposure during winters, I'd be confident in that. Again, the lab work will confirm.'

Lomond said to Linda, 'All trace of Scullion drops off the map five years ago. A few weeks after Taylor Clark was murdered. The fifth Sandman victim.'

Linda nodded. 'He hasn't been operational since then.'

'Until this week.' He asked Moira, 'What about the bones?'

She said free from any emotion, 'The subpubic angle and concavity, the ventral arc: it's a girl. Based on bone size, probably between five and seven years old. Dating her is much harder. There's not even an educated guess I could give that would narrow down–'

'Try me,' said Lomond.

Moira shrugged. 'Over a decade. Not likely more than twenty-five years.'

Lomond and Linda were both thinking the same thing.

Linda said it first. 'Maggie Belmont?'

'She was short for her age,' said Lomond.

'How old was she when she was taken?' asked Moira.

'Seven.'

She made a sound that verged almost on pleasure. 'Oh, that makes sense, then.' She wasn't happy about the death of a child. Of course. For Moira, it was all about the answered question.

Linda asked, 'Any indication as to cause of death?'

'Nothing so far,' replied Moira. 'We'll need to do some closer bone work to say. I can't see any bullet wounds or grazing from a knife.' She gave a withering look. 'I mean, I could speculate, but that wouldn't be helpful to either of us, would it.'

'I wouldn't dream of asking,' said Lomond, tongue firmly in cheek – which he thought Moira would be oblivious to.

'You know,' she said, 'I have never in my life found

anything amusing, Chief Inspector...' She paused, keeping Lomond on tenterhooks. 'But that was alright.'

'Thanks, Moira,' said Linda.

'Sure,' she replied. 'No problem.' She walked back to the forensics tent, barely moving her arms and leaning slightly too far forward, which, from behind, made her look like a zombie.

Linda sighed. 'Give me strength. If she wasn't a walking forensic biology encyclopaedia, I don't know what she'd be doing.'

'Probably a serial killer,' suggested Lomond. 'But she gets the job done. That's all I care about.'

It was in Lomond's nature to defend oddballs and misfits. He looked too normal – too totally average – to ever truly belong to any misfit subset. But Lomond's heart had always been with them. The misunderstood. And he had always had a terrible soft spot for people that were outstanding at their job. In Police Scotland, it was easy to feel like you were surrounded by mediocrity most days. The true geniuses, the original thinkers, had no ability to play the political game. It just wasn't in their make-up to care about any of that.

Like Moira, and Lomond, what they wanted was to solve the puzzle.

'What are you thinking?' asked Linda.

'Well, clearly Martin Scullion didn't take Jack Ferguson or knock Donna over the head.'

'Yet there's every chance he's lying there dead next to Maggie Belmont's bones.'

Lomond thought aloud, 'The Sandman suddenly stops killing around the time Martin Scullion dies. That's a wrinkle of timing we can't ignore. The problem with that: he also appears to have been a victim of the Sandman. That's a paradox we can't ignore.'

Trying to keep up, Linda said, 'So Scullion is *not* the Sandman?'

'We don't know yet. A lot will depend on what we get out of Sandy Driscoll. He's got a lot of questions to answer, that boy.'

'So have we,' Linda retorted. 'We have to face an uncomfortable question now: if Sandy Driscoll is the Sandman, and is also the person who abducted Jack Ferguson, and now we have Driscoll in custody...'

Lomond nodded dejectedly.

Linda asked, 'Who has Jack Ferguson now?'

CHAPTER THIRTY-SIX

A SEARCH TEAM had been assembled at the top end of Foxbar, pulling in every available body from the Major Investigation Team, and any spare in uniform – which wasn't a lot in Paisley after ten at night.

Forensics had been split between the Botanics site and the Foxbar properties seventy-thirty in favour of the Botanics, as there was deemed far more biological material to sift through there.

That didn't mean, though, that there wasn't anything valuable to be found in Paisley.

Ross had been stuck to Willie's side all night, taking in how a proper old-school inspector went about working a major crime scene. Although, exactly where the crime scene was had been hard to pin down for a start.

The first address at 72 had yielded no visible physical evidence. The signs at 116 were far more encouraging. Not least, the patch of Jack Ferguson's pyjamas, which had since been identified by Fiona Ferguson in person at Helen Street station with Linda Boyle.

Ross called Willie over, pointing out a black hoodie draped over the back of a chair. 'Recognise this?'

Willie pushed his lips out and nodded in encouragement.

'It's looking good, isn't it?' said Ross.

Willie replied, 'Let's not get carried away just yet.'

The flat itself had been preserved like a museum piece from thirty years ago. Rather than a Blu-ray player, there was a blocky VHS player. The TV was deep-bodied and weighed a tonne, not one of the modern anorexic numbers.

There was no evidence that indicated where Jack Ferguson or his captor might be.

Willie and Ross were outside 116, watching Donna standing on her own, pinching and zooming on her phone screen.

'Oh my god,' she said to herself, not realising that anyone else could hear.

Ross came over. 'What is it?'

Brandishing her phone, Donna asked, 'I need to show you something. Will you humour me for a minute?'

Willie and Ross looked at each other hesitantly.

Donna started walking back down the hill towards 71 Crowfoot Avenue, but she diverged from the main road and took a back lane for the bin lorries to cut onto Spey Avenue.

Sweating and struggling to keep up with his younger, fitter subordinates, Willie grumbled, 'What's this all about, Ross?'

Ross made a gesture for another minute of patience.

Sensing the dwindling goodwill behind her, Donna promised, 'Just another ten seconds, I swear.'

When the time was up, she stopped outside a block of low flats and gestured to the building. 'That's twenty-one Spey Avenue.' She held her arms out, awaiting credit for something.

Willie replied, 'Fuck me, you don't say. And is that twenty right next to it?' He turned to Ross, looking for an ally.

But Ross was pushing his way past, seeing what Donna had. 'I'll be damned,' he said. 'Of course.' He took another few steps towards the building, then turned around in wonder.

In exasperation, Willie looked at Donna, then at Ross. 'Will someone tell me what it is I'm supposed to find so fascinating?'

Ross told Donna, 'Tell him.'

She said, 'Sandy Driscoll's conviction was overturned fifteen years ago. As part of his new identity, he came to live on Crowfoot Avenue. Five years ago, Leanne Donnelly was snatched from Spey Avenue. She was the second victim of the Sandman.'

'How long was the walk to here, Donna?' asked Ross.

She held her watch up. 'A minute and forty seconds.'

For a few moments, no one spoke. They could feel the pieces of the puzzle starting to fall into place.

They had taken Driscoll.

Now it would be up to Lomond to break him.

CHAPTER THIRTY-SEVEN

DOUBTS ABOUT SANDY DRISCOLL's solicitor, Gordon Reid, started early when Lomond overheard him requesting access to see "Sandy Drummond". After the desk sergeant's suggestion, Reid double-checked his paperwork. He showed not even a hint of embarrassment at the mistake.

At a time when solicitors were boycotting legal aid right and left over pay – some, like Reid, weren't even making minimum wage on some cases – but it remained the solicitor's main source of steady income. He simply couldn't find the work in the private sector. Many in the trade would have called someone like Gordon Reid an ambulance chaser, but he thought of himself more as a hearse chaser. Murder trials were his bread and butter. Ninety per cent of the time all he had to do was tell his client to say 'no comment', then plead guilty (as his clients invariably were) or get to trial and hope that a key witness dropped out, or that the police screwed up paperwork or procedure somewhere along the way.

His clients weren't the kind to have thought their crimes through. They had acted impulsively, then panicked in the aftermath, when all the dumbest choices tend to be made. Their faces were caught on CCTV fleeing the scene. They left blood traces on their shoes. They blabbed to their pals about doing someone in. Or the police found internet searches on their phones from the week before for "how to kill someone with a knife".

Reid wasn't exactly dealing with criminal masterminds.

Their guilt was already sealed by the time Reid got involved. There was no legal advice he could give that would save them from a ten or twenty stretch. And when the fall is all that's left, Reid's job – as far as he saw it – was to find the shortest and least lethal route towards the rocky ground below.

Sandy Driscoll, however, was not Gordon Reid's norm.

He looked miles away when he was brought into the interview room. His gaze darted wildly around the room, looking anywhere but the eyes of DS McNair or DCI Lomond sitting across from him.

Lomond sat back in his chair, arms folded, trying to contain his anticipation. What he wanted was to shut the cameras off and get ten minutes alone with Driscoll. He'd been awake for twenty-four hours now. He was tired and eager for answers, and he wasn't going to leave the room until Sandy Driscoll had told him everything he needed to know.

It was clear early on that Reid wasn't going to be any impediment to them finding out where Jack Ferguson had been taken. When Ross asked Driscoll to confirm his address, Reid didn't even object or discuss it with his client, despite there being a MAPPA order protecting Driscoll's location. Any solicitor worth a damn would never have let them answer that.

Ross said, 'Sandy, we just want to know where the boy is, and if he's safe.'

Lomond scribbled something down, then shot Ross a sideways glance to draw attention to it.

"USE JACK'S NAME".

Ross turned back to Sandy. 'Jack's mum and dad are really worried about him. They just want him to come home. No one wants to get anyone in trouble.'

Sandy stared into his hands in his lap, showing no sign of responding in any way.

Ross presented the evidence bag containing the patch of Jack Ferguson's pyjamas. 'This was found in your bedroom. Do you recognise it?'

Sandy lifted his head for the quickest glance, but said nothing.

Lomond passed the findings of the forensics report across the table.

Sandy stared at it like a dog that had been shown a card trick.

'This,' Ross tapped the report, 'says that a patch of clothing we found inside one sixteen Crowfoot Avenue – your residence – belongs to Jack Ferguson.' He showed him the evidence bag containing the fabric. 'How did that clothing get in your flat, Sandy?'

Reid leaned towards Sandy. 'Remember what we talked about?' he whispered.

Sandy answered Ross, 'I...I don't–'

'My client has no comment,' Reid said.

'I'd like to hear your client say that, Mr Reid,' replied Ross.

Sandy could feel three pairs of eyes burning holes in him. He shook his head sadly at the fabric in the bag. 'I...I don't know.'

'Has anyone else been in your flat in the last forty-eight hours, Mr Driscoll?'

Sandy said, 'Yes.'

Ross and Lomond each felt a shot of adrenaline surge through their torsos – just a hint of what was to come.

'Who was in your flat?' asked Ross.

'The police. When I came home.'

Ross's posture relaxed again. 'Okay. So, apart from us when we came to arrest you, Mr Driscoll.'

'I...I...I don't–'

Showing his first sign of irritation, Ross cut in, 'You don't know. Okay. Fine.' He pointed to the forensics report again. 'This report, Sandy, tells us that DNA markers for Jack Ferguson were present in a bedroom in your flat. The chances of that DNA being there without Jack Ferguson also having been there are billions to one. We *know* he was there...' He noticed Lomond writing something down and moving it barely into Ross's eye line.

"Patience."

As soon as Ross had read it, Lomond folded the note over and pocketed it.

'Look,' said Ross, 'you seem like a decent guy to me. I don't know how Jack Ferguson ended up in your flat. What we want more than anything is to find him and get him home. That's all that really matters.' He leaned down to make sure that Sandy could see him. 'Do you know where Jack Ferguson is?'

Sandy mumbled something. Something no one could hear.

Ross and Lomond leaned forward.

'What did you say, Sandy?' asked Ross.

He said a little clearer this time, 'I just wanted to save the children.'

The adrenaline was flowing fully now.

'What children, Sandy?' asked Ross.

'The missing ones.'

Lomond circled Leanne Donnelly's name.

Ross said, 'How long have you lived in that flat, Sandy?'

'Oh...a long time now.'

'More than five years?'

'Um...' Sandy counted it out on his fingers, going across all ten fingers twice. 'Yes. More than five. More than ten.'

Ross showed a picture of Leanne Donnelly. 'Do you recognise this girl?'

Sandy smiled. 'Cute girl.'

Ross got a chill so sharp he felt like vomiting. 'She is, Sandy. She was. She lived around the corner from you. Did you know that?'

'Used to see her. Skipping. Always skipping with a pal. Chalk on the pavement. Jumping. Hopping.'

'Did you watch her a lot, Sandy? Did you like watching her?'

'I did. Yes, I did. I like watching the children.'

'Did she end up in your flat as well?'

Reid raised his pen like a lazy student who couldn't be bothered to raise his entire arm. 'I'd like a word with my client.'

'In a minute,' said Ross, keeping his eyes locked on Sandy. 'It's too late for Leanne Donnelly, Sandy. But there's still time to save Jack Ferguson. If you do the right thing.'

Sandy shook his head, his eyes wrinkling as if he might be about to cry. 'It's too late. She's in the land of dreams now. Always sleeping now.'

Lomond shot forward in his chair. 'What's too late, Sandy?'

'Is Jack okay? I tried to save him. That was my job.'

'Did you take Jack, Sandy? It's okay. I promise it'll be alright if you tell me, but you have to tell me now.'

He counted on his fingers again. 'So many children. They're all dreaming now.'

'Have you taken other children, Sandy? Like Keiran McPhee?'

Sandy shook his head. 'I...I don't know...'

Lomond had waited five long years to get an answer to his next question, which would essentially be the same as asking 'Are you the Sandman?'

'Sandy, did you kill those five children? Keiran, Leanne, Blair, Mark, and Taylor. Did you kill them?'

Sandy started to cry, putting his head in his hands.

Worried he was about to miss their chance, Lomond pressed him. 'You can tell me. Come on. Stay with me, Sandy. Did you kill those children?'

Sandy muttered to himself, 'It's my fault, it's my fault...'

Reid said, 'We're taking a break.'

'No, we're not,' Lomond snapped, then turned his attention back to Sandy. 'Just tell me, Sandy? Did you kill them?'

'Chief Inspector,' complained Reid. 'My client needs a break.'

Ignoring him, Lomond ploughed on. 'Where did you take Jack Ferguson? Where is he?'

Sandy spluttered into his hands.

'What about Jack Ferguson?'

Ross laid a hand on Lomond's arm, trying to reel him back in, but it was proving difficult.

'Is he still alive, Sandy?' Lomond demanded. 'Is he still alive? There might still be time!'

Sandy turned to Reid. 'I don't want to be here anymore. I want to go home. I want to go home...'

Reid stood up and encouraged Sandy to do the same.

Lomond kept on. 'Just tell me where he is, Sandy! Think about what Jack's parents are feeling right now. They think they've lost him for good. That he's never coming back and there's nothing they can do about it.' Lomond insisted, 'You can still do the right thing, Sandy. You can still save him!'

Reid put his hand up. 'That's it. I'm stopping this.' He turned to Ross. 'Is there a charge here?'

'You'd better believe it,' Ross replied. 'Sandy Driscoll, I'm now informing you that you are under arrest for the abduction of Jack Ferguson.'

ONCE SANDY WAS TAKEN AWAY, Lomond sat at the table for a long time by himself. He had often wondered on those lonely, cold, wet nights in his flat in Paisley, what it would feel like to finally catch the Sandman. To sit in a room with him and look into his eyes. And to have him actually admit his crimes.

He should have felt closer than ever to getting there. Instead, it felt like history was repeating itself all over again.

CHAPTER THIRTY-EIGHT

FORENSICS HAD BEEN HARD at work since dawn, erecting tents and sheeting to preserve the crime scene at Martin Scullion's flat in Govan. It might have been early morning, but the temperature was comfortably in the early twenties already.

DI Willie Sneddon was dressed head to toe in forensic whites, masked, and double-gloved, which, in the baking heat of a property where you couldn't open any windows or have any kind of draught running through it, was definitely a short straw as far as MIT tasks for the day went.

Willie's mask wasn't one of the loose blue surgical masks, either. He had on a tight, laboratory-grade face-clinger. He could feel sweat rolling down his face behind his mask, and he couldn't lose his discipline for even a moment and wipe it away.

Trying to analyse complex forensic details in a flat like Scullion's was time-consuming to say the least. It was almost impossible to tell what might be a significant marking or what was just neglect. The flat had been poorly maintained before Scullion's death, and had stayed that way. Filthy glasses and dishes littered the kitchen. The sink was full of what had once been soapy water for steeping dirty dishes. It was now a thick brown sludge. A layer of grease seemed to coat everything in the kitchen.

There was nothing about the flat that suggested there had been a murder committed there, but Willie found it hard to believe that a hard bastard and canny operator like Martin Scullion could have been lured to the Botanics tunnel or taken by surprise and killed there. Or that if Maggie Belmont had been killed in the flat that no trace had been left behind. No one in Scotland was better than the Gartcosh forensics team at unearthing the truth behind seemingly perfect murders.

What was of prime concern was some light blood spotting that had been found on the living room carpet, which had the classic smeared signs of an attempted clean-up. When they lifted the carpet to take a sample, Willie recoiled at what they found.

'Oh, jeez...' he said to himself.

The forensic manager said, 'We're going to have to stop, Willie. We need to take up every inch of these carpets. We're looking at really heavy blood loss in this room.'

Willie peeled off his mask and gloves when he got outside onto the street. He took in deep lungfuls of air, then called Lomond.

'I've got a very bad feeling about what's gone on in this

place,' Willie said. 'There's dried blood stains that have seeped through from the carpets.'

Lomond sighed. 'Shite. Okay, Willie. We're going to have to lift all the carpets in there. Get them to mark enhancement.'

'Already started.'

They took out all the carpets, room by room, and carefully packaged them up for analysis at Gartcosh. There, they would be sprayed with a mixture of Luminol powder with hydrogen peroxide and hydroxide.

Luminol detected minute traces of haemoglobin present in blood, which made it glow a bright blue-white as seen in a dark room. A carpet could look perfectly normal. But a few sprays of Luminol in a dark room could reveal a murder scene.

The forensic biologists in the Mark Enhancement Laboratory laid the carpet samples down one by one, so they could capture images in relative size to the photos already taken in Scullion's flat.

The senior biologist said, 'Okay, lights down, please. Photography, if you could give me a few seconds for my eyes to adjust.'

The room went completely dark, then the biologist started to spray the carpet with the Luminol.

She had seen a lot in that room in her time, but what she was seeing now took her breath away. Normally unflappable, she would perform her task without comment.

This time, she found herself saying, 'Good god....' She checked with the photographer, 'Are you getting this?'

'Yeah,' they replied.

Nothing else was said over the course of the next carpet samples.

When the lights eventually came up, the biologist was a little shaken. 'Let's get these to MIT. They're going to want to see these as soon as possible.'

The biologist's deputy was staggered. 'Have you ever seen any that bad before?'

The biologist scoffed. 'No. Never. And I doubt I will ever again.'

She stared at her laptop screen, which showed the uploaded photos of the Luminol demo. For the living room carpet, the sample was almost entirely bright white, with a handprint clearly visible in the middle of the blood.

At the centre of it all was a message, written in blood by hand.

It said: *"GOD FORGIVE ME"*

CHAPTER THIRTY-NINE

THERE WAS A RELATIVELY celebratory mood in the briefing room the next morning, tempered by the fact that Jack Ferguson was still missing. Pardeep, Donna, and Jason joined the rest of the MIT as news filtered through that Sandy Driscoll was being charged. The truth was that as police it wasn't always possible to save the day. Sometimes bodies were never found. The dead went to their graves unavenged. Often, the only thing left to call a victory was punishing the accused, and making sure they served their time. One way to ensure a person lost any belief in there being any justice in the world was to be a police officer for a year. Terrible people got away with terrible crimes all the time, and if you had a problem with that, then you were better off going to a seminary instead of police college.

Ross had been leaning back casually against a vacant desk, holding court as the most senior officer in the small group. The moment Lomond appeared, Ross let go of the desk and stood up straight.

'Do you know what I don't understand?' said Lomond from a distance.

Neither Ross, Pardeep, Jason, nor Donna knew who he was speaking to.

Ross chimed in, 'Why phones were getting tiny and then got massive again? I mean, what was that all about?'

Lomond paused. 'Well, I was being rhetorical, but not to worry. Do you know what rhetorical means, detective sergeant?'

Ross hesitated. 'I don't want to answer that, sir.'

'I was going to say, I don't understand how three young detective constables can look so knackered after having about three hours more sleep than Ross and I. Jason, you might have ironed your tie and shined your shoes, but you look like you spent the night with a finger in a plug socket. No more caffeine for this guy.'

Pardeep took on the task as spokesperson for the three of them. 'We never went home until three, sir.'

'Three?' said Lomond. 'What the hell were you doing? I sent you home.'

'We were working on background on Sandy Driscoll, sir. In case you needed it for further interview prep later this morning.'

'Who's we?'

'Jason, Donna, and myself.'

Lomond's eyes lingered on Donna. Good for you, he

thought, impressed at her immediate response to his advice about being a team player.

He headed to the front of the room by the whiteboard and called out, 'Okay, folks. Let's get started....For those of you who knocked off early doors yesterday, let me catch you up on some significant progress we've made since. We have a man in custody, Sandy Driscoll, and he is being charged with the abduction of Jack Ferguson...' Lomond braced himself, 'but we're building towards a charge of murder in the five Sandman killings we know about.'

Spontaneous applause rippled across the room.

Lomond was quick to put a stop to it. 'Our priority, however, must remain finding Jack Ferguson alive. And on that front, we're running a little quiet.'

After checking in around the room for updates with the various other sergeants and team leaders on what he'd asked for yesterday, the conclusion was that there were no good leads.

A situation that didn't sit well with Lomond. 'Are you really telling me that Sandy Driscoll – a guy who can barely tie his own shoelaces on a good day – has managed to abduct a child in the west end of Glasgow and we're not able to find where he's hidden him?'

A lot of people suddenly became very interested in their hands. And their notes. And their pens. Anything except John Lomond's eyes.

Lomond went on, 'I can tell you that there have been developments about a related murder. Yesterday, a source provided me with information that led to a property owned by a Martin Scullion. Which then led us to the scene at the Botanics railway tunnel that you'll likely be seeing on the news by lunchtime today. There, we found the remains of Martin Scullion, along with the bones of a child. Both had piles of sand in their eyes. We've now had it confirmed that those bones belong to Maggie Belmont, a long-time cold case some of you may remember. As for Martin Scullion, his name is probably a bit of a blast from the past for some of you. For those of you who don't know, Martin Scullion – all-around perv and sleazy dirtbag – was a sergeant in the old Strathclyde Police force who was fired on multiple corruption and indecency charges. What does any of this have to do with Sandy Driscoll and Jack Ferguson? The information that led to locating Scullion's remains was billed to me as being related to Sandy Driscoll. Despite the fact that we have still not named Driscoll to the media. Clearly, however, there is a Sandman connection here, and we have to explore it. That's going to be an issue for myself and my team today. For the rest of you, we need to be turning Sandy Driscoll's life upside down. I want a tick-tock on his movements in the past week by the end of today. Who does he associate with? Where does he spend his time?'

Lomond approached the whiteboard and pointed to the timeline he had constructed.

'Twenty years ago, Maggie goes missing. Her body is never found. Fifteen years later, the first known Sandman murder takes place. What does this have to do with Martin Scullion?' Lomond jumped to the end of his timeline, showing the major events in the Sandman murders, and below that, Martin Scullion. 'Five years ago, the Sandman killings stop, and we don't hear from him again until this week. Forensics at the Botanics place time of death for Martin Scullion there as five years ago. This is a question we've been asking ourselves for a while: why did the Sandman killer stop? We speculated that the real killer ended up in jail for some other offence, but the predominant theory has always been that he died.'

Jason raised his hand. 'Sorry, sir. If we're entertaining the idea that Martin Scullion was the Sandman, how did he end up dead with sand left in his eyes, too?'

'The answer to that, Jason, is simply we don't know.' Lomond pointed to the dates listed underneath one another. 'Can we fill in the blanks of Scullion's life, and how do they fit with what we know about the Sandman? We need to track down all known associates of Martin Scullion. Who did he pal around with? Where did he drink? What did he do? Somewhere in that background could be a location where Jack Ferguson might be being kept.' Lomond scored out on the board where it said "5 DAYS", and wrote underneath it "4 DAYS". He motioned at the dead space on the whiteboard between Maggie Belmont and the supposed start of the Sandman murders. 'Somewhere in there, Martin Scullion and Sandy Driscoll's lives intercept. When did that happen, and where were they? We have to find that out, because we're running out of time.'

CHAPTER FORTY

When he was done, Linda took Lomond aside.

'Good work, John,' she said. 'You almost had me convinced.'

'I'm sorry?'

'You'd never be so reckless and disloyal to say it in front of the others, but you don't think Driscoll did it, do you.'

'He confessed to taking Jack, Linda.'

'He's confessed before. But we need to park that for now. We need to talk about what Willie found at Scullion's place this morning.' She led Lomond up the stairs to her office.

Lomond shut the door behind him. 'What is it?'

Linda opened up the photos that had just been sent through from Gartcosh. 'They were taking carpet samples this morning when they found evidence of a botched clean-up. When they lifted the carpets they found old blood. A lot of it.'

'How bad are we talking?' Lomond asked.

She bobbed her head, considering it. 'Bad. Gartcosh have not long finished the Luminol photos.' She puffed heavily. 'They're are as bad as I've seen.' She beckoned him around to the screen, then clicked through the photos.

The first photo showed the regular image photographed at the scene in Scullion's living room. Then the next photo showed the results to scale of the Luminol spray on the same patch of carpet. It was illuminated like a Christmas tree, glowing bright white.

There had been blood everywhere.

Linda pointed at what had been explained to her. 'You can see toe marks where someone was walking through the blood. And then streaks here. Likely from a body being dragged.'

'To where?' asked Lomond.

Linda clicked to photos of the bathroom. It looked like any other ordinary bath. A little unclean, perhaps, but nothing major.

Cut to the Luminol photos, and the entire bath was practically luminous.

'Jesus,' Lomond muttered.

'Seeing as you mention him...' She pulled up the "GOD FORGIVE ME" picture. 'Willie says there are a lot of crucifixes around the place. I would never have figured Scullion as the religious type.'

'Wherever he is, he'll be finding out just how forgiving god really is.'

'As for the bath, it doesn't take a forensic pathologist to figure out what's gone on in that thing.'

'That is a serious clean-up operation. Is there any word on DNA?'

Linda clicked out of the photos to the email that Moira McTaggart had not long sent. 'Moira checked this all personally. The blood in the bath is Martin Scullion's.'

'No one else's?' asked Lomond.

'Not in the bath. But the living room...' Linda navigated to the results so that she had names. 'It didn't take long, because they had files on record.'

'Don't tell me...'

'Keiran McPhee. Leanne Donnelly–'

'Oh no.' Lomond shut his eyes in despair, then covered his mouth.

'Yeah. And the others. All five. We now know who the Sandman is.'

Lomond should have felt relief. Instead he felt anger. Scullion had got away with it. He had died before he could be arrested.

Lomond could barely comprehend the scale of what they were about to face from the media – to say nothing of the public. If someone had been challenged to come up with a worst-case scenario for Police Scotland, they still couldn't have dreamed up what was in front of them now.

Lomond didn't even want to say the words, but he knew that one of them had to. He removed his hand from across his mouth. 'So that's it. The Sandman was Martin Scullion.'

Linda said, 'An ex-cop. And if the evidence bears out with Maggie Belmont, there's every chance that Scullion killed while he was still in service.'

'But if Scullion killed Maggie twenty years ago, how does Scullion end up in the same place, killed by the same means five years ago?'

'We know that Driscoll lived near to Leanne Donnelly. He's obviously in the frame for Jack Ferguson now too. Can we really ignore those things?'

Lomond speculated, 'What if Driscoll murdered Scullion?'

Linda let the idea settle in her mind, waiting for a wrinkle in the theory to appear. 'That could actually fit.'

'Either way, I have to go to Arran to tell Sharon Belmont. We can't let this come out in the press, and I'm not sure how long we can keep it quiet.'

'Are you sure?' asked Linda. 'Why don't I send Ross?'

'No, it should be me,' replied Lomond. 'It's not just Scullion and his possible involvement in killing little Maggie. Driscoll's arrest will break by lunchtime too. Sharon should hear it from the man responsible for helping set him loose.'

'Driscoll admitted to snatching Jack Ferguson. Do you still think he's innocent of taking and killing Maggie Belmont?'

'He had an alibi for the night that Maggie was taken. With Jack Ferguson, there's stonewall DNA proof that he was in the parents' bedroom. But there's something else to this yet. Something we're not seeing.'

Linda took a beat to clear her throat, unsure of how Lomond would react to what she had to say next. 'John, we go way back. You'll always have a mile more rope than any other DCI who walks through my door. And you know that there's no one else I'd rather have in your position...'

'But?'

'I think you want Driscoll to be innocent, because that will mean you didn't make a mistake with Maggie Belmont. It just might make it easier to look Sharon Belmont in the eye if you believe he's innocent of all charges.'

Lomond stood in silence for a moment. The longer the silence went on, and his witty retort never materialised, he had to admit that Linda might be right.

She said, 'It's not your fault those kids died, John. You did everything that you could to–'

'That's the point!' he snapped. He felt five years of pent-up frustration and guilt and anger spill over. 'I worked every hour I could without keeling over, missing weeks at a time with Eilidh when she was pregnant and needed me. I did *everything* you're supposed to do to stop the bad guy. I followed the evidence. I spoke up when everyone in the force wanted me to shut up. I did the right thing. I helped set Sandy Driscoll free because he was innocent of abducting Maggie Belmont. And now Jack Ferguson might pay for that with his life. What's fair about that? You know, I wonder how I could have raised a child in a world this shitty. Some-times I'm even glad Eilidh and the baby don't have to live in it anymore. I'm grateful. Because the world showed me its true nature, its true meaning that night. Most people never find out.'

Linda was too stunned to reply at first. 'I don't think you really believe all that. I think you're tired. And I think you've been living with this for too long. You want to say that the world is callous and cruel, and your wife and baby son are better off out of all this? Okay. That's a valid way of looking at the world. But if it's true, John, then what are any of us doing here? What are we fighting for? Why bother getting out of bed?'

'Maybe this is all that's left,' he said. He checked his watch. 'I've got a ferry to catch. I can't give Sharon Belmont her only daughter back. But I can at least tell her the truth.'

CHAPTER FORTY-ONE

Ross stood with Lomond on the deck of the Ardrossan-Arran ferry, uneasy in his body language. The drive from Glasgow had been strained as he struggled to avoid firing a million questions at him. Lomond was obviously withdrawn, and Ross didn't want to push him.

He had assumed Lomond's quietness was because the pair now had to deliver the news that every police officer dreads having to do.

Ross said, 'I haven't done this before, by the way.'

'You're kidding,' he replied. 'A detective sergeant and you've not done a death call before?'

'I've done role play at college...' He trailed off, embarrassed at how weak his CV was when it came to death.

'You don't need me to tell you it's not the same.'

'If you've got any pointers, I'm all ears.'

It didn't take Lomond long to think. 'Be clear. If someone's relative is dead, then say that. Euphemisms and talking round things will just cause confusion.'

'I suppose you must be used to these by now,' he said.

'Don't ever let anyone fool you that they get any easier. They don't. Folk love to make out after they've done their first that they're immune to getting all cut up about telling someone their relative is dead. That they can just head home and eat their dinner in peace. I've seen DIs and DCIs do death calls, then be laughing and joking in the car five minutes later. Callous bastards who think they can block out the darkness. Trust me, those are the guys who end up drinking themselves to death in retirement, and can't get through a bowling match without flashbacks. It always catches up with them eventually.'

Ross speculated, 'It must be harder when you care as much as you do.'

'I wish I didn't, Ross. Honestly. Life would be a lot simpler.'

Trying to sound casual, but failing miserably, he said, 'I couldn't help but notice when I was doing some background work with Pardeep and Jason, all of the file upload times for the Sandman enquiries on HOLMES.'

'What about them?'

'Well, there's work uploaded under your name pretty much around the clock for months at a time.'

'You've been doing your homework. So tell me. What exactly goes around about me these days?'

Ross looked away for a moment. 'There was a nickname

going around at Mill that Donna told me about. The Long Dark.'

He scoffed. 'Christ, that one's just never going to die off...' He looked at what remained of the journey ahead. More than enough water to tell the story. 'It might be hard to imagine now, but in my teens I was a long-distance runner. Ten thousand metres, mostly. I didn't belong to a club or anything. I just ran. The only way I knew how was to go out fast and burn everyone off, then I'd simply outlast everyone. But as I won more and more races, the harder the fields got – until I reached a point where I couldn't burn the competition off anymore. They were too strong in the final third. Anyway, I found a coach, and he told me that I ran best when conditions were bad. When it was wet and windy and cold. I loved the dark. The rain. It wasn't always like that. It happened after this one race. I was heading for the start line with all those semi-pro runners when it starts pelting down with rain. I was moping about with my arms crossed, trying to keep warm when my coach says to me, what's the matter? I said I didn't feel like running. Dinnae feel like running? I says, aye. The rain was getting even harder. Look behind you, he says. So I did, and I saw about twenty guys who all looked stronger and fitter than I was. Coach says, those guys might be walking to the start line, but half of them just quit. I decided not to have a problem with it being dark and cold and wet. Everyone else was so busy fighting the weather, they didn't have any fight left for me. A guy I used to run with told the story when I was at Tulliallan one time, and somebody called me the Long Dark.'

'Why did you stop running?' asked Ross.

'Ach,' he said, 'my coach said I could have been good if I found another gear at the end. But all I knew how to do was go out really fast.'

Ross had also been told that Lomond's nickname, the Long Dark, had stuck during the Sandman investigations. When things got really dark, Lomond embraced it. If anything, it made him want to dive even deeper into his process – to set up camp there and live there, because in a place like the Sandman enquiries, no one else could outlast John Lomond.

IT WAS STILL EARLY, so the island wasn't nearly as packed as it would be come mid-afternoon. Now, it was mostly the retired in their multiple shades of beige, and serious hill-walkers in their practical clothing and stuffed rucksacks and wraparound sunglasses. They had to set off early if they were to scale the peaks of Goatfell and Cìr Mhòr and the like before the sun hit its peak and the temperature had properly soared. They wanted to be descending by then. The day-trippers from Glasgow and nearby would come later, having slumbered late into the morning, then rushed around ill-prepared for the day ahead which resulted in long queues in the Co-Op on the island which didn't carry half the stuff that they were used to in their supersize Tesco Extras back home. They were as bad as those Americans who landed on Skye or Harris and demanded directions for the "nearest shopping mall", always expecting their big-city luxuries to be available wherever they went.

The islanders didn't have it nearly so easy. When the Cal Mac service was disrupted due to urgent engine repairs to the MV Caledonian Isles ferry that operated between Ardrossan and the island, residents were left stranded there until it was fixed, or forced to go all the way from Lochranza to Claonaig on the Kintyre peninsula on the mainland via the island's secondary ferry service, a mere one hundred miles and three-hour drive to Glasgow. Food deliveries and residents who had hospital appointments on the mainland had to be prioritised. If such a situation happened in Glasgow, there would be riots in the streets. On Arran, there was a peaceful acceptance and community support for those who needed it.

Lomond and Ross were delayed on the way to the Belmont cottage by a group of cyclists. Their bikes were laden with bags velcroed to their handlebars and top tube, ready for a long day in the saddle, riding around the entire island on the coast road, always with mountain-scapes to the left and seascapes to the right. The twisting road out of Brodick made an overtake impossible, which was fine with Lomond. He wasn't in any hurry to get there.

When they pulled up outside the cottage, they found Sharon Belmont unloading shopping bags from the boot of her car, accompanied by the unmistakable *chinking* of lots of glass bottles inside. As soon as she spotted the car she knew it was police.

She left the bags in the hall then came back outside. Shielding her eyes from the sun, she said, 'Back already.'

Lomond introduced himself and Ross, then motioned towards the remaining shopping bags in the open boot. 'Can I help you with these?'

'Leave them,' she called from the doorway the moment Ross stepped towards the car. 'You found her, didn't you?'

Lomond said, 'Maybe we should go inside, Mrs Belmont.'

CHAPTER FORTY-TWO

SHARON WAS SHAKING as she sat down on the couch opposite Lomond and Ross. Tears were already flowing, and she kept a hand raised slightly, ready to cover her mouth should the worst be announced. In a way, she already knew. The only reason for the police to be back so soon was if they had found Maggie's remains, or they had arrested a suspect. Either way, Maggie wouldn't be coming home. If they had somehow magically found her alive, then Lomond and Ross wouldn't be looking as grave as they were.

Ross was perched on the front of the cushion, elbows resting on his thighs. Lomond sat forward too, but was more relaxed. He knew what to expect. Ross didn't.

'Mrs Belmont,' Lomond began. 'We've come here today because there's going to be some news coming out a few hours from now about a crime scene we've discovered in Glasgow.' Not wanting to drag out the agony any longer, he got right to it. 'At that scene, we have found human remains that have been identified as Maggie's. I'm sorry.'

Sharon just nodded at first. 'When did it...How long ago?'

'Our forensic team say it most likely happened within a week of her disappearance. That would be consistent with what we've seen in similar cases.'

She spoke through a trembling hand. 'How did it happen? How was it done? I mean, would she have been in any...would she have suffered?'

Lomond replied, 'It's very hard to assign cause of death in cases like this. But I can tell you that sand was found amongst her remains, similar to what was found in her bedroom by DI Sneddon and DS McNair. This leads us to believe that–'

'It was him, wasn't it?' Sharon said. 'This Sandman person.'

'We do have persons of interest, but I'm afraid I can't go into too many specifics.'

'That's it.' She dropped her hands on her lap. 'It's over. All these years, waiting for the phone to ring, or a knock on the door. Now it's over. She's dead. No more hope. That was all I had.' She paused to wipe her eyes.

Ross leaned forward and offered her a tissue.

Through choking back tears, Sharon said, 'At least, as long as she was still missing, there was a chance.'

Ross said, 'The Chief Inspector and I would like to offer our deepest condolences, Mrs Belmont.'

'I don't want condolences. I want you to find this bastard. Tell me...is it Sandy Driscoll?'

Lomond paused. 'I can't go into too many specifics—'

'Why?' Seeing Lomond's reluctance, Sharon tried Ross instead. 'Why?'

Ross answered, 'In an enquiry as complex as this, it's vital for information to be controlled very carefully.'

'You think I'll blab to the press?'

Neither Lomond nor Ross knew what to say to that.

Sharon went on, 'You'll protect whatever monster killed all these children. Who's going to protect me when Maggie's name breaks in the papers later th'day? Eh? I'll have them camped out at the end of the driveway again like twenty year hasn't passed.' She eyeballed Lomond. 'Just be straight with me: is it Sandy Driscoll?'

Figuring it was only a few more hours before it would get out, he confirmed, 'No. But we are charging him with a possibly related abduction.'

Sharon shook her head, feeling tears renewing behind her eyes. 'This is your fault, you know. You're the reason he was back on the streets. And if it wasn't for you, he'd be behind bars doing the time he deserved. You already caught him. Then some bollocks about CCTV comes up and suddenly he's being treated like Nelson Mandela.'

'Or Sir Walter Raleigh,' said Lomond. Realising the reference had gone over the others' heads, he added, 'There's a biography on King James the First over there.'

'My husband's,' Sharon said. 'He left them here when he left me.' She looked pointedly at Lomond. 'Try holding a marriage together when the press are hounding you, and the man who was arrested for murdering your child is released.'

Ross chimed in with the one contribution Lomond had told him to provide towards the end of the conversation. 'Mrs Belmont, we'd like to offer you the services of one of our Family Liaison Officers. This is someone who can keep you up to date with progress in the enquiry.'

'Like the last one you sent? Prick just sat where you two are and drank all my tea.'

Lomond stood up. 'The offer will always be there, Mrs Belmont. It might seem like a better idea when this is a little less raw.' He offered her his contact card. 'If you need anything at all, or if you have any questions, you can call me anytime on that number.'

Sharon made no move to take the card. 'You want thanks for the house call? If I need to talk, I'll talk to Maggie the way I have for the last twenty years.' Her voice turned to stone. Raw and ice cold. 'Thanks for coming. Thanks for telling me. Now fuck off and die, the pair of you.'

CHAPTER FORTY-THREE

JASON, Pardeep, and Donna were finding out what it was all about at the thick end of a major murder enquiry: intricate paperwork. Endless streams of it.

Piles of manila folders, and binders that refused to stack straight on top of each other, lay all around the floor on an area the three had cleared in front of the whiteboard.

One report, one enquiry at a time, they combed through Martin Scullion's documented movements, trying to find any link or consistencies with Sandy Driscoll. So far, they had come up with absolutely nothing.

It had been simple to check, as after relocating to a secret location under the MAPPA order, Sandy Driscoll didn't appear to have done anything for a fifteen-year period other than go to work at Shieldhall Recycling Centre on the edge of Govan and Renfrew, and come back home. He hadn't even bothered to change his name, as the three different employees that Pardeep spoke to on site all knew him by "Sandy Driscoll".

'They all said the same thing,' reported Pardeep. 'Quiet. A bit strange. They kept him busy in the section sorting the landfill waste. The guy I spoke to said it was the worst job they had. Driscoll volunteered for it every day for years.'

'What about before his arrest?' asked Donna. 'When does he move to Arran?'

Pardeep and Jason had teamed up on that one.

'That's where things get a little murky,' explained Jason, sifting through a mountain of paperwork that had told them very little. 'He lives in sheltered housing in the east end of Glasgow from eighteen years old, and does odd jobs for the next ten years. He collects trolleys at B&Q at Parkhead for a few years. The manager there couldn't even remember him. I had to show him a picture. Then stacking shelves overnight at Tesco in Maryhill. Waste collector for Glasgow City Council. Every time it's the same answer: he seemed like a nice guy. Quiet. He gets a job as a litter picker on Arran, and moves there permanently after three months on the job – moving into a tiny cottage a minute away from the Belmont cottage. Driscoll's old boss went on record as saying "he was the best employee I ever had. Never late, and never asked for holidays."'

Pardeep nodded his head at the familiar story. 'The guy is clean. And we can't tie him to any Sandman victims, except living a minute away from the second victim Leanne Donnelly.'

Donna insisted, 'But we agreed that that can't have been a coincidence.'

'I know that's what we said,' said Jason. 'The fact is, we don't have any physical evidence linking Driscoll to a Sandman victim. Not even circumstantially.'

The three of them assembled in front of the whiteboard, which looked depressingly similar to how it had started that morning.

'Have you got anything?' asked Pardeep.

Donna replied, 'I think I've got something on those two Foxbar flats. We couldn't work out how Driscoll ended up linked to two properties on the same street, right?' She stuck paperwork on the board that she had found in the Maggie enquiry. 'Driscoll has been living at one-sixteen Crowfoot Avenue since his conviction was quashed. That flat has been owned by him since he was eighteen. The interesting thing is that when Driscoll is released from jail, the property that he chose to keep hidden behind the MAPPA order wasn't the flat we found him living in. It's number seventy-two.'

'Why?' asked Pardeep.

'Exactly what I thought.' She reached behind her for further paperwork then held it aloft. 'I checked through all police records on the property, and there were two separate complaints about noise by residents in number seventy-two. All relating to flat six.'

'That's Driscoll's,' said Jason.

'Look,' Donna said, pointing to the date on the report. 'That's two nights after Leanne Donnelly went missing.'

A hush came over the three. The worst thing about being

police officers with such information was that it wasn't hard for them to imagine what the neighbours might have been hearing.

Pardeep asked, 'What about complaints around the time of the other abductions?'

'I thought of that too,' replied Donna. 'Nothing.'

Jason took a much closer look at the board. Still facing it, he asked, 'What's the story with Sandy Driscoll's dad?'

Donna said, 'He was a property developer and a private landlord. The two Foxbar flats were his until he divorced his wife. She got everything, and he disappeared. I mean, without a trace. Totally off the map.'

'What happened to the mum?' asked Pardeep.

Donna retreated to the desk where she had been working. She picked up a piece of paper like it was a smoking gun. 'Janet Driscoll. She died when Sandy was eleven. Half the property was left to Sandy, which he inherited when he turned eighteen. The other half went to his sister Jean, who quickly disappears into the care system with Sandy, which goes as well as that normally goes.'

'Where is she in all this?'

'Never heard from again,' said Donna. 'No bank accounts, no taxes paid. Just another one of thousands who disappear every year.'

Jason said, 'So we have no explanation why Sandy kept number seventy-two hidden instead of one-sixteen.' He remonstrated at the board in frustration. 'He didn't even change his name! Why bother?'

Donna felt an answer coming to her. 'It was an opportunity,' she said. 'The MAPPA order gave him the opportunity to keep a property totally secret. He chose a flat that was completely empty and hadn't been lived in for months. Maybe years.' She grabbed her suit jacket off the back of her chair, then headed for the doors.

'Where are you going?' asked Pardeep.

Before he got an answer, Jason was setting off after her.

'For fu–' Pardeep ran after them. 'Ho! Wait for me...'

CHAPTER FORTY-FOUR

THE THREE OF them were in the living room of seventy-two Crowfoot Avenue. Donna and Jason were hunting with a renewed sense of purpose, while Pardeep was trying not to get sweat on his gloved hands as he wiped his forehead. They all had on disposable gloves and masks.

'Forensics have been through here already,' Pardeep said, doing a good impression of someone half-heartedly looking for something.

Donna buzzed about the place, knocking on walls to check for hollow sections. Checking inside cupboards for false doors. Stepping on floorboards to see if any had give in them.

But there was nothing.

Pardeep put his arms out. 'Happy?'

'Do I look happy?' asked Donna. She paused, staring at one of the walls. She turned quickly to Jason. 'We got a floor plan of this place, right?'

Jason took it out of his immaculate leather shoulder bag. 'Right here.'

Donna squinted. 'What's this?' She pointed at a section of wall that on the floor plan showed a flat wall at a ninety-degree angle.

Jason looked at the wall, then the floor plan in confusion. 'That can't be right.'

Donna pointed. 'What's through this wall?'

'Neighbours, isn't it?' suggested Pardeep.

'No,' said Jason, taking out a second plan. He showed it to them. 'Look. This is ours. Then this is the original floor plan here.'

The wall in front of them was at a forty-five degree angle to the adjacent wall, rather than ninety degrees.

Jason said, 'This room's been altered.'

'Where did you get that?' asked Donna.

'The National Records of Scotland's general register house in Edinburgh. They know me there, so I had someone take a scan of it for me.'

'What the hell do you do there?' asked Pardeep.

'Maps!' Jason declared with delight. 'I like looking at old maps.' He could tell his colleagues weren't as enamoured. His enthusiasm drained. 'You know, comparing town plans over the years...that sort of thing.'

Pardeep paused, then looked at Donna. 'Are we sure that he's not a serial killer?'

'Don't judge him too harshly,' she replied, inspecting the wall again. 'If it wasn't for his mad hobby we'd be walking out of here empty-handed.'

A look of trepidation came over Pardeep's face. 'Then what's behind this wall?'

Giving up on the wall itself, Donna looked to the side where there was an electrical socket. She got down on her knees, then took out a Swiss army knife.

Pardeep lunged towards her. 'Whoa! What are you trying to do? Break the Olympic long jump record with zero fucking training?'

'Trust me,' she said, poking a short blade into one of the pin holes. With a turn of the knife, a panel with a wooden border released from a latch, revealing a hidden door. 'There was no wiring behind it.' Down on her hands and knees, she pointed a small torch attached to her car key inside.

The sound she made told Pardeep and Jason everything they needed to know about what she had found.

'Oh god...' She sounded sick. Unwell. 'Oh, no...' Disgusted.

She stood up and held the torch out.

Pardeep was reluctant to take it.

Jason went next, crawling through into a hidden room.

'What is it?' Pardeep asked Donna.

She was still shaking her head.

He crouched down and called through the door. 'Jason? What is it?'

'There's a bed,' he replied gravely. 'A bare bed with an old mattress. And...and...' His voice cracked a little. 'I'm coming out.'

When he emerged, he and Donna looked at each other.

'That's not a hidden room,' she said. 'That's a prison cell.'

'It makes sense,' Jason added. 'No neighbours beyond that room. And the sound insulation on the walls would stop any...' He didn't want to finish.

Pardeep said, 'Yeah.'

'So what is it, then?' wondered Donna. 'Driscoll keeps this place empty so the children can be kept here in private?'

'Did you see his interview tape?' asked Pardeep. 'Sandy Driscoll isn't juggling multiple properties and hiding kids in a busy residential area without getting caught.'

Jason concurred.

Donna said, 'Then who's helping Driscoll?'

Pardeep shrugged. 'We've spent all day looking at the same things you have. Driscoll doesn't go anywhere except to work, where he doesn't talk to anyone. He doesn't even have internet up the road.'

Donna was first to suggest a solution. 'What's the one place we know he's been that we haven't checked yet?'

Jason answered, 'Prison.'

'And how are we going to look into that?' asked Pardeep. 'It's fifteen years since he was put away.'

After doing some quick calculations in her head about timing, Donna said, 'I might have a way. Can you guys call this in to the gaffer?'

'Where are you going?' asked Jason.

'I'm going to talk to someone that I think can help.' She took out her personal-use phone, then paused as she was about to send a message. 'Anyone who wants to retain deniability of illegal activity should probably let me do this next part on my own.'

CHAPTER FORTY-FIVE

LOMOND HADN'T EVEN MADE it to the car at the end of Sharon Belmont's driveway when Ross asked him, 'What was all that stuff about Walter Raleigh?'

'I was hoping you would pick up on that,' Lomond replied. He waited until they were both in the car before elaborating. 'I think she knows more than she lets on. Like that husband of hers.'

Ross hung onto his seatbelt. 'What's that supposed to mean?'

'I think she knows where he is.'

SERGEANT DAVIE MUIR recognised Ross as he entered the station, and seemed to linger somewhat on Lomond who was trailing behind.

Muir's relaxed posture stiffened, and he hurried back

behind his desk, as if he needed something physically between him and Lomond to stop him doing something rash.

Ross introduced the sergeant to Lomond.

'I was wondering if we could ask a few questions, Sergeant,' said Lomond.

'That depends,' Muir replied. 'What's it about?'

'I don't know if you've followed what's been happening in Glasgow.'

'We do get the news here, Chief Inspector. We might be islanders, but we're not completely behind the times. Dalmarnock have even given us tasers now.'

Taken aback at the adversarial attitude and tone, Lomond said, 'No. Of course.' He took a quick look behind at the sound of passing traffic and hikers. 'Is there maybe somewhere private we can have a sit down and chat?'

'Not really,' Muir answered. 'My only other officers are dealing with a road accident over on the String.'

Lomond turned his head ever so slightly. 'The...?'

'The B880. It runs across the middle of the island. Links the west side to the east.'

'Okay,' Lomond said, uncomfortable at having to deliver the news in the reception. 'There's been some progress in an enquiry relating to human remains found in a tunnel in Glasgow. DS McNair and I have just been at Sharon Belmont's cottage to inform her that we have confirmation the remains are Maggie's.'

Muir sighed. 'Right. That's...' His head dropped. 'How was she?'

'Prepared, I think. The longer it went on, the more likely

it was going to be about recovering remains rather than finding a missing person.'

Muir's expression tightened, turning to barely restrained frustration. 'That's going to make a lot of people here very angry. Very angry indeed. I mean, it makes *me* angry.'

'That's understandable, Sergeant,' said Lomond. 'The thing is, when we were talking to Mrs Belmont, she mentioned her husband. Can you tell us anything about him?'

'Like what?'

'Where he was on the night of Maggie's disappearance.'

Muir seemed stunned. 'It's all in the report, isn't it?'

'It's actually not,' Ross interjected. 'There's a statement about Sharon Belmont's movements, but not her husband's.'

Lomond added, 'It was a while ago now, but I remember at the time a lot of discussion about where the husband had been.'

'Aye, by that prick reporter, Colin Mowatt.'

'Do you know where Mr Belmont was that night?'

'Mick was a fisherman,' said Muir. 'He was out on the water.'

'On his own?'

'Aye. But three other boats saw him, and he radioed twice from the boat to give his location. Facts that were left out of the *Glasgow Express* story. That reporter's got blood on his hands for what he wrote about Mick Belmont.'

Lomond did a double-take. 'Blood?'

Muir pointed in the direction of the water. 'They found his boat drifting out there the day after the press conference.

We found his body face-down in the water two days later. He never wanted to do that press conference to begin with. Said that everyone would say that he did it because Sharon had a stronger alibi.'

'And who was that alibi?'

Muir hesitated. 'Look, no one ever said Sharon was perfect, right. So her fella was off working, and she went out to the Ormidale – the hotel in Brodick. It's got a nice bar. She met someone and got chatting. The cameras behind the bar showed them talking for over an hour, and one of my own officers on his night off saw them going into his car in the car park.'

'Who was the guy she was with?' asked Ross.

'She said she never got his name, but we managed to trace him to Kilmarnock. I was the one sent to his house.'

'He must have had some face on him when you pulled up.'

'And he had an entirely different one on him when he had to explain to his wife what it was all about.'

'Can you walk me through the timings, Sergeant,' asked Lomond, 'because I don't understand how anyone knows Maggie wasn't taken after Sharon Belmont was seen going into the guy's car.'

'My officer saw them together, and he checked his watch because he was surprised to see Sharon out so late with the wee one at home. The poor lad blamed himself for not having a word with her or going back to her place to check on Maggie sooner. A neighbour saw Sharon leaving her cottage, and Maggie was inside, waving goodbye from her window.

Sharon ended up ejected from the hotel bar. In the end, the constable went by the house and Maggie was gone. Sharon Belmont wasn't out of the hotel CCTV the whole time she was there.'

Lomond's line of questioning had clearly got the sergeant's back up, his tone growing more and more irritated as he'd gone on.

Muir said, 'If you want to find guilty parties, Chief Inspector, you might want to take a look again at the guy who actually confessed to taking Maggie and didn't have an alibi on the night in question.'

'He actually did have an alibi, Sergeant,' retorted Lomond.

'Then he had someone else helping him,' Muir fired back. 'I don't care what anyone says. That Driscoll boy was up to his neck in this thing.'

Ross was shocked at how Muir was speaking to a Chief Inspector, but that was nothing compared to how much Lomond's restraint was being tested.

'This was a courtesy visit,' Lomond pointed out. 'My office will keep you abreast of any further developments in the Maggie Belmont case.'

As Lomond strode back to the car, taking his anger out on the gravel driveway, Ross dallied behind a little.

'Something the matter, Ross?' asked Lomond.

'Did you really need to go after Mrs Belmont like that?'

'Innocent until proven guilty is fine for a courtroom, but it's a shitty way to approach a murder enquiry. If you want to be good polis, son, do yourself a favour: don't ever take any name off the table until you're certain.'

Lomond felt righteous in his indignation, but deep down he knew that Sergeant Muir was partially right on one point. When he found out that Driscoll had copped to taking the five Sandman victims, and was up to his neck in the Jack Ferguson abduction, Lomond knew that he would be lucky to ever be allowed back on the island again.

CHAPTER FORTY-SIX

DONNA STOOD at the corner of a small shopping square in Broomhill in Glasgow's west end. It was one of the many places in the area where working class collided with middle class. Almost every street offered some variation in housing. On one side of Broomhill Drive were expensive tenements that had ballooned in value in the last ten years, while directly across the road were high flats that routinely had police vans pulling up outside them.

Donna was surrounded by just as many residents of the high flats as from the nearby tenements. You were as likely to pass a recovering junkie in a tracksuit heading to Boots for his methadone as you were some lawyer who had just parked their Audi TT.

The real engine room of the Broomhill shops was Greggs and a small Co-op supermarket. Throughout the day it fed the men in their white vans; the kids on their way to school; the lone drunks who shuffled over from the flats before shuffling back with a carrier bag filled with only wine and ciga-rettes; and everyone in between.

Donna finished off a Greggs sausage roll and was reminded why she ate there so rarely. No one actually liked Greggs, did they, she wondered. It just so happened that they were absolutely everywhere and you could get some-thing hot in the middle of the day without having to wait very long.

Once she'd rubbed the grease off her fingers down the front of her trouser legs, she took the SIM card out of her work phone and removed the battery. She didn't want anyone tracking where she was going, or ever find out where she had been.

What she was participating in took place hundreds of times across Glasgow every day, and most people hardly ever noticed.

It started with a text message to an anonymous number. The number changed every week, and you only found out what it was through personal contact with someone on the inside of the "Broomhill Taxi Service".

You never asked for what you wanted or how much. If you did that, you never got a call back. You did exactly what Donna had done – and only that. You texted asking for a taxi along with your meeting location and what you were wear-ing. Then you received a reply saying what time you would be picked up at.

If it was your first time, it could be a scary business. You were climbing into a drug dealer's car, and you had no idea where you were being taken, or what would happen. It could have been a complex police sting operation. But they didn't have the resources necessary to hoover up such low-hanging fruit.

As far as the trade went, the drugs sold via the Broomhill Taxi Service were fairly soft. A bit of weed, opioids, maybe ecstasy nearer the weekends. There was never any smack – the dealers didn't want proper hardcore junkies stinking up the interiors of their rides.

It was easy to spot cars operating in the Service. They were the gleaming, kitted-out Mercedes and Audis and BMWs that pulled into the high flats car park, picked up someone who didn't have any bags, drove around the block a few times, then deposited the passenger back where they came from. The passenger normally jogged back inside, eager to consume whatever they had just bought.

Donna knew it was the car before they even pulled up.

A black Mercedes with sparkling rims, the suspension dropped far lower than was practical in a city with so many potholes, and the sound system thumping so loud it could be heard from the other side of the Clyde.

Donna couldn't actually hear anything other than the bass when she opened the door. 'How you doing?' she asked, unsure of protocol beyond the phone call.

The driver, so low in his seat that he could barely see over the steering wheel, didn't look at her. The front passenger dealt with everything.

'Get in,' he said, irritated that she didn't know what she was doing. He hated dealing with newbies.

Both the men were in their early twenties. Handsome in

an obvious kind of way, and exceedingly well groomed. Especially their intricate little beards and their hair.

The front passenger was white, and wearing mostly North Face sportswear and a massive gold chain around his neck.

The driver was Asian, looked bored out of his face and smoked a cigarette. As soon as Donna closed her door, they drove off slowly, not drawing any attention.

'What d'you want?' asked the passenger.

'I want to talk to Higgins,' Donna answered.

The passenger eyeballed her via the side mirror. 'The fuck you say?'

'You heard me. Higgins.' She took out her ID. 'Now.'

She didn't show it, but inside Donna was shaking like a leaf. If she had gone rogue in taking off on her own before on the Sandy Driscoll address lead, then she had gone completely off the reservation now. She was unarmed polis in an area she didn't really know, and had tricked two drug dealers – both with semi-serious time under their belts already – into picking her up for a score.

'I think you've made a mistake,' said the passenger. He indicated to the driver. 'Pull over, man. Pull the fuck over. Can't believe this amateur entrapment shit...'

Donna didn't budge when the car came to a stop, diving into an empty space on the narrow road behind the shops. 'I'm not here to search you or the car,' she said. 'I'm not here to make any arrests or confiscate merchandise. I just want to talk to Higgins.'

The passenger tossed his phone over his shoulder,

landing in the backseat. It was a cheap burner. 'There's a phone. Knock yourself out, sweetheart.'

Donna reached around both sides of the seat in front of her, grabbing for the area that was most exposed by the passenger's woeful posture.

'When you make your balls so easily accessible, it doesn't always end well,' she snarled.

The driver was too busy laughing to intervene.

Through anguished cries, the passenger implored him to do something.

The driver casually waved her to sit back. 'Let him go, man. Chill. Fuckin' hell...'

Donna stopped crushing the passenger's balls, then tossed the phone towards the front dashboard. 'I want to talk to Higgins,' she said. 'In person.'

'Alright, alright,' the passenger groaned. 'He lives at Glasgow Harbour. One of the penthouses.'

'Great,' she announced cheerfully. 'Take me there. We're two minutes away.'

He muttered something under his breath, then snapped at the driver. 'Fucking go, dude. Before she turns them to mush.'

The driver shook his head. 'Higgins is going to have a fit, man.'

'Don't worry,' said Donna. 'He knows me.'

CHAPTER FORTY-SEVEN

GLASGOW HARBOUR TERRACES was one of the most prestigious new-builds in the city when it was being built. Set on the banks of the River Clyde, and offering spectacular panoramic views of the city, Harbour Terraces appeared to be Glasgow's answer to the kind of upscale apartment blocks that were springing up all around London and Manchester at the time.

Everyone that drove past them wanted one. The penthouses were all snapped up by Celtic and Rangers footballers who thought they were buying into a fashionable new address.

But months after residents started moving in, the prestige quickly disappeared.

The problem was that they had been massively overpriced, leaving only a small group of successful professionals who could afford to live there. After a few years, developers were still sitting on dozens upon dozens of vacant units.

With no end in sight to the drought, and in a desperate bid to cut their losses, the remaining units were sold off at cut-down prices, which invited in a raft of predatory landlords who filled the fancy flats with the one group guaranteed to rile up the existing property-owners.

Students.

Snapping up the cheap rent offers, the savvy students rammed three-bedroom flats with five people. They partied around the clock, blasting dance tunes until the early hours of the morning. The paper-thin walls that surrounded the flats didn't exactly help matters. A neighbour shutting a kitchen cupboard door too loudly could be heard next door. There were running battles in the hallways in the middle of the night with water soaker guns. Barely a morning went by where vomit wasn't discovered on staircases or in the lifts.

As residents fled, accepting bargain offers, the up side for drug dealers like Barry Higgins was penthouse apartments could be had for half of what they cost five years earlier. It was one of dozens he kept in his portfolio. And even a guy like Higgins who brought in over £20,000 a week was on the lookout for a bargain.

The passenger escorted Donna to Higgins' door on the top floor.

'If he knocks us both the fuck out, remember whose fault it is,' he told her.

Higgins said, 'Hello?' from the other side of the door.

'It's Donna,' she said.

There was a pause, then a flicker of light at the peephole as he checked it.

Then the chain on the other side slid off and Higgins opened the door.

He was in his sixties, had his thinning grey hair in a ponytail, and was wearing a silk bathrobe over a pair of boxer shorts and a Partick Thistle football jersey for the current season.

'Well, well, well,' he said. 'Am I under arrest?'

'No,' she said, brushing past him. 'We won't knock for that.'

Higgins held his hands out as if to say "what the hell is this?"

The passenger pleaded, 'She said she knows you.'

Higgins slammed the door shut and made his way to the living room.

The entire flat was in darkness, which hadn't been done as an aid to keep the searing heat out. It was like that every day, all year.

'I like what you've done with the place,' Donna said, recoiling from the stench of strong grass. 'What the hell are you smoking?'

In her day, a bit of weed was a casual thing. All of her friends did it, and she most certainly did it – almost every night as a teenager.

'It's all that laboratory-enhanced shit, loaded with THC,' Higgins explained. 'Back in the day, you could just light a spliff and watch *The Big Lebowski,* nice and relaxed. Now everyone wants their joint to be like getting hit by a bus. Fucking degenerates.'

Donna pointed at the silk bathrobe Higgins was wearing.

'It doesn't seem that long ago you were slashing folk in Gallowhill. Now you're poncing about a penthouse dressed like Elton John – apart from the Partick Thistle top, of course.'

'Just living the good life,' he replied. His eyes were red raw from the potent weed he'd been smoking since early that morning.

A one-hundred-inch TV dwarfed everything else in the living room. It was currently playing a Blu-ray of *Scarface*. The part where Al Pacino is cuckoo on cocaine, getting high on his own supply.

'For how much longer?' Donna asked.

'Have you come here to arrest me, or convert me to your little piggy cult? Or are you wanting to rip off my stash?'

'I know you're not stupid enough to leave merch in the flat. And you know that I turn a blind eye to what you do for a living.'

'I don't need any charity, Donna.'

'No, but you could do with some advice.'

He was all ears.

'It took me two phone calls to get inside your little operation. How hard do you think it'll be for Frank Gormley once he gets out?'

'What you talking about?'

'I've heard word that he might be getting out soon. I know we don't really have a relationship anymore, and that's how I want it. But right now, we could use each other.'

He took a joint out of his bathrobe pocket and showed it

to her. 'Do you mind? Or would you rather we kept up the pretence?'

'I'd rather you didn't because I'm going to leave this place smelling like I spent the evening at a Pink Floyd gig, and my SIO's expecting me back soon.'

Higgins put the joint away and scoffed. 'What are you going to do for me?'

Donna saw through the tough guy act. She had seen it a thousand times from him growing up. She knew all about the terrible things that he was capable of. She had seen it first hand, and that it took a lot more than business acumen and good timing to last even five years as a semi-big drug dealer in Glasgow. Barry Higgins was getting into his fourth decade.

'How much longer do you think you can keep getting away with this before someone nails you again like last time?'

'What are you talking about?' he asked.

'The five-year bit. It was because you fell out with some street dealer of yours. Didn't like the cut you were giving him. The problem is, the bigger you get, the more money you take away from people like Frank Gormley. And his people are starting to notice.'

He smirked. With just a tinge of fear. 'Who told you that?'

'I work in Paisley CID, dad. I hear things.'

Dad. It had been a while since he'd been called that.

'Is there something in it for me?' he asked.

'I need some information about someone who was in Bar-L at the same time as you.'

Higgins laughed. 'That was fifteen years ago. You don't

need me. You need a DeLorean and enough road to get up to eighty-eight miles an hour, because you need a time machine.'

'I've come to you because you knew everyone. Heard everything.'

'Who are you looking for?'

'Sandy Driscoll.'

'The kid killer? I remember him.'

'What do you remember?'

'I remember everybody thought he was guilty. The governor was fear't for the boy, so they stuck him in E Hall with all the other beasts.'

Donna's skin crawled at the thought of it. Over two hundred of Scotland's most serious sex offenders housed together. The other inmates called them "the Beasts".

'Do you remember anyone Driscoll hung around with?'

'That's easy,' said Higgins. 'There was only one. Peter Lee.'

'The paedophile?'

'You say that like he was just some disgraced Geography teacher or something. The guy was a proper beast. And he took Driscoll under his wing. Looked after him. Made everyone assume Driscoll was guilty. We were all stunned when he was let out.'

'There was no one else?' she asked.

'Not while I was around.' He took the joint out and lit it.

She started towards the hall. 'I'll let you get back. Lovely life you've put together for yourself here.'

'Better than being a pig,' he remarked.

Donna told herself that she should just leave. She got the information she wanted. But she couldn't let it lie. Not again.

'As if it wasn't hard enough having to watch you beat my mum half to death, do you know how hard I've had to fight just to get into uniform because of your name? Your reputation? There are officers at Mill Street that don't want to work with me.'

Higgins gestured at the surroundings. 'To think, you gave up working for me to join that shite.'

'That "shite" saved my mum's life that night. That constable is the reason I joined the polis. He showed me what a life was really worth.'

'What's it worth?' he asked.

'Far more than you think.'

As she reached the front door, he called after her, 'You'll let me know about Gormley getting out?'

'Quietly,' she replied. 'No one can ever know this meeting happened.'

CHAPTER FORTY-EIGHT

BACK AT HELEN STREET STATION, Jason and Pardeep were back poring over anything they could think of to track down Robert Driscoll – or at least confirm that he was dead, and thus not a suspect.

'I'm telling you,' said Pardeep, 'I like this guy for it.'

'He would certainly tick plenty of boxes,' Jason replied. 'Someone with some authority over Sandy. He could look after the practical concerns that Sandy couldn't.'

After things had lulled again, Jason waggled his pen. 'What do you think Donna's up to?'

'Don't know,' said Pardeep. 'Don't want to know.' His eyebrows suddenly furrowed at the files he had been combing through. 'I was just clearing this old file on Scullion off my desk. It's his arrest reports. Have you seen this name come up a few times?' He showed it to Jason.

'Now you mention it, I have, actually,' he said. He considered a large pile of folders on his desk, then thought

for a moment, and took out the one he needed. 'Here...
Charlie McBain. Over and over again.'

'They spent seven years together in Drumchapel CID,
before McBain moved on to Specialist Crime.'

'Doing what?'

'Cyber Crime Unit.' Pardeep recoiled. 'Fuck that. You
couldn't pay me enough to do that job.'

As a father of four, the idea of working in Cyber was
particularly repulsive to Pardeep. They were the team that
tracked down paedophiles with images and videos of child
pornography.

Pardeep said, 'If there's anyone that can fill the gaps in
on Martin Scullion, this guy's worth a punt.'

Having called Lomond on the road and been left hanging, Pardeep instead tried DI Sneddon, who was still working
through the final forensics report from Scullion's flat.

Pardeep put one of the files down to show Willie the
signature. 'Have you ever heard of this guy?'

'God, old Bainy,' said Willie. 'That's a name that takes
me back.'

Pardeep said, 'Personnel says he's retired. How would
you go about trying to track him down?'

'If he's still alive, there's only one place Bainy will be at
this time of day.'

THE LEGENDARY COBBLED Ashton Lane in the west end of

Glasgow – with its ceiling of fairy lights and village atmosphere – was home to the equally legendary restaurant and bar, The Ubiquitous Chip.

As Jason and Pardeep arrived, the first of the early evening drinkers were beginning to assemble on the front patios of the various bars that lined the lane. It was busier than usual for that time as the sunshine had brought everyone outside instead of sitting in dingy, dark pubs.

For Pardeep, who was always either working or looking after his children, it was a rare glimpse of Glasgow nightlife. Indeed, his glimpses of it only ever happened now when on duty.

Pardeep and Jason headed for the upstairs bar in the Ubiquitous Chip. It was hard to think of an establishment more loved by Glaswegians.

The pair struggled through the dense crowd that had already assembled inside. A prime spot in the upstairs bar was often treated like a sun lounger by a holiday resort swimming pool, with folk showing up well before their friends to secure it.

The bar's pokiness was part of its charm, and it also made spotting Charlie McBain much easier. Exactly where Willie said he would be: on a bench tucked up against the wall, nursing a pint. There was a wooden shelf above McBain's head. After taking a slurp of beer, he seamlessly – and without having to look – lifted the pint glass over his head and placed it on the shelf without spilling a drop. The action was so ingrained in his muscle memory, in his sleep he could often feel a phantom limb lifting a glass above his head.

Pardeep introduced himself first. 'Mr McBain?'

Charlie's eyes narrowed, unsure yet if he was dealing with a friend or foe. 'That depends. Who wants to know?'

Pardeep showed him his ID. 'I'm Detective Constable Pardeep Varma.'

Jason followed suit. 'I'm Detective Constable Jason Yang, sir.'

Charlie grumbled under his breath, then said, 'Does retirement not mean anything to you lot anymore?'

Pardeep said, 'We just need a few moments of your time. We have some questions for you about one of your old colleagues.'

With heavy eyelids, Charlie said, 'Let me guess. Scully?'

Pardeep and Jason looked at each other quizzically.

'It is, actually,' said Jason. 'How did you know?'

'Pfft...' Charlie reached for his glass. 'I've been waiting for one of you to show up for a while now. I knew it would happen eventually.' He motioned to the two free seats that had just opened up in front of him. 'Take them, quick, before they go. I'll get youse a drink.'

Pardeep pointed at Charlie's glass. 'Same again?'

'Aye,' he said. 'This might take a while.'

'Jason?'

Jason turned towards the bar, weighing up his options. 'Do you think they do any protein smoothies?'

Pardeep gave him a withering look that said it all.

'Okay, okay,' Jason said to mollify him. 'Just a water. But

from a bottle. And can you check it's definitely sealed? And that there are no fingerprints on the glass? I hate that. And ice that's very cold, but not, like, rock hard.'

Pardeep stared at him. 'Anything else? Would you like the building moved slightly to the left? I bet you're one of these people who wash their dishes before putting them in the dishwasher.'

'I'm just specific about what I like.'

Charlie McBain remarked, 'Aye, that's one way of describing it.'

Pardeep explained to Charlie, as if apologising for a small child, 'You'll have to excuse my colleague here. He's only with us to fill our quota of the anally retentive.'

<hr />

WITH DRINKS BOUGHT, the portrait of Martin Scullion that then emerged from Charlie's testimony was consistent with everything they had gleaned from his personnel file.

Charlie explained, 'This was back in the Strathclyde Police days, remember. It was a different time. There were none of these disciplinary panels where an officer's every move is analysed and discussed. I mean, not like it is now. There wasn't any taking of minutes. No real process. If you messed up, you were just hauled up to the Chief Super's office for a bit of the old hairdryer treatment. No one was looking at patterns of behaviour. An allegation would be made, and the bosses would just pack him off to somewhere out in the sticks, and it would all be forgotten about.'

'You two worked together for a while in CID, right?'

'Yeah…' The memory of it didn't seem a happy one. 'I requested a transfer after a few years. I couldn't take it anymore.'

'Couldn't take what?'

'It started off small. It always does. You'll get to find that out, boys.' He nodded sagely. 'You see it with those guys who kill young women. There's always something there in their past. A charge of indecent assault. Exposure. Whatever it is, it's relatively minor in the scheme of offences that we're used to dealing with. Then it escalates. Scully was the same.'

'What did he do?' asked Jason, steeling himself.

'Little comments to start with,' said Charlie. 'We'd be in the car together, and he'd see some school girls walking along and he'd say something. I put him in his place but…he just gave me the creeps is the best I can describe it. When I moved to Cyber, that was what broke it.'

Pardeep said, 'That must have been a rough job. I take my hat off to anyone who can stomach it.'

'Do you know what they do in Cyber? I mean, really?'

'I have an idea.'

Charlie shook his head. 'Then you've got no idea. Every time we arrested some paedo, someone had to look through the thousands of images and videos they had on their computers to track down victims. Having to look at that stuff…' He pushed his lips out in disgust. 'There's no going back after that. It changes you. That's why I drink. Building that wall, brick by brick. To keep me away from my own thoughts.' He took a moment. 'It was at Cyber that I finally snapped with Scully.'

Pardeep asked, 'What happened?'

'He came by one day, saying he had an extra ticket for the Rangers match that night. I said I couldn't, I was working an enquiry. I went away to make a coffee, and when I came back I found my computer screen was on. There was a folder open that hadn't been before. One look at him, and I knew he'd been looking at images. The folder had kiddie stuff in it. It wasn't an accident. It wasn't curiosity. I just knew.'

Jason asked, 'Did you make a formal complaint?'

'I took it as high as I could, but it never went anywhere. Turns out he was already on a final warning. A week later he was booted out over allegations of grooming some kid online, but they couldn't make any charges stick. That day was the last I saw him.' He drained the last of his pint. 'What's he done this time, then?'

Pardeep leaned closer, mindful of keeping anyone else from hearing. 'Mr McBain, Martin Scullion is dead. We've found his remains under a tunnel in the Botanics.'

Charlie nodded slowly, thinking through his response. 'Good,' he said. 'I mean, I've got no problem saying that. Some people are just born bad.' He stopped, tilted his head to one side. 'Is that why there's police all over the Botanics, then?'

'That's right,' said Pardeep.

Charlie turned away, his head suddenly somewhere else. 'It's funny...'

'What is?'

Charlie blinked heavily, bringing himself back to the present. 'It's just, when you said the Botanics and Scully...it's so funny the stuff you remember only once you've been prompted. You ever get that? If you asked me to tell you everything I could about Scully, I could have sat here for another two hours and not remembered this. Until you mentioned the Botanics.'

For the next ten minutes, Pardeep and Jason barely moved a muscle, rapt with attention to Charlie's story.

When he was done, Pardeep checked, 'Are you sure?'

'I might be a drunk, Detective Constable, but I'm not a liar. And I'm not mistaken. I'm telling you, that's exactly how it happened.'

———

PARDEEP AND JASON were still slack-jawed at Charlie's anecdote when they got outside.

'What are you thinking?' asked Pardeep.

Jason replied, 'I'm thinking I want to see it in black and white before I believe it. You?'

'I think the old man's onto something.'

———

BACK AT THE STATION, the pair trawled for nearly an hour through months of HOLMES reports and hard copies to find the one that Charlie mentioned. He hadn't been sure of the exact time frame. Pardeep and Jason couldn't take any chances of missing it. They both knew they were close to the sort of break they'd been looking for.

Pardeep was sitting on the floor with a laptop, his face illuminated by the bright screen in the murky room. His eyes lit up as he found the report that Charlie had described. 'I've got it, Jason.'

He rushed over.

They read the report together in stunned silence.

When they were both done, Pardeep said, 'We have to get this to the gaffer.'

CHAPTER FORTY-NINE

As they rushed past the records room, Jason and Pardeep spotted Donna languishing on her knees on the floor, deep in concentration.

Pardeep called to her, 'Donna!'

She jumped a little and put her hand to her chest.

Suspicious at to what had made her so jumpy, he told her, 'The gaffer's just back. Are you coming?'

'Be right there.' She kept the file close to her chest until Pardeep was out of sight again. She didn't show it, but her heart was beating like a jackhammer. She opened the folder which was bore a sticker down the side that said, "LEE, Peter."

But the file inside was sealed, stamped with "MAPPA order".

Wherever Peter Lee was now was a mystery.

In the rush of the moment, Donna slid her finger towards the thick sticker that kept the file sealed. How easy it would be, she thought, to just slip it open and have a quick look. At that point, she didn't think about her career. All she could think about was that constable who had saved her mother all those years ago.

She saw his face clearly in her head. He had broken the door down in order to get in. Once her animal of a father had been restrained and cuffed, the teenage Donna told the constable thanks.

'*Hey,*' the constable replied, to let her know it was all part of the job. '*Whatever it takes.*'

She had already taken it to Linda, who had bumped the matter up to CSU Reekie as a matter of urgency.

She shook her head, telling herself to stop being crazy. To wait for the proper channels to open up and have Reekie give them access to the encrypted digital version on the intranet system.

With a puff of her cheeks, she returned the file to its place on the shelf, then dashed upstairs for Lomond's briefing.

LOMOND WAS in deep consultation with Ross in front of the whiteboard when Donna ran in, the last to arrive.

'Right,' said Lomond. 'We've got some catching up to do here. Willie, where are we with Scullion's pad?'

Willie looked beaten up psychologically. It was an oppressively grim place to spend an entire day. 'Outside of the blood forensics, there's not much, John. The place is a dump. It will take weeks to run down any marks in a place like that. We do have something, though, on Jack Ferguson.' Willie showed a photograph on his phone taken at the scene.

Underneath a table in a bedroom was a plastic tub containing glass vials.

Willie said, 'According to forensics it's a paralysing agent. And yes, it's exactly the kind that could have been used on the Fergusons.'

Lomond thought it through. 'Then who administered it? It certainly wasn't Scullion.'

'That remains up in the air.'

'Okay, let's get that up on the board,' Lomond said, then redirected to the others. 'On the Maggie Belmont issue – the Chief Super will be conducting a press conference tomorrow morning where he'll announce the discovery of her remains at the Botanics site. We're going to have to get ourselves ready for a heap of press about the connections to the Sandman enquiries as well as Jack Ferguson. Sharon Belmont has been informed, so we can at least relax about the news getting leaked. She took it about as well as you would expect. I think it's highly likely that we'll get some media blowback over Sandy Driscoll in the next few days. But we can't concern ourselves with that right now.' While Lomond picked up a steaming cup of coffee, he said, 'Do you have anything to add, Ross?'

'As far as possible accomplices go for Sandy Driscoll, we've ruled out Maggie Belmont's dad, who had an alibi and died in rather tragic circumstances not long after her disappearance. And Sharon Belmont is in the clear as well.'

'Out of interest, what was her alibi?' asked Pardeep.

Lomond answered, 'She was on a bar's CCTV all night until it was discovered that Maggie was gone.'

'Then who discovered she was gone?'

'A local off-duty constable saw Mrs Belmont at a hotel bar and decided to run past her cottage to check on Maggie.' Lomond turned to Willie. 'Can you imagine that happening here?'

Willie flashed his eyebrows up as if to say "no chance."

After exchanging a tense look with each other, Pardeep mouthed to Jason to say something that was on his mind. 'Go on,' he urged him.

'Who was the officer?' asked Jason.

Lomond paused. 'There was me thinking that I was the most cynical bastard in the room, but no.' He announced like a TV game-show host, 'Step forward Detective Constable Jason Yang!'

Donna could already see what he was getting at. 'Martin Scullion was never based on Arran, Jase.'

But Jason insisted, 'Pardeep and I spoke to a contact who worked with Scullion through the years, and he told us that Scullion would regularly get, quote...' Jason consulted his notepad, '"sent out to the sticks" when disciplinary matters flared up.'

It was enough to give Lomond pause. 'Maggie was taken in July. Arran always gets seconded officers to deal with peak summer season.'

Ross said, 'We checked Scullion's records already, though.'

'You did? Or did you farm it out?'

He hesitated. 'I gave it to one of Sutherland's guys.'

Lomond huffed. 'Secondments don't flag on the first page of an officer's record.'

'I'm sure they didn't only look at the first page,' Ross said, checking the files. He held his gaze on a particular page, then said, 'Shit...He was sent to U Division for six weeks.'

'That was North Ayrshire in the old Strathclyde system,' said Lomond.

Willie said. 'And Arran was under North Ayrshire.' He raced through the Maggie Belmont file, then stopped suddenly. 'Christ on a bike. It was him, John. First on the scene, PC Martin Scullion.'

Ross said, 'Sergeant Muir on Arran told us the officer checked on Maggie at Mrs Belmont's home and said she was still there. He could have taken her then.'

Willie added, 'He could have had an hour, maybe more, to hide her.'

Lomond could see how it might have worked. 'This is great work, but it still doesn't get us any closer to finding Jack Ferguson. We need to work locations.' He turned to Pardeep and Jason. 'What about this hidden room at Crowfoot Avenue?'

'Forensics haven't found any trace of Jack or anyone else in there,' said Pardeep. 'They're still looking, but they say it appears to have been thoroughly cleaned. Maybe we'll get something overnight.'

There was silence as everyone waited for Lomond to announce next moves. But he said nothing. He stared at the whiteboard – the section concerning the known details about Sandy Driscoll's childhood.

Lomond wagged his finger at it, then turned to his team. 'And we're sure there's nothing on the dad? He can't have just disappeared.'

Pardeep gave an "I don't know what to tell you" gesture. 'That's exactly what it looks like.'

Jason was busy scribbling down notes from the briefing. He raised his hand without looking up and said, 'Unless he changed his name.'

There was a long pause while everyone waited for an explanation.

Jason looked up. 'It could have been done by deed poll.'

Lomond said, 'You don't say much, son, but when you do you make it count, I'll give you that.' He turned to Willie. 'Can we check that?'

'It's extremely hard to verify,' Willie replied. 'We could try going through the National Crime Agency. Maybe they could forward it to GCHQ.'

'I might have a theory on that,' Donna offered. She brought the file she had on Peter Lee to the front. 'I have a source who was in Barlinnie at the same time as Sandy Driscoll. He said that Sandy kept to himself, but he did pal about with one guy on the inside.'

While Lomond skim-read the file, Donna explained, 'He was in on a twelve-year sentence in E Hall.'

Lomond looked up from the file in disbelief. 'Is this right?'

Donna nodded. 'For sure.'

'What was the charge?' asked Willie.

Lomond showed him the file. 'Attempted abduction of a minor.'

All the air seemed to rush out of the room. If there was a single red flag offence they would be looking for in a suspect, that was it.

But Donna wasn't done yet.

'There's more,' she said, producing more files. 'I attempted to trace back Peter Lee's movements before he was locked up. I couldn't find anything. Until I figured out this...' She approached the whiteboard, taking the pen and started drawing two columns. One marked "PETER LEE", the other "ROBERT DRISCOLL". She said, 'I think Jason's right.'

Where one column ended with question marks, Peter Lee's column began, showing his record of arrest and when.

Donna said. 'Peter Lee appears at the same time that Robert Driscoll disappears.' She clicked the pen shut with finality, giving it a satisfied waggle. 'I think Peter Lee is Sandy Driscoll's dad.'

CHAPTER FIFTY

Lomond raised his hand and shut his eyes as he thought it through. 'Wait a minute...You're saying that Sandy Driscoll ended up in Barlinnie's E Hall at the same time as his estranged dad?'

'That's exactly what I'm saying.'

Pardeep asked, 'Why would he have changed his name?'

Jason chimed in, 'If you look at when Peter Lee was arrested, it's around the time of the Sex Offender's Register coming into law. When I was studying at Glasgow, I read a case study about offenders changing their names in the run up to that, to avoid their new names being linked to any old crimes. It meant that they could re-enter communities without anyone knowing who they were.'

Impressed, Pardeep asked, 'You studied law?'

'Yeah,' Jason replied.

'And yet you joined the police?'

'I did,' he said, like he thought nothing of it. 'Peter Lee

was charged with attempted abduction. That's not a very typical first offence. What if Peter Lee is a cover name, and somewhere in his past is a catalogue of other offences that we know nothing about?'

Lomond told Donna, 'Get me a list of every Peter Lee in the central belt. I want to be kicking in doors tomorrow morning.'

'There's one problem with that, sir.' She showed him the screenshot she had taken from the protected area on HOLMES. It showed a digital MAPPA stamp on Peter Lee's file.

'Then take it to Reekie,' said Lomond.

'I did. He already rejected it.'

Lomond turned his head away in disgust, barely able to hold in his rage. 'Wait here,' he said, before marching up the stairs to Linda's office.

'What is this MAPPA order bullshit?' he yelled from the open door, before slamming it shut.

The rest was muffled to the others downstairs, but the way that Lomond's arms were windmilling about the place made his thoughts on the matter pretty clear.

He went back downstairs. When he reached the white-board, he pulled out a seat and collapsed into it. 'Apparently,' he said in mock officiousness, 'the link between Peter Lee and Sandy Driscoll is not substantial enough to approve overriding the MAPPA order to give us Lee's last-known address.'

Willie was in a rage too, but did a better job of hiding it. He stabbed a finger towards the floor. 'This is Reekie covering his arse because Assistant Chief Constable will open up next year and he doesn't want the approval he gave for this MAPPA order hanging around his neck. Being the man who decided to help keep a possible Sandman accomplice's location hidden isn't exactly a good look in his position.'

Lomond shook it off. 'Fine,' he said. 'We roll with it. Donna, I'm giving this to you. Find Peter Lee's address. Get onto Barlinnie. Check visitor records. Talk to prison officers, the fucking governor. I don't care how you do it.'

Pleased to be entrusted with something so significant to the enquiry, she affirmed, 'Sir.' Then she rushed out of the office.

Lomond then turned to Ross. 'Get Sandy Driscoll into an interview room. I want to know what he knows about Peter Lee, Robert Driscoll, whatever his name is. Tell him if he gives us an address we'll be lenient. But only if Jack Ferguson is found alive.'

Jason raised his hand again, before Lomond could break up the briefing. 'Excuse me, sorry, sir? Pardeep and I might have something else.'

'Like what?'

'We spoke to an old colleague of Martin Scullion's, who mentioned a strange episode involving Scullion.' Jason gestured for Pardeep to continue, seeing as he had found McBain in the first place.

Pardeep said, 'We spoke to Charlie McBain, who was a constable at the same time as Scullion. McBain said that their sergeant brought them a call to check out. A wire cutter had walked in off the street one day, saying that he saw two people dumping what he thought was a body in the tunnel at the Botanics.'

'When was this?' asked Lomond.

'The file we found puts it at twenty years ago exactly. Two weeks after Maggie Belmont was taken.'

Jason put his arm across Pardeep. 'Hang on,' he said. 'You're skipping over the part that really matters. Tell him.'

Pardeep shook his head, acknowledging his mistake. 'Right. So. This wire cutter–'

Ross interrupted, 'What is that you keep saying? Wire cutter?'

Lomond answered, 'The guys that go around the city centre with shopping trolleys full of waste electric cable and piping left by construction workers.'

Willie added, 'They hawk it to scrappies for a few quid, and it keeps them in booze and dope for a few days.'

Lomond gestured in apology to Pardeep. 'Carry on, son.'

Pardeep struggled to find his place again. 'Okay, so the wire cutter goes to the police the next day and sits with a sergeant who takes a description, and tells the guy that he'll have one of his officers check it out. According to Charlie McBain, one constable volunteered for the task.'

Lomond only needed one guess. 'Martin Scullion.'

'Correct. Scullion reported back that nothing was found except fly tipping.'

'Just so we're clear, this guy said that he saw *two* people dumping a body in the Botanics tunnel.'

'That's right, sir.'

'Well, the first one was likely Scullion. Maggie's DNA was all over his flat, and we know now that he had access to Maggie on the night she disappeared.'

'Which leaves the second person.'

Sensing that they were on the cusp of a big lead, he said, 'We need to find them.'

Willie demurred. 'John, it was twenty years ago. You're talking about a guy who's possibly dead already. Even if we find him, even if he could make a positive ID, how could we put someone like that forward as a witness at trial?'

'I don't care,' said Lomond. 'If Martin Scullion was in league with someone else in killing Maggie Belmont, then whoever else was in that tunnel that night could now be Sandy Driscoll's accomplice in taking Jack Ferguson. I think we owe it to Jack to worry about finding him, rather than worrying how a witness might be deposed.'

Pardeep said, 'We're having trouble finding anything concrete, sir. We're dealing with a lot of homeless shelters and hostels. There's no computer system, no–'

Lomond whipped around from the whiteboard. 'Just *try*, Pardeep. Can you do that? Just try! You and Jason stick at that. Willie, you keep them on the straight and narrow. Ross?'

'Yes, boss,' he answered.

'Get Gordon Reid on the phone. Tell him I've got an offer I want presented to his client tonight.'

CHAPTER FIFTY-ONE

DONNA KNEW EXACTLY where to go to find Peter Lee's sealed file that would contain his last-known address. She was shocked at how ready she was to rip it open.

After all, Lomond had said it himself: "*I don't care how you do it.*"

Opening up a sealed file like that without proper approval would be an extremely serious offence. She didn't even know exactly what would happen if she was caught. All she knew was that she wasn't going to waste all night trying to squeeze an address out of someone at Barlinnie for an inmate from fifteen years ago.

True, any address inside the sealed file was a long shot as well, but if their odds of finding Jack Ferguson alive shifted from one in a thousand to one in nine hundred and ninety-nine, then she was willing to do it.

She took out the file, and held her finger out, ready to dig a nail into the tape, when she heard footsteps behind in the dark.

'Are you sure you want to do that?' asked Lomond.

He walked slowly towards her.

Instant panic. As an otherwise honourable police officer, Donna Higgins was a shitty liar. 'I just came down to...'

She couldn't even come up with an excuse. She just left her sentence hanging there in mid-air.

There was no excuse she could give. There was no other reason to be down there.

'This isn't exactly what I meant when I told you I didn't care how you did it.'

Donna opted for attack rather than defence. 'The DCI Lomond I know, in my position, would be doing the same thing.'

Lomond kept walking slowly towards her. 'You know me that well, do you? Have you thought about what happens if you open that file and we find Peter Lee? How do we get a warrant to enter the building?'

'We don't need one,' she replied. 'There's an immediate threat to life.'

'Okay, great. We arrive at Peter Lee's house and save Jack Ferguson. How do we explain how we arrived at the address? And what happens to Peter Lee after that? Jailed or set free?'

Clutching at straws, Donna said, 'At least we would have Jack Ferguson back.'

'Maybe,' Lomond accepted. 'But you'd be out of a job, and I'd be down one massively talented detective constable.'

'If that's what it takes.'

Lomond pondered her. 'Why does it mean so much to you?'

Donna shook her head like she couldn't bear to answer.

Feeling the need to backtrack, Lomond said, 'Why don't we go back up–'

Donna then said suddenly, 'Because I don't want them to get away with it. That's why it means so much to me.'

'What happened?'

'My dad was a coke addict. He would go on these three-day benders. When he came home, he'd go after my mum and me. He chained her to a radiator. The old-style one with the bars. He beat the shit out of me, then I lay on the floor bleeding and watched him beat her half to death. The person who saved her life was a police constable. You ask me why it means so much to me? Because if every day I'm not doing everything I can to save all the other Donnas out there, then I don't even know what we're doing here.'

Lomond took the file out of her hands.

Just as she thought he was going to put it back on the shelf, Lomond took out a penknife and slid the blade down and through the tape.

'If anyone asks,' said Lomond, 'it was me and me alone. When you find the address, put the file back on the shelf and don't say a word to anyone. You got the address from the same source who told you about Lee in the first place. He just needed his memory jogged. Got it?'

Donna nodded, too scared to speak.

Lomond handed her the open file. 'Be quick.'

CHAPTER FIFTY-TWO

ON THE WAY across the car park, Lomond gave Donna the sort of look that only two people with a dark secret can share.

She wanted to be one of the officers to go through the front door and find Jack Ferguson safe and well. But Lomond had ordered her to do some digging on prison records relating to Sandy Driscoll. If the Peter Lee lead was a dud, then they were rapidly running out of time – heading into night three of a possible five.

And night five was when Sandman victims met their end. Lomond knew they could have as little as thirty-six hours left. Maybe less.

The rest of the team marched with purpose towards the two other cars that would be making the journey.

Lomond decided to bring Pardeep and Jason with him for some safe hands. They had proven themselves in stellar fashion in the Sandy Driscoll raid, and there was a bit of

Lomond who wanted to reward their detective work with a little action.

If Pardeep and Jason had any hopes of roaring through Helen Street's sizeable security barrier in a blaze of flashing lights and deafening sirens in a massive convoy of patrol cars and armoured vans, they were sorely disappointed.

The only uniform officers that could be spared fit into a regular police Transit van. Lomond's modest saloon containing himself, Pardeep, and Jason completed the 'convoy'.

THE SUN WAS SETTING, turning the clear sky over Dumbarton a pinkish orange. Once they were on the transitional stretch of road between city and countryside on Stirling Road around Milton, the atmosphere in the car grew tenser. More charged.

Pardeep and Jason took their cue from Lomond, who had his game face on. The jokes and sniping had dried up.

None of the men knew what they would be walking into. Lomond had told them to be prepared for anything. Which was well-intentioned advice but ultimately useless.

Because nothing could have prepared them for what was waiting in Peter Lee's cottage on the remote east bank of Loch Lomond.

CHAPTER FIFTY-THREE

Ross KNEW that in many ways the interview would be not only a strategic gamble, but a high-risk play with potential to backfire messily. The strategy was Ross's, to keep the dialogue emotionally charged, and appeal to Sandy Driscoll's innocent nature.

Lomond disagreed with the strategy, but in the end it would be Ross in the room. And an interview room can be a lonely place when you're pushing a strategy you don't believe in.

Sandy's lawyer, Gordon Reid, arrived late, the smell of a glass of wine from dinner on his breath. He had received Lomond's proposal and was currently discussing it with his client.

From what Ross had managed to overhear when the interview room door opened and shut during Reid and Driscoll's consultation, Reid was very much in favour of encouraging Sandy to take any offer that was on the table, and to give the police any information he had.

With Willie at his side, Ross opened the conversation gently. But that wasn't necessarily the start of the interview.

Fifteen minutes earlier, long before any recording began, Ross had placed Peter Lee's mugshot on the table facing Sandy's side of the table. Each time Willie wanted to go in and get started, Ross held him back, telling him 'just a few more minutes'.

Ten minutes in and one of Sandy's legs was tapping rapidly up and down in a nervous beat. He stared at the photo. Wouldn't take his eyes off it, even as Gordon Reid tried to give him advice on how best to answer questions.

Emotionally, Sandy wasn't in the room. He was way back somewhere far darker.

The past.

Childhood.

Ross started by saying, 'Sandy, our enquiries have progressed quite a bit since we last spoke.' He placed a photo of Martin Scullion on top of Peter Lee's. 'Do you recognise this man, Sandy?'

'No comment,' he mumbled.

'This is Martin Scullion. But I think you know that. We know Martin did some very bad things in his flat, Sandy. We know the children that went missing were all there at some point. We know that for a fact. Did you help him take them? Is that how it worked?'

'No comment.'

'Did you take them, but he killed them? Is that it?'

'No comment.'

'Because if that's what happened, it means you're not in as much trouble as you might think. We can talk about it, then. Is that why you said you tried to save them?'

Sandy began to cry, silently.

Ross continued, 'Did he trick you into taking them, Sandy? Surely you saw the papers when the bodies were found.'

'I tried to save them,' he whispered.

'You know what I think? I think you and Martin were working together. But something happened. You had a falling out. He found religion and wanted to stop. So someone killed Martin – except this was bloodier than what happened to the children. Did you kill him, Sandy?'

Sandy tried to compose himself, then managed to say, 'No comment.'

'Five years went by and no more children were taken. It stopped when Martin Scullion died, Sandy. Then you decided to start again, with a new partner this time. That's what I think.'

Reid interjected, 'Is there a question there, Sergeant McNair?'

Ross didn't take his eyes off Sandy. 'Are you working with someone else this time? You'd need the help. Like you needed it before. Someone to look after the details. Like where to take Jack Ferguson. Or where to source a paralysing agent. Because someone is out there right now with Jack. Who is it, Sandy? Who's working with you this time? Is it this man?'

Ross removed the photo of Scullion, revealing Peter Lee once more.

Sandy looked away. His tears fuller now. His cries louder. It was as if it hurt to look at Lee's face.

Ross said, 'We've been looking into some of your relationships when you were in Barlinnie. It seems that there was one man in particular that you were close friends with.' He tapped a finger on the photo. 'In fact, some people have said he was your only friend in there. I'm not surprised. It's not easy for a first-time offender in a place like Barlinnie. In all honesty, being housed in E Hall with the beasts was the best thing that could have happened to you. From a safety standpoint. Those wild boys in general population would have eaten you up and spat you out every day you were in there.'

Sandy said nothing. Kept staring at the photo. Now both his legs were going like the clappers.

'Do you remember this man's name?' asked Ross.

No reply.

'His name's Peter. Peter Lee. Thing is, Sandy. I think you knew him before you ended up inside. Is that right?'

Sandy's mouth started moving, mumbling to himself, inaudible to the others in the room.

Reid leaned towards him, asking if he was okay. Did he want to continue?

Sandy didn't answer.

Ross kept on. 'It must have been a shock when you first saw him in there. You couldn't have seen him since you were, what? Ten? Eleven? Younger?'

Sandy's agitation was building.

As he had done through some of their consultations, Reid resorted to writing in his notepad and showing it to Sandy: "ARE YOU OK?"

Again, no answer.

'Peter Lee wasn't his real name, Sandy. He changed it at some point.' Ross leaned closer across the table. 'You know what I think? I think you saw a lot from a very young age. We found the nook in the flat at Crowfoot Avenue. Is that where he'd take you, Sandy? Somewhere private. Where no one could hear you?'

Even a tough old bastard like Willie Sneddon thought Ross was laying it on thick. He could see how agitated Sandy was getting, and Ross's approach wasn't having the desired effect.

Willie decided to step in. He was softer than Ross. More approachable. 'Sandy, all we want is some help in finding this man. I don't know if anyone has put you up to all this stuff with the Fergusons. But whoever it is, I don't think they really told you the truth about what was going to happen. Is that right? If it is, there's still time to save Jack Ferguson. If you know where he is, you have to tell us before something really bad happens to him.'

Sandy finally spoke again. 'I don't want bad things to happen to him.'

'Good, Sandy,' said Willie. 'That's good. The best way to make sure bad things don't happen is by telling us where he is.'

Sandy muttered to himself, 'I couldn't save her, I couldn't save her...'

Ross crept forward in his chair. 'Couldn't save who, Sandy? Who? Maggie?'

Sandy started to cry. He told Reid, 'I don't want to be here anymore. I don't want to be here anymore.'

Reid shook his head at Willie. 'I think we're done here. Detective Inspector, a word outside, please.'

Sandy was left rocking in his chair, staring at the photo of Peter Lee.

Ross was last to get up, reluctantly joining Willie and Reid out in the corridor.

'Nice work, Joey Essex,' sniped Willie. 'He's practically frothing at the mouth in there.'

'I rolled the dice,' Ross replied. 'It was worth trying to see what sort of response we got.'

Reid balanced his briefcase on a raised thigh, putting away his notes, then he felt down the pockets of his suit jacket and trousers. He said to Willie, 'About DCI Lomond's deal. Is there a ticking clock on it?'

'Tomorrow morning,' answered Willie. 'Ten o'clock. After that, I can't make any guarantees. About Jack Ferguson's safety. Or your client's future.' Distracted by Reid still patting down his pockets, Willie asked, 'Have you lost something?'

'I don't have any business cards with me. I was going to write down my mobile for you...'

Ross turned in horror from the two men back towards

the interior window of the interview room. He saw what was about to happen before it had truly started.

He yelled out, 'No!' He lunged for the door handle.

When he reached the centre of the room, Sandy Driscoll was already on his feet. He had dunted his chair back as he stood up, and was now clutching Gordon Reid's cheap biro pen, and pointing the tip of it at his neck.

As he plunged it in, his head trembled. Every vein in his neck was standing up. When he retracted the pen from his neck, a geyser of blood came shooting out. Through a rictus of tears, he cried out, 'I won't go back!'

Ross charged at him, but was unable to disarm Sandy before he got off a few lesser blows

Ross shouted, 'Help me! I need help in here! Get an ambulance!'

It felt like he'd been in there alone with Sandy for twenty minutes. It had been all of five seconds.

Sandy kept trying to speak, but all that came out was gurgling.

Ross put his ear to Sandy's mouth. 'Just tell me where Jack is, Sandy. Please. You can still save him. That's what you wanted!'

Willie rushed in behind and tried to help stem the flow of blood, but between him and Ross there still weren't enough hands.

Ross had never seen so much blood. It was like something out of a Quentin Tarantino movie. He couldn't even tell where the wounds were on Sandy's neck. The blood was just pouring out like a dam that had broken.

It spilled across the linoleum floor, turning the surface as slippery as ice.

Ross got a hold of Sandy's neck. 'Hey, stay with me, Sandy. Stay with me. Please...just hold on...'

He could feel Sandy slipping away in front of him as his eyes closed. It felt like Jack Ferguson was fading away with him behind those eyes.

CHAPTER FIFTY-FOUR

THE HOUSE WAS on the east bank of Loch Lomond, on a remote stretch of the B837 beyond Balmaha. Eventually, the road was a dead-end, culminating at Rowardennan. The end of the line for traffic, at least, but walkers still had plenty of miles they could put in on the West Highland Way footpath beyond it.

As settings went, and after another long day of the sun splitting the skies, it would have been a spectacular back-drop. But Lomond and the others couldn't think about that. Or the sweat running down their backs.

Their focus was on whether Jack Ferguson was inside Peter Lee's house.

The house was set in the middle of one of the few long breaks in the forest, which gave unobstructed views across the loch. It was peaceful. Remote.

Lomond pulled up a good distance short of the house, still under cover of trees. He adjusted his stab vest and did final radio checks with the uniform officers in the van behind. They were to go in quietly until they breached the front door. Lomond didn't want to take any chances in giving Lee an opportunity to do something rash if Jack was in there.

The officers' shadows lengthened along the road, stretching towards the house's short driveway. A grey Renault Kangoo van was parked there.

Lomond's immediate thought was that it looked exactly like the kind of vehicle they'd sought in the aftermath of Jack's abduction. He also noted that there was a cage between the rear cargo hold and the driver's seat.

For safety? Or protection? Lomond wondered.

He directed the officer with the Enforcer to the front, bypassing the heavy gravel driveway in favour of the front lawn to maintain silence.

The house was now surrounded by two detective constables, a detective chief inspector, and five of Govan's most physically capable constables.

Lomond held up a hand, then counted down from three by showing his fingers. When he had no more showing, he called out, 'Police!'

The constable with the Enforcer swung it through the front door, knocking at least five heavy-duty chains off the inside.

As the officers swarmed in, they each were knocked back on their feet as soon as they reached the hall.

Lomond knew the smell. You never forget it. All it takes is one time.

The stench was too strong for it to have been Jack Ferguson.

The constables called off the rooms as clear one by one.

Each room except for the living room. Pardeep was the first there. When he saw Lee in the armchair, he took a full step back.

The room was full of bluebottles and horseflies, a steady pink noise of buzzing in the thick air.

Pardeep pushed his stab vest up around his mouth, which took none of the edge off the stink.

Lomond and Jason joined him quickly.

'He's long gone,' said Pardeep.

Peter Lee was in a slumped seating position in an old armchair with worn armrests. His throat had been cut, and his shirt had been ripped open. The word "BEAST" had been carved into the skin.

If that had been all, it would have looked like a nasty case of vigilantism.

But that wasn't all.

His eyes had been gouged out and replaced with piles of sand.

Lomond wearily directed the others to check the rest of the house thoroughly.

'I thought we had him,' Jason said.

'Me too, son,' Lomond replied, heading for the front door.

There wasn't time to process the bad news that their only major, active lead to find Jack Ferguson was dead, because DS McNair was calling Lomond with the only news that could have made things worse.

Sandy Driscoll was being taken to intensive care, and it was a flip of a coin whether he was going to make it or not.

Lomond needed a moment to himself. He crossed the front lawn and stopped on the road, looking out across the loch. The only thing he could think was that the last chance of finding Jack Ferguson alive had just gone up in smoke.

CHAPTER FIFTY-FIVE

Ross was slumped in a chair in the incident room, covered in Sandy Driscoll's blood. His knees were still soaked through, and he had streaks of blood across his temples and cheeks that he didn't know about yet.

Pardeep and Jason were also crashed out – though not as heavily decorated as Ross was.

Everyone else in the other teams had gone home, giving Lomond's crew the run of the place.

'I'm done,' Ross told Lomond. 'They'll can me for this.'

'No one's going to can you,' he replied.

'If we find Jack Ferguson dead I'll kill myself.'

Lomond scoffed.

'I'm serious,' Ross insisted. 'No one does the honourable thing anymore these days. If you're responsible for the death of a child, you should just kill yourself. No questions asked.'

'This isn't all on you, Ross,' Lomond told him. 'We didn't get to Peter Lee in time either.'

'What now? Our two main suspects in this case are either dead or hospitalised. If Driscoll speaks again it will be a miracle.'

'I don't know,' said Lomond. 'Peter Lee had been there far longer than three days. I think someone got to him before Jack Ferguson was taken.'

Jason, ever the optimist, pointed out, 'What about that wire cutter?'

Pardeep waved it off. 'There were five other officers chasing that guy down tonight. They can't find him anywhere.'

'We're not going to find him on some database somewhere,' said Jason. 'If he's a wire cutter, he'll be on the streets.'

'You think he's still doing that? After all this time. It's a bit of a long shot, don't you think?'

'I'd say that long shots are all we've got left.'

Lomond smiled. It was the sort of line that could have come out of his own mouth a decade or two ago. 'That is true,' said Lomond.

Jason went on, 'My mum used to say, life isn't what happens to you. It's how you handle what happens to you.'

He had been referring to the enquiry, but the words landed in a powerful and personal way for Lomond.

'Jason's right,' he said. 'Anyone feel like giving up yet?'

No one answered.

Lomond held up a framed photograph in an evidence bag. 'This was in Peter Lee's living room. We know him. And we know the boy. Sandy.' He pointed to a girl next to

Sandy, who was a few years older. 'We don't know the girl, but it's probably safe to assume it's Sandy's sister.'

'Is she in the fold now?' asked Pardeep.

'Put it this way,' Lomond answered. 'That wasn't a murder back there. That was an execution. Peter Lee was killed before Jack Ferguson was taken. Which means Sandy Driscoll's accomplice is still out there. We're not giving up on Jack Ferguson. Not yet. Everyone go home and get some sleep. This isn't over.'

CHAPTER FIFTY-SIX

EVERY CONSTABLE IN the city centre had been briefed that morning to be on the lookout for a man in his forties pushing a shopping trolley full of metal pipes and wiring. Lomond wasn't satisfied leaving it at that, though.

He had been out driving around the city centre since dawn, circling any blocks that had ongoing construction or open skips. So had Pardeep and Jason, while Donna chased down more leads on Sandy Driscoll's life in Barlinnie.

The problem Lomond had was that the nature of transient life made it very hard to find people like Archie Hanlon.

His job had had many names through the years. Midgie raker. Wire cutter. Wire burner. Sifter.

What didn't change was the nature of the work. Archie searched through bins for anything valuable that could be resold. Back in the old tenement days – the real tenement days – a midgie was a bin, or with the tenements, the shelter at the back court where everyone's bins were kept. The midgie man was a bin man. A midgie raker was someone who rummaged through the bins.

Archie's quarry was a little more specific than mere rubbish, though. He collected copper for scrap by burning off the plastic cover on electrical wire. Copper was the bread and butter of being a midgie raker, but Archie would happily collect any kind of metal if it paid. He could identify types of metal from across the road, and could tell the weight just by looking at them.

Archie had been a jack of all trades since his early teens. He used to run onto golf courses and steal balls – their owners were 200 yards away, and the fat bastards couldn't run that fast. He got to learn what the best golf balls were, then would sell them back at fifty per cent cost price to golfers the next week.

The members swore to discourage the trade, but when no one was looking, they couldn't resist the bargain. It was a dangerous game for Archie, though. Some golfers pretended to be interested, only to reveal that they themselves had been victims of Archie's plundering, and proceeded to boot the shit out of him.

He didn't mind. The profits were decent enough to make it worth taking a kicking every now and then. He'd had a kicking so many times in his life, he was used to it. And at least he was making some money from it.

One day, Archie saw a man pushing a shopping trolley

full of copper wiring past the Italian Centre, a haven of luxurious designer-label stores like Versace and Armani. After asking a few questions, Archie decided to give wire burning a shot for himself.

His first batch netted him fifty quid. More money than he'd ever seen in his life before.

He couldn't believe that so much stuff that was literally left in bins could be so valuable. But stripping down wire housing was time-consuming, and no one had the patience for it on busy building sites.

The foremen and labourers liked Archie because he emptied their bins for them, which saved them money and time, and cleared space. Archie left them bottles of Buckie and fags in return for a big haul, never forgetting to keep everyone happy up the chain.

Members of the public would even point out where a good haul could be found. It was part of the nature of Glasgow – everyone helping each other out. It was in the city's DNA.

The police didn't mind, either, because he wasn't a thief. He had no criminal record and never took drugs – unlike a lot of other wire burners. For them, the job was a means purely for buying heroin. In Archie's neck of the woods in the east end, it was rife.

He did his work on a patch of scorched land called the Fire Place at the back of a hostel. It was covered in syringes and bottles and cans. All empty, of course. Nothing went to waste in the Fire Place. Every last dreg accounted for.

Scored. Shot. Drunk.

Never leaving an ounce of a buzz behind.

LOMOND HAD BEEN DRIVING for hours. For so long, he was going to have to refuel soon. That was when he saw the shopping trolley. It was sitting on its own on the pavement off Blythswood Square, next to a rubbish chute leading into a construction skip filled with rubble.

Inside the skip, tossing aside anything unprofitable, was Archie Hanlon.

Lomond didn't have a photo to go on, but the rough description his contacts around the city had given him told him that he had found his man.

Archie emerged from the skip carrying two giant sheets of aluminium. He placed them down on the pavement, then looked towards St George's Tron Church at Nelson Mandela Place at the bottom of the hill. Even that looked far. And he was going nearly two miles beyond that.

After parking up quickly, Lomond put down his window. 'You're going to need a bigger boat.'

'I don't use boats,' Archie replied. 'This is a shopping trolley.'

'Aye, I know,' said Lomond, trying not to roll his eyes. 'It was a–'

'Clever reference to *Jaws*. Aye. What can I do for you, officer?'

Lomond chuckled. 'That obvious, huh?'

'I mean, you could always get "POLIS" tattooed on your forehead.'

'It's Archie, right? Archie Hanlon.'

He paused. 'I don't steal. And I don't do drugs.'

'It's alright, Archie. You're not in trouble. I'm hoping you could help me with something. It's about something you saw a long time ago in the Botanics.'

CHAPTER FIFTY-SEVEN

LOMOND ACCOMPANIED Archie to the Fire Place, where he set about stripping down the wire he'd salvaged that morning. His shopping trolley was burned to a crisp from using it as a kind of fire pit to burn off the wire housing. The fumes were horrendous, and it was dangerous work. Archie had burn scars all over his hands and up his arms to prove it, like a chef branded by hot pans and roasting trays.

'I just want to know what it was you saw,' explained Lomond.

Archie put on a pair of gloves and used a broken umbrella to prod the burning wire stacks in the shopping trolley. When he'd taken as much smoke as he could, he dived back and took in deep gulps of fresh air. 'It's what I told that other cop. I was down in the tunnel, raking, when I saw two people carrying what I thought was a body. I never liked going down there anyway, so I ran off before I could be sure what it was, but I reported it to the polis the next day.'

'Why did you wait until the next day?' asked Lomond.

'I had to book into a hostel for the night or I'd be sleeping rough. You tried sleeping rough in this city?' Archie made a "phew" noise. 'Dodgy, mate. Well, dodgy.'

'You're in the station. What then?'

'I told the cop what I saw. He took my statement, I signed it, and he said he'd check it out. I told him I'd sit with a sketch artist if he wanted, but he said it wasn't necessary yet. I thought that that was a mistake if it turned out I'd actually seen two murderers, and no one would have a picture of it. So I went home and drew them.'

'You draw?'

'I'm a bit of an amateur artist.' He swooped back in towards the furnace in the shopping trolley. He was pouring sweat.

No one could accuse Archie of not earning his money.

Lomond took out his phone, and showed an old personnel photo of Martin Scullion. 'Do you recognise this guy?'

Archie pointed at the screen in an aggressive stabbing motion. 'That's the guy, mate. That is the guy! How did you find him?'

'You know how good you are at finding the best wire?'

'Aye.'

'Well, I'm really good at finding people who do bad things.'

'I told that cop the next day, you've got to check it out. What was his name...The cop called him Tully or–'

'Scully?'

'That's it! Scully. He said a constable of his checked it out. Didn't find anything. Just fly tipping.'

'Did you ever go back to the tunnel to check?'

'No way, mate. Too many junkies down there shooting up.' He nodded his head in the direction of the trees a short distance away.

Three people were huddled around bits of foil on the ground.

Archie said, 'I don't mess with that shite, mate. That's how I got a house. Well, a flat, you know. It's up the highrise.'

'You said there were two people there that night, Archie. Could you describe the other person?'

'Ooft, it was a long time ago now. It was a woman, I know that.'

'A woman?'

'Aye. But I couldnae describe her face. Not now.'

Lomond's heart sank.

He was about to say thanks and get away from the toxic smoke and the heat, when Archie said, 'I could just show you the picture.'

Lomond couldn't believe his own ears. 'You've still got the drawing?'

'Oh, aye. It costs money to buy charcoal. I'm not going to just chuck a drawing away after spending the time oan it.'

Lomond turned from one side to the next, trying to get his bearings. And a visual on the nearest high flats. 'Where abouts do you live, Archie?'

LOMOND CALLED Pardeep and Jason to watch Archie's trolley of goods at the foot of the high flats nearby. Calls rang out across the balconies of 'Polis!'

Jason asked, 'How do they know?'

Pardeep smiled. 'They just do.'

In Archie's flat, a dozen floors up, he showed Lomond inside. The flat was immaculately clean and tidy. The kitchen had been kitted out with salvaged appliances: kettle, toaster, microwave. 'All in perfect working order,' Archie informed him, while making them tea.

He then set to rummaging through a vast stack of charcoal sketches. He was almost at the bottom of the pile when he made an 'aha' sound.

He brought the picture to Lomond. 'That's her. That's the one, mate.'

Lomond's mouth fell open. 'Of course,' he muttered under his breath.

How could he not have seen it until now, he thought.

He phoned down to Pardeep and Jason. 'I've got it, boys,' he told them. 'You'll never guess who I'm looking at right now.'

All the pieces of the puzzle fell into place now.

The information might have been a revelation, but for Jack the news couldn't have been worse. If Lomond's calculations were right, little Jack had even less time left than he'd thought.

CHAPTER FIFTY-EIGHT

DONNA CAME FLYING up the stairs to DSU Boyle's office, taking two stairs at a time. She stood at Linda's door, out of breath, her cheeks flushed, her face sweaty, and holding up a brown folder with a look of anticipation.

Linda waved her in. 'What's going on?'

Still catching her breath, Donna explained, 'I'm just back from Barlinnie, ma'am...I was looking into Sandy Driscoll's visiting records to see...' She took a beat to get more air into her lungs. Instead of explaining why, she just handed over the records. She pointed to the relevant entries. 'Look who visited Sandy Driscoll on four separate occasions.'

Linda stared at the visiting records, trying to make sense of the name listed. 'Fiona Ferguson? What was she doing visiting Sandy Driscoll?'

'I can't explain it,' said Donna. 'Not yet. But I think she's the missing daughter. The girl in the photo from Peter Lee's. I think Fiona Ferguson is Sandy Driscoll's sister.'

Linda stared at the records. 'This has got to be some mistake.'

'I just called the FLO at the Fergusons. He says that Fiona wasn't in her bedroom this morning. She took off in the middle of the night. No one knows where she is.'

LOMOND HAD ONLY JUST JUMPED BACK into his car, and was currently speeding his way along London Road when his phone rang. 'Linda,' he answered. 'We've got it. Or should I say her.'

'I know, I know,' Linda told him. 'Donna's here. She's got it as well.'

'Eh?'

'She found her name all over Sandy Driscoll's visiting records. The FLO at the house said she wasn't there this morning. The bedroom was empty. He thinks she did a runner in the middle of the night. I want to send Pardeep or Jason there now.'

'Hang on, hang on...' Lomond needed a moment. 'You're talking about Fiona Ferguson?'

'Yeah. She visited Driscoll at least four times...' Now it was Linda's turn to second-guess herself. 'You're *not* talking about Fiona Ferguson?'

'I've uploaded a picture to HOLMES,' said Lomond. 'I just left Archie Hanlon. He drew a bloody picture of the woman who helped Martin Scullion dump Maggie Belmont's body in the tunnel.'

Linda clamped the landline phone between her cheek and her shoulder. 'Hang on,' she said, logging into HOLMES. When she saw the photo of Archie's drawing, she gasped. 'Oh no...'

'Oh *yes*,' Lomond emphasised. 'You said Fiona Ferguson wasn't in her house this morning?'

'Yeah, the FLO's there right now. The husband hasn't seen her either.'

'Right,' he said gravely. 'In that case, I think she's got herself into a lot of trouble. And right now, there's only one place where this could end.'

'Where?'

'The same place where it all started.'

'Look, hang up just now. Donna's here. Get back in one piece and we'll figure this out.'

When she hung up, she told Donna, 'It's not Fiona Ferguson.' She turned the computer screen towards her.

Donna put a hand to her forehead, kicking herself for missing it.

Staring back at her was a charcoal drawing of extraordinary detail. Although the face was twenty years younger, Archie had caught all of its nuances.

It was unmistakably Sharon Belmont.

CHAPTER FIFTY-NINE

TECHNICALLY, the A737 was the shortest route to Ardrossan from Glasgow, but the patrol car escort that was accompanying Lomond in his car could travel at a far higher speed and clear a path ahead on the M77.

The two cars stayed in the fast lane the whole way there, spearing through the mid-morning traffic. The panoramic expanse around Kingswell all the way down to Fenwick moor showed a sky that was no longer clear. Clouds were gathering in the distance, and they looked angry.

Ross was in the passenger seat of Lomond's car, in a fresh shirt provided by Lomond – which was two sizes too big – but the rest of his clothes were still stained with Sandy Driscoll's blood. He was shellshocked and had said little since they had raced out of Helen Street.

Donna was in the back seat, coordinating on the phone with the Dive and Marine Unit, channelling the bluntness and aggression Lomond told her to use if necessary.

She remonstrated in her most aggressive, roughest Paisley snarl, 'We're not trying to cut down travel time for a day trip, Sergeant. A boy's life is in the balance!'

Willie, Pardeep, and Jason were in the patrol car ahead, liaising with Sergeant Muir, who was facing an operation like no other he'd encountered on the island.

Lomond glanced in the rear-view mirror to check that Donna was otherwise occupied before he spoke. 'Try not to think about it, Ross,' he said quietly. 'We've still got a job to do.'

'Sir,' he said, giving a stiff nod. He didn't want Lomond to think he was falling apart.

He was glad that Lomond hadn't bothered with any "It wasn't your fault" stuff. Ross and Lomond both knew that it absolutely *was* his fault, and telling him otherwise wasn't going to do him any favours.

When one of his officers fucked up, Lomond wanted them to know it. Major Investigations wasn't sports day at primary school. Not everyone got a medal just for participating.

Lomond said, 'I'd be angrier if I thought it cost Jack Ferguson his life. As it stands, there might still be time to save that.'

Donna tapped out of her phone call. 'Dive and Marine Unit have got a boat on the way for us. They should be at Ardrossan by the time we get there.'

There was no time to faff about with ferries. If they got their timing wrong and just missed a departure, it would be over an hour before the other ferry reached them. Then there was the travel time – another fifty-five minutes. The prospect of not getting to the island for two hours when the Dive and Marine Unit could get them there in twenty minutes was unacceptable to Lomond.

Now that she was done with phone calls, Donna said, 'I can't believe that the woman we sat with is capable of doing that. To her own daughter.'

Ross added, 'And all the other kids. God knows how many she and Scullion have been responsible for over the years.'

Lomond said, 'I've found in this job that it's best to adjust what I think people are capable of. It makes it much easier to get to the truth, because it's so often much worse than you initially thought.'

Lomond hit the horn, then made a turning gesture with his hand at the patrol car ahead. He told Ross, 'Text Pardeep and Jason. Tell them to remind the driver we're not worried about conserving fuel here. They can drop down to eighty if there's a sharp bend.'

Donna asked, 'How do you think they did it? With Maggie, I mean.'

'Scullion had the time and opportunity,' said Lomond. 'I think he would have waited for Sharon to come home. Or maybe she didn't want to be around. When it started.'

'Sergeant Muir said the island was sealed off. All the cars going to the ferries were searched.'

'A police constable on a summer secondment, who was there as a favour? All he would have had to do was flash his badge at whatever constable was at the port. There might be paperwork on it. If there is, I'd be stunned if Scullion's car wasn't logged getting on a ferry within twenty-four hours of Maggie's disappearance. I checked. He had the day off the next day. I'll get one of DI Dagley's boys to run it down.'

'How does Sandy fit into all of this, though?' asked Ross.

'His alibi that quashed his conviction was right. He wasn't there. I'll bet it was Sharon that got him to Arran. Why she sought him out, I don't know. It had to have been something personal. Only Sharon Belmont knows why.'

'You mean Sharon Driscoll,' remarked Donna.

'I suppose so.'

'What about the husband? Do you think Sharon was involved in that?'

'Anything's possible. But the poor bastard had been through the mill, thanks to Colin Mowatt's innuendo that he'd been involved in his daughter's disappearance. When Sandy was released it must have...' Lomond broke off at the thought of it. 'It must have sent him over the edge.'

Ross assured him, 'You did the right thing, boss. It wasn't your fault he didn't believe Sandy was innocent.'

'Yeah, well...with him out the way, the decks were clear for Sharon and Martin Scullion.'

Donna said, 'If Maggie was the first, why the long gap between the next murders? Keiran McPhee wasn't taken until fifteen years later.'

Lomond shot her a piercing look in the mirror. 'Who says there weren't other murders between them? There's miles of tunnels under the west end. It took us this long to find Maggie. Who knows how many other bodies are languishing under there. We'll need to sweep them. Every inch. But that's for another day.'

Ross looked out his window, still in disbelief. 'Why the sand? Why any of it?'

'We always want reasons for these things. Hoping that it might somehow explain how someone can do the unthinkable. For now, all I care about is finding Jack Ferguson.' He looked up the road with concern as the Arran mountains came into view. For the first time in over a week they were now bathed in shadow. Lomond added, 'And his mum.'

Ross asked Donna, 'And she's definitely not involved?'

'She was doing pro bono work for inmates that had potentially been wrongly convicted. I wonder if she'll see the irony in offering representation to the man who would end up abducting her as-yet-unborn child.'

'Didn't she recognise the name when the FLO told her who we had arrested?'

'It was twenty years ago, Ross,' said Lomond. 'She visited a dozen other inmates either side of when Sandy Driscoll was jailed.'

'Why has she disappeared then?'

'Pardeep managed to trace the phone call she received late last night. It came from Arran. I can only assume Sharon Driscoll has plans for her here.'

Ross said, 'But Sandy Driscoll definitely abducted Jack Ferguson. Right?'

'Abducted or saved? He seems to think it's the latter. God knows how Sharon pitched it to him. But it would have been her plan. Without Scullion there to take care of the physical stuff, she had to refine the method that she and Scullion had crafted over the years. It won't take long to check the cameras at Brodick port. Anyone care to bet that Sharon Driscoll isn't captured getting the ferry to Ardrossan in the twenty-four hours before Jack Ferguson was taken?'

That was a bet no one was willing to take.

'Forensics are all over the van in Peter Lee's driveway. I'll give you odds on that Sharon Driscoll's DNA is all over the driver's side.'

Again, a bet no one would take.

'She killed Martin Scullion, and I'm damn sure she killed her estranged dad, both in cold blood. She's got an endgame in sight now. Wrapping up a sordid story that must go back all the way to her and Sandy's childhood.'

Ross said, 'The way he was looking at that picture of his dad...It was pure terror.'

'Yeah,' Lomond agreed. 'She wants this one to be the last. This one isn't about bloodlust. I think she came back for a reason.'

CHAPTER SIXTY

THE EMERGENCY BOAT from the Dive and Marine Unit was waiting for them in Ardrossan Harbour. It had already been in transit around Wemyss Bay, which cut the travel time south past Largs and Millport significantly.

In ironic timing, the ferry to Brodick was idling, about to start boarding. Although Lomond couldn't help noticing that it was running ten minutes late.

As he followed the patrol car into the parking area, he said, 'The water's calm, and there's only been a handful of crossings today. How come they're so far behind already?'

The ferry staff were locked in conversation around the hull, with one of them pointing out a solitary car still parked on the vehicle deck.

Sergeant Muir was waiting for them, having crossed on the previous ferry. 'Chief Inspector Lomond,' he said, hurrying over.

Lomond flicked his head in the direction of the commotion. 'What's going on?'

'A car's been left onboard, and they can't find the driver,' he said. 'I don't think they're going to find them. That's Sharon Belmont's car.'

'Did anyone see her jump in the water?' asked Ross.

Lomond wandered towards the ferry, thinking it through. 'Bollocks,' he muttered. He retuned shaking his head. 'She's stalling us. She's still on the island. She didn't go to all this trouble just to jump into the Firth of Clyde with no one watching. She wants us all paying attention now.' He asked Sergeant Muir, 'How quickly can they get us over?'

Muir glanced at the patrol boat. 'About twenty minutes. The wind's up and helping.'

'Good,' he said, setting off towards the boat. 'We're going to need a bit of luck.'

ONE OF MUIR's Ford Ranger off-roaders was waiting at Brodick port, along with a Ford Transit van. Lomond and the team didn't pause for breath from the moment the patrol boat met the dock.

The island had never heard multiple sirens overlapping each other the way they were, the vehicles charging through Brodick's Main Street.

Tourists and locals alike stood on the packed pavements, wondering what could be happening on such a peaceful island.

Lomond had insisted on driving the Ford Ranger, but Muir managed to talk him down by telling him he knew the roads better. Which was true. Muir was no slouch, and went much faster than Lomond could ever have hoped to travel on such tight, twisting roads.

Panicked cyclists on hired bikes who weren't used to riding on open roads hurled themselves towards the grass verge when the police vehicles came roaring past.

'Bloody idiots,' Lomond commented, hanging on to his seatbelt. 'There are cows in Campbeltown that can hear us coming.'

In the back seat, Ross and Donna kept their mouths shut, holding on to anything to stop themselves being flung about.

Both vehicles ignored the natural sweep right of Main Street, and instead went straight onto the String road at high speed. Their momentum took them rapidly up the steep hill, but no sooner were they on the B road when they dived right onto a tight, single-track country road that led through a small wood worthy of Tolkien's most romantic imagination. Then up to the Belmont cottage on the hillside, and beyond that the Glen Rosa trail and campsite.

Lomond was confident of where Sharon would be by now, but he wasn't willing to bet Jack Ferguson's life on it.

When they reached the Belmont cottage, the Transit van containing Willie, Pardeep, Jason, and Muir's most trusted constable peeled off and stopped with a skid at the driveway, while Muir and the others kept on further up the hill.

THE RAIN really started when they cleared the short run of cottages and farms, and they reached the single-track road that ran past Glen Rosa campsite.

Situated down a steep bank off the road, it was ordinarily an idyllic, quiet setting by the riverside, where the only violent beings you were likely to encounter were midges at peak summertime.

Muir took them as far as he could, stopping at a fork in the road.

'You'll have to go on foot from here,' he told them.

Lomond threw his door open and beckoned to the others to keep up.

It had all started at Goatfell, Lomond told them. The site of Sharon's annual pilgrimage – which in retrospect, had now taken on a much darker meaning than what Ross had earlier encountered with DI Sneddon.

He and Willie hadn't interrupted the pilgrimage of a grieving mother. They had found a murderer basking in the memories of where Maggie Belmont had in all likelihood met her end.

Ross was much faster than the others, leaving Lomond and Muir behind. But it was Donna who broke clear once Ross began to tire.

'I can see her,' she called over her shoulder, arms pumping like pistons. Spurred on by a rush of adrenaline, and the sight of what appeared to be Sharon and the tiny figure of Jack Ferguson standing by her side, right next to the river's edge. Almost dangling.

The closer Donna got, she realised that Jack wasn't standing there freely. Sharon was holding him by the collar of a filthy t-shirt. If she released her grip, he would fall straight into the water ten-feet below.

Fiona Ferguson looked on helplessly, a good fifty feet away. 'Please,' she pleaded, 'I came just like you told me to. Please don't hurt him.'

Sharon shouted to Donna, 'That's close enough!'

Donna slowed her run step by step until she came to a stop. She leaned on her knees, trying to catch her breath.

The rain was pounding down now, streaming down everyone's faces. It was the first time the heat had broken in over a week.

Sharon was smiling. 'I wanted you to see this,' she told Fiona. 'Because this will be the last one I ever do. I wanted you to see him being taken. To bear witness. Now I want you to see him die. That's how we all escape this existence. Do you see that? That's what Martin showed me. That's how we escape this miserable world that you all have to live in.'

Fiona was sobbing her heart out, her hands clasped together as if in prayer. 'Please, don't hurt him! He hasn't done anything.' She put her arms out in front of her, wrists pointing up as if offering to be handcuffed. 'Take me instead. You can kill me. If you really have to kill someone, please, let it be me...'

What parents were willing to do for their children never failed to amaze Lomond.

Ross, his chest still heaving from the long sprint there,

told Lomond, 'There's something in her hand behind her back.'

He was right.

Sharon told Fiona, 'When I cut your boy's throat and throw him into the river, I want you to tell me how it feels.'

Lomond had been in close contact with his fair share of killers over the years. But watching a killer actually reveal themselves in front of his own eyes shocked even him. Gone were the innocent eyes of grief. In their place was a coldness of stare that could freeze the sun.

Fiona turned her attention to Jack, who was sobbing. Mostly because he was shivering, and he was upset at seeing his mum crying so hard. 'It's okay,' she told him. 'It's just a game that mummy's playing. We'll go home soon. I promise.'

'No, you won't,' said Sharon.

Lomond stepped forward, edging closer. Slowly. 'Sharon, it's over. There's nowhere to run. We don't know everything, but we know a lot of what's happened. Why don't you come in with me, and you can tell us. I think you're unwell. I think you need help.'

Sharon took a stronger grip of Jack's collar. 'I think you need to stop coming any closer.'

Lomond showed her his hands. 'I have to check Jack's okay. That he's not hurt, Sharon. Just let me get close enough to do that...' As he crept past Fiona Ferguson, he whispered to her, 'Trust me.'

Sharon shouted, fiercer this time, 'Stop!'

Not wanting to push it too far, Lomond did as he was told.

He assessed the ground between them, not sure if he was close enough. 'I don't know what your dad did to you and Sandy, but I'm sure I can get a solicitor who could plead a case for you.'

Sharon cackled. 'Me and Sandy? He never laid a hand on Sandy. That was the problem. I was always his special one. Always the subject of his...attention. Sandy was too slow. Wouldn't play along with his games. He didn't like that.'

Lomond took the opportunity to get in another step. Even half a metre could make all the difference.

Sharon yelled at him, 'Last warning, John!'

Lomond raised his hands again. 'Is that why you roped Sandy into helping you take Jack? As punishment? Did you tell him he was saving him? Maybe that it was a way to get Maggie back?'

'I had Sandy exactly where I wanted him: rotting in jail. You really ruined that one for me. Having dad in there at the same time, well, that was the sort of perfect thing you can't plan for. The things he did to me all those years. In that hidden room at Crowfoot Avenue. And all those years Sandy watched and did nothing. Stupid little Sandy. Poor little confused Sandy.' She glanced at Jack, whose legs were trembling from fear and the cold rain. 'They're so innocent, aren't they. So happy. They don't know what the world really is...' She looked away, back towards Lomond. 'Do you know what my dad did to me? Him and all his friends? That's why Martin and I took the children. Before the darkness of the world, of men, could swallow them up. We were saving them from the world. Sending them to the next life. Where they could always sleep. Always dream.'

'But at some point, Martin didn't want to do it anymore,' said Lomond. 'He wanted to stop, didn't he? When he found God.'

'He wanted us to stop. Well...I couldn't do that,' Sharon said. 'I didn't have a choice. Like now...'

Lomond threw open his suit jacket the moment he saw Sharon let go of Jack's collar.

Jack screamed as he fell towards the water, his arms out wide. He only narrowly avoided the rocks below.

Lomond pulled out the taser he'd been hiding inside his jacket and fired it at Sharon, who had the knife raised to her throat.

'It's not the same without him,' she cackled.

Lomond fired the taser, which stopped Sharon's arm. Two fishhook probes dug into her skin, delivering an electrical charge that stunned her entire body into suspended animation, before dropping to the ground.

Fiona Ferguson ran to the river's edge, calling out Jack's name. When she couldn't see any sign of him she jumped into the water.

Following close behind, Ross dived off the grass verge into water. He stayed underwater as long as he could in search of Jack, then he came up for air. Gasping and spluttering, he saw a glimpse of Jack's hand break the surface of the water. He swam after him as fast as he could, grabbing a piece of Jack's shorts.

The effort to keep himself and Jack afloat without Jack

swallowing any more water was arduous. It was only the presence of Donna, who had also jumped in, that allowed Ross to keep Jack's head out of the water.

She and Fiona Ferguson helped them all to a high grass verge, which Ross managed to push an unconscious Jack onto.

Donna delivered CPR, urging him to come around. With each second that passed, life seemed to be leaving his body. Then, with one more pump of the heel of her hands on his chest, Jack convulsed. He lurched sideways to throw up the water that had been in his lungs.

The first thing he saw was his mum, hauling herself up out of the river, taking Ross's hand to help her out.

Donna slumped back in relief, turning her head towards the sky. It had never felt so good to have rain on her face. 'It's okay, Jack,' she told him. 'You're safe now.'

Lomond was left alone with Sharon, who was shaking from the electrical shock. 'I told you it was over,' he said.

Then, echoing the bloody message that Martin Scullion had scrawled on his living room floor, Sharon whimpered, 'God...forgive us.'

'No,' he said, pulling her hands behind her back. 'I'm arresting you. For the murder of Martin Scullion. The abduction and murder of Maggie Belmont. Keiron McPhee. Leanne Donnelly. Blair Forbes. Mark Whitehouse. And Taylor Clark. And the abduction and attempted murder of Jack Ferguson.'

Hearing him say the words out loud felt surreal to him.

After so many years, after so much loss, for himself, and five other grieving families, it was over.

The Sandman had finally been caught.

Both of them.

CHAPTER SIXTY-ONE

LOMOND STOOD at the interior window of Sandy Driscoll's private room in Major Trauma in the Queen Elizabeth hospital, listening to the steady blips and bleeps of the monitoring equipment and drips hooked up to Sandy.

Linda joined him. 'The doctors say he'll make it.'

'So I heard,' said Lomond.

'Reekie's pencilled you in for the press conference this evening. If you're up for it.'

'It's not really my bag, that kind of thing.' He checked his watch. 'Is Ross finished up with Sharon Driscoll yet?'

'Not long ago,' she replied.

'What does she have to say for herself?'

'"No comment". The solicitor must have got to her.'

'It doesn't matter. Willie told me that Moira found Sharon's DNA all over the inside of Peter Lee's van. Along with Jack Ferguson's. She'll be going down for that at least. Pardeep's taking Archie Hanlon's statement just now. That should seal a conviction on Maggie Belmont's murder. As for the other Sandman murders, we'll need to wait and see. Either way, the Sandman's done for good this time.'

'It must feel good to finally say that after all these years,' said Linda. 'I just hope we didn't lose you in the process.'

———

THEY WALKED out of the ward together, taking an exit that led them out next to the Maternity unit.

Lomond held his gaze on the front doors, watching a couple leaving for the first time, carrying their wee one in a car seat that made the baby look like even tinier than it was.

Linda wanted to say something to take the edge off the moment, but she couldn't think of the right words. In the end, she didn't need to.

Lomond said, 'It's funny...all this time I was chasing the Sandman, I thought it proved how cruel and unfair the world was. Because why should some family lose their child, while another family gets that?' He motioned towards the happy new parents. The dad with his arm around his wife, struggling with the weight of the car seat in just one hand. The man had been told plenty about expecting a lack of sleep. No one ever mentioned how damn heavy everything was with a newborn.

Lomond said, 'Maybe it was a lie I had to tell myself. To get through the day, to keep going. That way, I wouldn't miss them both so much.' He turned to Linda. Struggling to keep it together, he said, 'I mean, how can you miss someone so tiny, and who you hardly got to know? Someone I didn't even get a chance to...a chance to hold while they were alive.'

Linda laid a hand on his back.

He went on, 'When Sharon Driscoll said something about cutting Jack's throat, I got a flash of what he might have looked like at Jack's age. My boy. We were going to call him James...' He broke off, trying to keep a little composure. 'Jason said this thing earlier: life isn't what happens to you. It's how you handle what happens to you. I'd never thought of it like that. And if he'd told me a year ago, I don't know that it would have meant anything to me. But after everything I've seen, everything that's happened, I understand it now. Without the darkness, you can't see the stars.'

She led him past the building where so much hurt had been buried for so long. 'Come on,' she said. 'There's some people waiting for you back at the station.'

WHEN LOMOND and Linda got back to the incident room, they found Willie, Pardeep, Jason, and Donna, using a battered Police Scotland laptop to watch a live feed of Reekie's press conference.

It was the first time Willie had seen Lomond since everyone left the station for Arran. He shook Lomond's hand.

Neither man said a word. They didn't have to.

Sitting next to Reekie at the press conference were Fiona

and Maitland Ferguson, and between the couple, little Jack Ferguson.

Lomond folded his arms, telling Donna, 'I'm surprised you didn't snap up my place seeing as it was going spare.'

She smiled. 'Team effort, sir. No victory laps in MIT. Right? In any case, I wouldn't want to sit next to the man who deleted Sandy Driscoll's MAPPA file from the system. He could have cost us a chance at finding Jack.'

Lomond said nothing, but a hint of a smile crept onto his face.

Donna went on, 'It *was* him, right? It must have been. He didn't want anyone finding Driscoll ever again. The force's biggest mistake in the last twenty years.'

Lomond looked at Linda, nodding his head in Donna's direction. 'She's going to fit right in, isn't she.' Lomond noticed Pardeep and Jason draining their plastic cups of water, making moves as if about to leave. 'You two got some place else you'd rather be?'

'No, sir,' answered Pardeep. 'It's just...we've got an early start tomorrow.'

'Yeah,' said Jason. 'We're going to start clearing the tunnels under the park.'

'Are you joking? Leave it for uniform.'

Neither seemed comfortable with the idea.

'We want to make sure it gets done right, sir,' said Pardeep.

Lomond leaned back against a desk. Before the two men reached the double swing doors, Lomond called after them. 'Ho! Boys!'

Pardeep and Jason stopped.

Lomond said, 'Good job this week.'

Linda remarked to Willie mockingly, '"Good job?" Should we check his temperature?'

Willie replied, 'I think someone's replaced the miserable bastard we all know.'

Lomond said, 'Oh, I wouldn't go that far.'

He took a few steps towards the laptop and shut the lid just as Reekie was in mid-sentence: "...*I would like to pay tribute to the efforts of the Major Investigations Team, led by Detective Chief Inspector John Lomond...*"

LOMOND WAS BACK in the car not long after the press conference. He had ended up leaving after sunset, which was in its last throes just as he reached the Kingston Bridge. The dark clouds had broken for a few moments to let the final beams of light through, piercing across the city.

Mogwai's "Golden Porsche" was playing through Lomond's Spotify on his phone via the car speakers. It had come on through the "shuffle" play, which Lomond had accidentally selected. He hadn't heard the song in years, and tried to place where he had last heard it.

Then he remembered. Eilidh was on her pregnancy ball in the living room, bouncing gently on it as the two of them constructed a playlist for her to listen to in the labour ward.

Lomond took his foot off the accelerator to enjoy the view over the bridge. First east. Then west.

He listened intently to the melody of the piano, the melancholy cello, and soft brushing of the drums. Then, with the last dregs of sunshine gone from the clear night sky, Lomond said, 'I wish you two could see this right now...' He blinked heavily to try and get rid of the tears that were filling his eyes. He said, 'It's not bad.'

In a way, the city was all he had now. But he was okay with that.

And in that moment of music and darkness creeping across the sky, Lomond could see the stars coming out.

THE END

**DCI Lomond and the team
will return very soon...**

ACKNOWLEDGMENTS

This book is dedicated with love to LJD.

This book would not have been possible without the incredible support of my loving wife and editor. May I never ever write 'waiting on' instead of 'waiting for' ever again.

For my own sake...

Thank you to the many police sources who offered their time and expertise.

Thanks to Les Virlogeux for the last-minute editing suite.

I'd also like to pay tribute to DCI Mark Bell of Glasgow MIT, whose work inspired me no end. A true Glasgow hero.

Finally, to you dear readers...

If you enjoyed the book and have a spare minute, I'd really appreciate it if you could leave a review. Even a sentence or two or just a star rating is great. Every single one honestly helps writers a lot.

Thank you for all of your lovely emails, Facebook comments and messages, and anything else. They are truly appreciated. As I always say, a writer is nothing without readers, and you lot are the best out there.

Your good humour and encouragement really keep me going.

- Andrew

ALSO BY ANDREW RAYMOND

Printed in Great Britain
by Amazon

12446733R00215